ST. MICHAEL'S SCALES

ST. MICHAEL'S SCALES

Neil Connelly

ARTHUR A. LEVINE BOOKS
An Imprint of Scholastic Press

Library of Congress Cataloging-in-Publication Data

Connelly, Neil O.

St. Michael's scales / by Neil Connelly.

p. cm.

Summary: Keegan Flannery, fleeing responsibility for his twin brother's death and his

mother's mental illness, believes he must atone by committing suicide before

his sixteenth birthday, but he gains new insight when he joins his school's wrestling team.

ISBN 0-439-19445-8

[1. Family problems — Fiction. 2. Guilt — Fiction. 3. Suicide — Fiction.

4. Wrestling — Fiction. 5. Catholic schools — Fiction. 6. High schools — Fiction.

7. Schools—Fiction.]

I. Title.   ·   PZ7.C76186 St. 2001   ·   [Fic] — dc21   ·   00-046367

10   9   8   7   6   5   4   3   2   02   03   04   05   06

Printed in the United States on acid-free paper

First edition, April 2002

Acknowledgments

I need to express my deepest thanks to Adam Johnson, Keegan's uncle from Day One. Without Adam's sharp criticism and constant encouragement, this book would simply not be. I am also especially indebted to George Clark for his camaraderie and enthusiasm. I thank Robert Olen Butler for his invaluable guidance and John Wood for his endless insights and relentless compassion.

Over the course of the seven years since Keegan appeared in my life, I have been fed, advised, housed, and otherwise supported by an astonishing number of wonderful people. I thank my sisters Ceil, Kayte, Mary, Ticia, Susie, Jeanne, Eileen, and Beth, as well as my brother John. I thank the Beauchamp family, the Smith family, the Naddeo family, the Hummel clan, Amy Fleury, Lisa Graley, Pam Chozen, Dan Daly, Hans Merkel, BJ, Monsignor Ed Coyle, and Brian and Jerrod Weida. Also for understanding my hang-ups and pretending I was funny, thanks to Kathy, Shirley, Jill, Dan, Hill, and Marilyn at Cape Fear Community College, and all my colleagues at McNeese State University, especially Morri, Jacob, and yes, Keagan.

Finally, special thanks to Beth for being on that porch on October 6, for every minute before and every minute since.

I dedicate this book to my parents.
To my father for showing me how to tell stories
and to my mother for listening to me tell them.

IT'S NOT SO BAD BEING DEAD. People generally tend to ignore you. Like today in Rocker Hall, down in the depths of Our Lady of Perpetual Help High School. There I was, flat on my back just off center court, and the paramedics and the student nurses were stepping over me like I was a muddy puddle. Everyone except Angela Martinez, who knelt suddenly at my side in her shiny white sneakers, setting down a white box with a red cross. After checking the index card in my shirt pocket, she rested her hand on my chest and held it there, waiting. For a heartbeat or two I thought I might have a chance, and the hope of salvation through mouth to mouth brought my eyes up to her thin lips, but there was no smile. Looking straight into my eyes, she said what I've known for a long time. "This one's a goner."

St. Michael's Scales

Angela wrote something across a piece of cardboard, and behind her the big light that hangs over center court, above even the balcony bleachers, cast a halo around her dark hair. Last month one of the million smaller lights up there came crashing off a rusty girder. Nobody was hurt, but it got the old talk going about tearing the school down. They have all those lights up there because Rocker's a basement gym, completely below street level — no windows and no sunlight. This also explains the faded yellow signs scattered along the walls proclaiming it a CERTIFIED CLASS B BOMB SHELTER. Nowadays, I doubt it could handle a rowdy pep rally. The whole school is falling apart. To raise money for repairs, they force the students to participate in fund-raisers with snappy names like "Peanut Brittle to Pave the Parking Lot!" and "Wind Chimes for New Windows!" But really, everybody knows this place is a lost cause.

Angela finished and gently set the cardboard on my chest, then rushed off to diagnose another "victim." I lifted my head. Even upside down, the big, black Magic Marker letters she had written were clear. D-e-a-d. No underline, not all in capitals, not even a lousy exclamation point.

Maybe the only thing saving Rocker from caving in on itself is the good grace of its very own guardian angel. Hung high on the wall above the baskets, higher than all the frayed sports banners with things like 1953 FOOTBALL, 2ND PLACE, so high He almost touches the ceiling, is the Wrong-Hearted Jesus. He watches everything from up there, the basketball games and the graduations and the little fake masses. The life-size statue has gold streaks beaming out of His head, and His heart is on the outside, showing how wounded He is and everything.

But the problem is, His heart's on the wrong side. I heard some ritzy church in Philly paid for it, but when they saw it wasn't perfect, they didn't want it hanging in their church, so Father Halderman told them to ship it here. We have an open-door policy concerning misfits.

There was some movement close to my body. Tony Dickert and Adam Marshall, the only other ninth-grade boys who got drafted into coming to school on a Saturday, were being checked out beneath the basketball net. Tony went to St. Joe's Elementary like me, and his mom always used to volunteer to come along on field trips. Sometimes on Sundays, if I go to mass alone, I see the Dickert family at church. Mr. and Mrs. Dickert hold hands when they pray.

Tony flashed his cardboard sign to Adam, boasting SEVERE HEAD TRAUMA. Two paramedics rolled him onto a stretcher and raced him toward the girls' locker room — today's emergency room. Laughing to Adam, Tony shot a thumbs-up and yelled, "To boldly go where no freshman has gone before!"

"Dickert. Shut up. You're in shock." This came as the stretcher passed Mr. Strubek, Head Football Coach and Health Instructor Supreme at Our Lady. He played football back before they thought up face masks. He held his clipboard, the one he always seems to have, and was pointing out something to a guy in a long white lab coat, the doctor who helped plan this Authentic Disaster Simulation. I guess the two of them were making sure the catastrophe was running smoothly.

Last week, Mr. Strubek cornered me by the first-floor water fountains and told me if I wanted to pass my health class I would need some extra credit. I got a thirty-five on my test of human sexuality. Out of a hundred. He also reminded me of my well-below-average performance during the school's participation in President Carter's Youth Fitness Achievement Test.

So this morning, when I should've gotten off the bus at Hamilton and walked down to Jerry's International Newsstand like I do every Saturday, I stayed on till Sixth, where the bus comes closest to school. Jerry puts the new comics out on Saturdays and by Monday it's hard to find a clean copy. But today, while all the clean copies were being ruined, I walked in the freezing November rain to school and Mr. Strubek poked an index card in my shirt pocket and told me to lie down on the court until someone came to see just how bad my "condition" really was.

About half the victims had been seen to, and some were sitting behind me on the bottom row of bleachers. Jen Riley and Lisa Carlson, both Mild Shock, were just a few feet from me, twittering away about nothing at all. I heard every word because they weren't whispering. Nobody whispers around me, even when I don't have a dead sign on my chest. Moving through the hallways between classes, I keep my head down. The tiles pass beneath my feet and I notice which ones have cracked corners and which ones have petrified gum. I don't look at anybody and don't talk to anybody and I'm sure they all figure I'm some kind of zombie, which may not be altogether wrong.

But if people don't notice you, they can't give you a hard time. And more important, they can't blame you for anything.

Another one of the nice things about being a zombie is that people don't watch what they say around you. So I hear more than people think I hear. That's how I know things about this school. Like what Jen and Lisa were talking about. Jen's mom and dad took her car shopping this week because she just turned sixteen, and she fell in love with a used VW Bug. Her brother's going to help fix it up. I pictured her whole family standing in some sunny driveway, with buckets full of sudsy water, washing the car together. Then I imagined the four of them hunched inside, smiling as Jen eased the VW out into traffic. I'm turning sixteen in two weeks, but nobody in my family has said one word about it.

While I was leaning my head back to eavesdrop on Jen and Lisa, I noticed some guy in wrestling sneakers walking among the dead. He looked familiar, but I couldn't place him because he was still at the far end of the court and for some reason he had a black wool cap on his head. Then I caught a dirty look from Mr. Strubek. I didn't want to get yelled at for not playing my part, so I dropped my head and closed my eyes quick and went back to being dead, wondering about my birthday.

I lay perfectly still and tried to slow my breathing, concentrating on moving my chest just enough to get air. I relaxed the muscles in my face and tried to shut out all the sounds of the gym. After a while I felt peaceful, and I started to slip away, thinking about the day I'll turn sixteen and what a big deal it's supposed to be and how probably nobody will even notice. You'd be surprised the things that occur to you, on the twilight of sleep, when you're just about dead. I suddenly imagined I was on my back in a coffin, only for some reason there wasn't any top, so as they lowered me down I could read part of the headstone: HERE LIES

LITTLE KEEGAN. I couldn't quite see the date. As I sunk deeper into the grave, I looked up at the people along the edge. Big Keegan, Dad, was there, and Mom was next to him. In one hand I saw her fingers working the worn beads of her rosary, and her lips twitched with prayer. She had her arms crossed like she was hugging herself, or was strapped in a straitjacket.

Dad wasn't even looking at her. Patrick and Andrew and Sean stood by, all with the same blank look on their faces as Dad. And as my coffin disappeared into the darkness I heard him speak. "Well," my father said, "that took longer than we thought."

Then dirt was coming in on me, one shovelful at a time, dropping down from the blue sky a hundred miles up. Little by little I was buried, like when you get covered in sand at the beach, until I couldn't move my arms and I couldn't move my legs and only my face was left exposed. I knew I should be trying to move, trying to break free. And I felt just a second of panic and I think I was about to come to, and that's when I heard the voice. It sounded so familiar at first that I couldn't place it. But Michael's voice was crystal clear, as if he were whispering in my ear when he said, "Don't fight it."

For some reason his voice calmed me, and once I realized who it was it made perfect sense because he was right there next to me, one grave over. Our coffins were no farther apart in the Consolata Garden Cemetery than our incubators had been at Queen of Heaven Hospital sixteen years ago. Twins born six weeks premature. Too small to live. Bad hearts. Even though I came out first, he was bigger, and they thought he'd be the one who might live. But then he turned for the worse and nobody knew why. I can imagine Father O'Donnell with his hand cupped on Mom's shoulder. *Best pray that God takes them quickly.* So in charged the priests, and we were baptized and confirmed and we both received Anointing of the Sick. Only Michael got Last Rites, but you can bet they kept the page marked for me.

After that, I was alone under the glare of the incubator. Through my eyelids I could sense the shine from the light above me, could hear the light's steady buzz. I could feel the strange warmth, warmth they thought was saving me. I realized I wasn't breathing and searched in the void for my heartbeat. Its pumping rhythm slowed like the wheels of a train coming to some unstoppable end. The currents of my blood waned and then froze and there was no movement in my body. I waited for the rising I felt was just ahead, the rising that would set me free and the pure white light that would transform me, and I was almost there; I was so close, and then I heard the words, "Hey, Lazarus."

My eyes popped open and I looked straight up into the big gym light that hangs over center court. I felt the sweat on my cheeks. My heart was beating. The light was bitter and I turned my head and saw the black-capped wrestler standing over my body, staring down at me with his hands on his hips. Up close like that I recognized him as Nicky Carpelli, a sophomore who sits behind me in Sister Teresita's freshman religion class. He flunked it last year.

I sat up and looked around feeling kind of dizzy. The disaster drill was over. The wounded were up and staggering off the court. Nobody was coming for the dead.

Nicky said, "You Keegan Flannery?"

I got to my feet. I couldn't tell if he was pretending not to know me or really didn't.

"Morgan wants to see you. In his office. Pronto."

Morgan's the wrestling coach. He teaches sophomore social studies, but I hear he can't spell medieval. Nicky went left toward the wrestling room and I went right toward the lockers.

I dumped my Dead sign in the garbage can by the pay phone. Coming up the stairs were Mr. Strubek and the doctor. Both were staring at the clipboard and smiling so I guess the disaster was a big success. I wanted to know if I did okay being dead, but Mr. Strubek brushed past me like I was invisible. You'd think he would at least tell me if I might pass health now, or if he was going to send the file off to Washington and tell the president I was the only kid in Allentown, Pennsylvania, who couldn't do ten pull-ups.

9

I was real sick for a long time after I was born, so I never grew quite right. By the time Mom finally let me go to school, I was two years older than everybody else. So it's not bad enough I'm the smallest freshman, I'm also the oldest. Not that I broadcast this embarrassment. If things were right, I'd be a junior like Jen Riley. Then again, if things were right, a lot would be different.

When I was a kid, I didn't mind so much that I was small. I didn't care that year in and year out I got all the lousy parts in the Christmas pageant, always a shepherd or an innkeeper with no room. I couldn't picture myself as a wise man or an angel. Angels aren't short and skinny. And to tell the truth, I don't care now. The fact is that sometimes I wish people would stop pretending that I'm normal. Two months back, on my first day of high school, everybody acted like I was Flannery Boy-Genius Number Four. Father Halderman patted my head and Sister Regina tried to pinch my cheeks. Only senile Sister Cecilia Agnes, who's misfiled half the library and who always ignores fire drills, let anything slip. When I was introduced to her she shook my hand and looked me square in the eye. "Of course," she said. "The sickly one."

Mr. Strubek disappeared and I walked down into the locker room, shuffling toward the coaches' office. The whole locker room is beneath the home-team bleachers, so the ceiling angles down and you can see the metal underbelly of the steps. The top of the door to the coaches' office is cut at a forty-five-degree angle, which is about the only thing I've figured out in geometry class. Coach Morgan was standing in the crooked doorway talking to our janitor Mr. Dan, who's so thin he seems like a scarecrow.

As I came close, I heard Mr. Dan say, "When a boiler's as beat up and old as that baby, you may as well write 'grenade' on the side. It's just a matter of time."

The boiler broke down again yesterday and we had to wear our coats during classes. They'll probably have us selling Christmas candy next month as part of a "Band-Aids for the Boiler" campaign.

Morgan saw me over Mr. Dan's shoulder and said something that made him look back at me and slide away on those long legs. Then Morgan reached his hand out to shake mine. No adult shakes your hand unless he wants something. He crunched my knuckles and his smile widened. Across his T-shirt, in two rows, was printed, A LITTLE PAIN NEVER HURT ANYBODY.

Morgan's not too tall, but he's thick. He graduated from Our Lady fifteen years ago, but came back after Vietnam. They say this place has a gravity to it.

He led me into the office, ducking beneath an angled

girder. He sat at a wooden desk scarred with forty-odd years of graffiti history. I LOVE MY JOB was knifed in deep in one corner. It looked fresh. I grabbed an aluminum chair and folded it out across from him. Right away I knew one leg was short because the chair tottered back and forth, so I had to sit real still.

"You know Bill Miscio?" Morgan asked.

I know Miscio from biology and geometry. He's small like I am, but he's really fast — the kind of guy that gets picked early in gym.

"He called twenty minutes ago. Sick as a dog. Can't make our match today."

I thought about Bill and wondered if he was at home on the couch watching TV like I did back in first and second grade on those days Mom kept me home because of a fever or sore throat. She'd cut up a watermelon into little squares and pick the seeds out, then bring the juicy cubes to me in a big bowl, and we'd watch cartoons and soap operas. Sometimes I wouldn't even feel all that sick, but she'd still keep me home. That's how lonely she could get.

Morgan picked a manual off the desk and started flipping through it. The cover was a cartoon of some kid running into the end zone, a football in one hand and a textbook in the other. He asked me, "What do you know about AA sports regulations?"

I wasn't sure where all this was going, and I guess Morgan saw that in my face, because he stood up and closed the door.

"Look," he said, "Halderman — Father Halderman — has cut my wrestling budget to the bone. He says there's no interest. Talks about starting a golf team. Golf. Now that's a manly sport."

A vein bulged on his neck.

"It's bad enough I have to forfeit my 185-pounder every week. But Bugalski's a pound and a half over and he's not gonna make it. Now Miscio's out. If I can't field ten wrestlers, we have to forfeit today's match. And if that happens, we'll have one foot in the grave."

He planted himself on a corner of the desk and leaned toward me. "Ever wrestle?"

I told him I hadn't.

"That's okay. We can teach you. And look, Miscio said you're a nice kid so I'll be straight with you. I don't need you to win. I just want a warm body who can make ninety-eight to weigh in. I don't care what happens after that."

Keegan Flannery: Warm Body. Finally a position I was perfectly suited for. Here was someone who wanted nothing more from me than to be a loser.

Morgan stood up. "Let's check your weight."

Over in the corner was a beat-up scale. He set it at ninety-eight and told me to slip out of my shoes. When I stepped on, the metal pointer arm didn't move. The coach tapped the countermeasure back, reading the numbers off. "Eighty-nine . . . eighty-seven . . . eighty-five . . ."

Finally the end of the metal arm rose gently and hovered in the air. "Eighty-four and a half," he said, then turned back to the desk.

I looked closely at the scale. "Three-quarters."

"What?" He came back and squinted at me.

"My weight," I said. "I weigh eighty-four and three-quarters."

His face was close to mine now. His eyes shifted to the scale, and he reached up and barely touched the counter-measure. "Sure," he said, "eighty-four and *three-quarters*."

He sat on the edge of his desk again and I put my shoes back on.

"If you did this," Morgan said, "I would consider it a personal favor. Do you know what that means?"

I had no idea, but nodded my head.

Morgan started talking again, saying he'd give me a ride home after it was all over, and I heard some bit about not having any trouble passing his social studies class next year.

I kept thinking about what had happened on the court, and that shining warm light and Michael's voice.

The coaches' office was small and I didn't want to say no to Morgan's face so I figured I'd tell him I had to use the bathroom and disappear. The words were right in my mouth when I heard him say, "Besides, Three-Quarters, we'll make a man out of you."

And it occurred to me at that moment that the whole time we were talking, Morgan never used my name. He never once called me Keegan. For some reason I liked that, and I took a quick breath and found myself saying, "I'll do it."

So that's how I ended up standing on the edge of the wrestling mat, rolled flat across the same basketball court where two hours earlier I'd been declared dead, staring at Benedict the bulldog and wondering if he could get loose. Benedict is our school mascot. Our Lady of Perpetual Help Bulldogs. Other schools call us the Perpetual Dogs. Benedict was alongside the mat, and the cheerleader who was holding his leash didn't seem to notice that he was snapping and growling at me. Somebody had put a big piece of white tape on the front of Benedict's collar so it looked like a priest's. Morgan stood on one side of me and told me I'd do fine. Just before Morgan pushed me out, Angela Martinez walked out and sat on one of the chairs behind me, back with the other wrestlers. She had changed into jeans and was carrying the same white box with the red cross on it, and it reminded me of the plastic first-aid kit Mom always had under the front seat of the station wagon.

When I reached the center of the mat, I stood in the stance that Morgan had shown me and looked down at the mat in front of me. I listened to Benedict barking and the rumbling chant rising from the Bethlehem Vikings' bench. It went faster and faster and stopped with three loud shouts and all at once my opponent's leg was across from me, twitching with short quick beats, his knee wrapped inside a bruised knee pad. Just above, a muscle rose like an island on his thigh.

No part of my opponent's body was still; he dipped and swayed on the spring of his knees. His hands floated in the space between us, waiting to reach for me. I remember Morgan telling me to focus on his waist and not look him in the eyes because then it's easy to get faked out. But even as I was thinking this, I felt my gaze rising to my opponent's face. His eyes were waiting for me.

They were clear and sharp and he didn't seem to notice that I was looking straight into them. He stared at me, stared through me, and though I wanted to look away, I couldn't. His head weaved and rolled, and all the while his eyes held mine. I felt the sharp pinch of my chin strap biting into my jaw and realized I had sucked my lower lip into my mouth and gripped it between my teeth. I couldn't make my eyes blink.

The referee came over and leaned in between us, and when he said, "Shake hands, gentlemen," his voice told me his view of the scene. He looked at my frozen body with my hands planted on my legs, and he saw the medical tape pulling the straps together in the back of my singlet so it wouldn't fall. Then he looked at my opponent. We must have seemed strange reflections of each other. Here was a body almost the same height and weight as mine, but everything my body was not.

I held out my hand and my opponent slapped at it and there was a sting in my palm and the sharp shot of the whistle and suddenly his face was gone and I could see the other team's coach standing straight across from me off the edge of the mat. Something rammed my gut and I thought I was falling but instead I started coming up, away from the mat completely. I looked down at the top of my opponent's head, tight to my stomach. His arms wrapped around me and I felt the squeeze of air leaving my body. For a second I was taller than the referee, but then came this spinning of colors. The back of my head bounced and my teeth caught a piece of the inside of my cheek when I smashed into the mat. I caught a flash of the ceiling and the center-court light before he was on me. His chest across my chest. One arm shot around my neck and the other scooped behind my leg and he brought his hands together and my nose whacked my knee as I was yanked beneath him into the darkness. My spine curved and he began tilting me back and forth, trying to get my shoulders flat to pin me.

I couldn't move. It was my fault I was about to be pinned, but I knew there was nothing I could do. So I just closed my eyes and waited for the end of things. But in that rocking darkness, I felt Michael's presence once again. I felt the strange slickness of my brother's embrace, and the wet warmth of his unborn body in my arms. Then the white light split the sightless void and he began slipping away, rising toward the escape. But my hand caught hold of his ankle, and it was soft like jelly and I pulled him down as easily as a balloon on a string, but only because he did not struggle. Even when my hands pulled on his shoulders and pushed him down, away; even when I stood on his body and shoved myself up to be born, my brother never fought.

As I was drifting toward that brightness a horn blasted and a smack cracked the mat next to my head. I got up off the mat, defeated, and Morgan waved me back to the bench. He sat me down and told Angela to get me some water. Then he looked in my face and yelled to bring the bucket too.

I was glad when they finally left me alone, and I slumped to the floor behind the bench, beneath the accusing eyes of the Wrong-Hearted Jesus. To escape His stare I hung a towel over my head and tried to sort out what I'd seen. I'd always had a feeling I was to blame for my brother's death. I'd just forgotten how. And I was happy in a way, to finally know the details. Because then I understood that the mess in my life isn't just some accident but the result of something I did. And once I knew it was my fault, once I knew *how* it was my fault, I became overwhelmed with the idea that I could make up for it. That somehow I could fix everything.

By the time Morgan drove me home and dropped me off after the match, the understanding inside me felt ready to explode. The old urge to spill my secrets to Dad about what I'd done and what I was going to do rumbled in my gut. I pictured the two of us alone, talking out problems the way we used to. Even when I saw Andrew and Sean's rusted Mustang in the driveway and remembered they were home for the weekend, I still stayed excited. I came through the front door and stormed straight to the dining room and found my brothers finishing off some Shake 'n Bake pork chops. Dad's chair was empty.

I said, "Where's —" but Andrew cut me off with a finger to his lips and a "shhh!" He nodded to the kitchen, where I saw the wall phone was off the hook.

"Of course," my father said. "Whatever you think is best, Carl."

Dr. Carl Becker looks after Mom at Hellman House. I met him once, a few years back.

"No," my father said. "Don't worry about that. It's not a

concern. . . . I understand. Thank you for calling. Thank you."

He hung up and stepped back into the dining room. Part of me was desperate to know what news he'd learned of Mom, but part of me just wanted him to ask why I was home late, so I'd have an excuse to explain all that had happened. Instead, Dad sat down and said, "Your brothers made pork chops." He picked up his knife and fork and started sawing at a corner.

Still standing in silence, I watched him lift the meat to his mouth and pull it off his fork. Andrew looked at me and said, "Me and Sean got most of the yard in shape. How was your field trip?"

I didn't even waste a look at him. I sat down looking at Dad, still hoping.

"Maybe you can strain yourself tomorrow and help with the woodpile," Andrew said. "We come back from college, and you take a vacation."

"Enough," Dad said, waving away the insults. Again the room fell into silence as the three of them ate. Looking at the two empty chairs, one next to Dad, the other at the end of the table, it was hard for me not to think of the days when Mom and Patrick were both still here. When dinner meant our stories of the day and Dad's game of "King Solomon" when we finished. He'd explain some case he was working on or make one up, then ask each of us what we would decide. Like the farmer who sold his neighbor a cow but then found out it was pregnant. Who did the calf belong to? Or the man who lied to get a job but then did good work. Should he still get paid?

Nowadays, on the rare nights we even sit down together, dinner is the sound of the knife across the plate, the ice tinkling in the glass, the creak of the wooden chairs. But tonight, out of nowhere, Sean suddenly broke our code of silence. "Do you think we could go see her?" he asked. "Maybe for Christmas?"

Dad's hands stopped cold, his knife and fork frozen in the meat. He inhaled deeply, let the breath out, and said, "We'll see."

He finished cutting, lifted his fork to his mouth, chewed, swallowed. "You should eat something, Keegan," he said to me.

I looked at the plate set out for me. "No, thanks," I said. "I don't have much of an appetite."

Safe inside my room, I closed the door and rolled onto the bottom bunk. I reached under my pillow and pulled out Patrick's drumsticks, the ones he left behind when he took off. His drum set is still set up in his room. But nobody goes in there. I've slept in this bunk bed for as long as I can remember, and always on the lower mattress. Before me,

Andrew and Sean used to sleep in this bed. And before that, Patrick and Andrew. I've always slept in it alone.

But when Mom used to change the sheets on my mattress, she'd change the ones on the top bunk too, and even though nobody ever used that bed during all those years, I knew she was making it for Michael.

Most kids conjure monsters from scratches behind closet doors or deep breathing beneath their bed. When I was little, my nightmare sounds came from above. Nothing like growls or roars, just soft sighs and the easing of springs, like someone was gently sleeping. If I woke up in the darkness to those sounds, I'd tug the blankets over my head and lie frozen until Mom came in to get me up for school. As a dead brother, Michael was a comforting angel in Heaven, but on Earth he became the worst of all terrors.

In the wooden slat above me, I found a swirl that looked to me like an eye, and I imagined Michael watching me here. I searched the silence for some sign of him, wondered what would happen if he were suddenly right there above me, right on the other side of that mattress. I began to feel dizzy and tired, and that eye began to grow larger. As the top bunk slowly descended, lowering on top of me like the lid on a coffin, I remembered Michael's words — "Don't fight it." I lay frozen, not thinking about calling out for help, not trying to roll off the side of the bed. I waited for it to press down onto me, and just before it was about to crush me, my world went completely black.

After a time, I heard distant sounds in the darkness, and then foggy shapes began to form, and even before I recognized them, I knew I was back at my grave.

It was different the second time. I wasn't in my body anymore and my burial was complete. Invisible, I stood across from Mom and Dad and the boys, all of us standing over the mound. I sensed a swelling in the fresh soil. My halo rose up through the ground, beaming so bright I couldn't see my new face at all. Wings, white and pure, sprang from the muscles in my shoulders. They barely pulsed, and the rest of my body, hard as oak, lifted easily from the earth and hovered. It was clean and naked, the body of an angel.

Dad had his arms around Mom and her head was pressed to his chest. He reached into his pocket and offered her a white handkerchief. Patrick had come home, and he and Andrew and Sean all crowded around Mom and Dad, like one big, happy family.

And Michael was there too, standing with Mom and Dad, the whole family now embracing. His body wasn't like the earthly body I had; it was small like mine, but healthy, strong. Seeing him there, standing over my grave, I understood that Michael was supposed to have lived and I was supposed to have died. And with that realization all the disasters of the Flannery family made sense. From the very first day of my life, when I grabbed my brother's ankle, I had upset the balance of God's plan, of what was supposed to be.

My heavenly body rose out of the scene, but none of them saw it, and even I didn't follow its ascension. If I had, I would've missed the whole reason Michael granted me this vision. Because I know now that Michael wants the same thing that I do. He wants the balance restored, and like a good brother he's giving me a chance to right my own wrong. Just before the vision faded, my eyes fixed on the headstone, where I saw the date carved plainly in stone.

I don't know why I'm hesitating, why I don't just close my eyes and whisper an acceptance to Michael's offer. After all, it's the answer to all my prayers. And that's why part of me is almost grateful to know my brother Michael wants me to die on the day before my sixteenth birthday, just fourteen days from tonight.

Holding my hand, Mom leads me to the sea. We pass a half-finished sand castle and Mom squeezes my hand to keep me from kicking it. She guides me around islands of whole families huddled beneath beach umbrellas, hiding from the sun. It's just the two of us here, no Dad or Patrick or Andrew or Sean.

I've never been to the beach before. When the sand gets wet my toes squish in deep and I'm afraid of being swallowed up, but I keep walking because Mom's holding my hand and I don't want her to know I'm scared. Just ahead, waves curl over kids twice my size, crash to white foam and ripple past. The water laps at my feet and there's a pulling on my legs, some current urging me into the waves. I don't want to go any farther.

But then Mom steps between me and the waves, blocking the sun as she bends over and scoops me up. When she straightens I'm out of the water and in her arms, though now she's wading into the deeper water. I turn away from the first wave, burying my head into her chest. We rise up, slide down, and I hear Mom laughing, a sound so rare it opens my eyes. And I look up at her and smile too and we're happy, riding the waves and laughing together, just like all the other people.

But when the little boy starts crying behind us, Mom is the first one to turn toward shore. He's pointing out past us, to the sea. Coming up behind him are a lady and a man with a hairy chest. Mom backs us out of the waves until she can stand clear of the water. We see a small yellow raft, now riding the top of a wave, now behind one, like it's playing peekaboo. The little boy's mom is pointing too, and the dad squints into the sunny water. By now the raft is past the waves, wandering into the open ocean. The dad dives into a wave or two, then starts swimming arm over arm. His muscles are big, but something stronger has a hold of that raft, something that's drawing it away, and soon it's just a yellow nothing bobbing along. Then the lifeguard whistles the dad back to shore.

I watch the yellow raft until it disappears, like a balloon gone too high. Mom's watching it too, and once it's gone completely she smiles a funny smile, as if something good just happened. I ask her why the lifeguard stopped the dad from rescuing the raft.

"He tried his best," she says. "But the water out there is too deep."

Mom carries me back into the ocean and she tries tickling me, but I don't laugh. Now each wave seems to be smashing into us, trying to rip her away from me. I wrap my arms around her neck to protect her. But I know I'm too small, and if she gets drawn out into the sea, there'll be nothing I can do to save her, and that thought makes me start to cry but I try to hide it.

But soon we're heading out of the waves, up onto the beach, and Mom is whispering to me that everything will be okay. Just as we reach our towel she says, "How about we dry off and go to the boardwalk? Maybe we can find you a present. And then we'll have some lunch and you can have anything you'd like for dessert. Anything at all."

"A birthday cake," I say, even though my birthday's not until November.

Mom seems to freeze. When we drove past the exit for Consolata Garden Cemetery on our way here, she didn't pull over and make us lean into the dashboard for a quick "Our Father." That was the first time.

I go on. "My own cake. With candles and just my name on it. Just for me."

She kneels and cups my shoulders, then bends her head and I think she's about to pray, but then she says, "Keegan, I love you. I'll buy you a cake, a birthday cake, but we'll make this our special secret day, okay?"

"Top secret," I say, and she smiles.

Then she lies down and when I settle in on top of her, my face nestles into her belly like it's a pillow. Her skin is already warm from the sun and that warm on the side of my face is the best warm I've ever felt. I can hear her heart beating, and when she pats my back the two sounds run together in perfect rhythm, and my eyelids grow heavy and I'm drifting in the dark with that gentle pulse, dreaming of my birthday cake and the one wish I always wish for.

Lᴠɪɴɢ sᴛɪʟʟ ᴜɴᴅᴇʀ ᴍᴠ ᴄᴏᴠᴇʀs, more asleep than awake, I heard the sound outside my bedroom window of metal pounding metal. I pictured a machine sent by Michael to finish me off, something with steel claws and an iron skin. Rolling over onto my stomach I leaned out of the bed, one hand reaching for the floor, the other for the window and the metal sound outside. I slid back one side of the curtain to look out into the Sunday morning. Andrew and Sean were at the far end of the yard, under the oak, splitting the winter wood. Sometimes I think the only reason they ever come home from East Stroudsburg University some weekends is so they can break things. They like macho jobs like chopping logs or ripping up dead bushes.

Andrew leaned the sledgehammer onto his shoulder and

stepped up to an upright log like a baseball player stepping up to the plate. I couldn't see the metal wedge spiked into the top, but I heard it ring when he connected with the sledge. Pulling back to swing again, he pounded the metal wedge deeper. On the third steady swing, the log split in two even pieces.

Sean bent and stood the two pieces up, then split each one with a small hand ax. This of course is the same ax that years ago decapitated all my *Planet of the Apes* and *Space: 1999* action figures. A guillotine would be a quick death I guess, right at the last moment. But I'd hate to wait for that sharp slice.

Dad wasn't outside, but that was no surprise.

I got out of bed and reached up onto the top bunk for a pair of jeans. These days I keep my laundry pile up there. The sheets haven't been changed in two years.

I headed downstairs, part of me wishing for the smell of Mom's French toast. But the kitchen was empty, and I opened a fresh box of blueberry Pop-Tarts and poured myself a Coke. While the Pop-Tart was toasting, I remembered those big breakfast mornings when Dad would wake us all up early and command Patrick and Andrew and Sean and me out into the yard like his own private army. Together we attacked gutter cleaning or wood splitting or leaf raking, which was always my favorite. Dad would lead the charge

with the leaf blower, dispatching orders to Patrick and Andrew, lieutenants raking neat piles. Me and Sean brought up
the rear, Hefty bag patrol.

The best part about leaf raking was when Dad got to the
side yard. That's when he'd call me over. I'd step in between
him and the blower and reach my hands up and grab the bar.
Then his hands, warm with work, would fold over mine and
together we'd blast the rest of the leaves out into the street.
That battered blower sounded like a tank, so we couldn't talk
much. But that was okay. What needed to be said?

A steady stream of smoke twisted from the toaster, and
when I flipped the lever my Pop-Tart hopped out, the edges
burned black. Mom used to throw burned toast out for the
robins. I put my Pop-Tart on a paper towel and got my
Coke, then headed for the TV room to catch some bad cartoons. The new Tarzan is goofy — talking apes and aliens in
the jungle — but it's something to watch while you're eating
a burned Pop-Tart.

I got about halfway there when I heard radio static coming from Dad's study. I stuck my head in through the crack
of the door and saw the clock radio humming on his desk.
He was leaning back in the chair, one hand forward on the
desk, wearing the same clothes he had on last night at dinner.
His tie was draped around his neck like the stole of a priest.

Instead of just closing the door, like I know I should have, I slid inside.

I put my Coke and Pop-Tart down on the small wooden table that used to be my homework desk. At night after dinner, Dad would sit at his big desk and I'd sit at this table and he'd catch up on paperwork from the office or read the newspaper while I plowed through history and new vocabulary words. I used to call out ones I thought he wouldn't know: epistolary, transubstantiation, onomatopoeia. But from behind the folded newspaper, he'd spell the word, recite a perfect definition every time, then say, "Try again, professor."

Quietly, I stepped past the homework table and the antique liquor cabinet, then past bookcases filled with law books thick as encyclopedias lining the wall. I passed an empty space where a book was missing, and the shelf there had dust on it. Closer to Dad's desk, I came across the old statue of Lady Justice on a shelf by herself. A blindfold is across her eyes to show she's blind, and she's holding scales to weigh both sides of anything. I remember me and Dad balancing marbles and pennies on it when I was a kid. But the chain is broken these days so the scales don't work anymore.

As soon as I clicked off the radio, I heard my father

breathing. His head was tilted over the back of the leather chair, so he was facing the ceiling. His mouth was open.

I smelled morning-after cigar smoke and saw ashes sprinkled down his shirt. The ashtray on his desk, one of a hundred he's received for Christmas and birthday presents, was empty. I didn't see the cigar itself but figured it was on the carpet. It's a miracle we've never had a fire.

I wondered what it would be like to die wrapped in flames. How long can you burn before you pass out? What's it like to have your whole body sting like that? Fire has got to be the worst way to go, except maybe being eaten by a shark.

Dad's glasses weren't on and I looked around for them, then found them on the desk, cupped by his open hand. We've both got the same bony fingers, the same veins crisscrossing and sliding into the valleys made by the knuckles. When I was little, people were always telling me I had his eyes or his smile. And when Dad used to take me to Mr. Frederick's to get our hair cut together, the old barber would always say, "You've got your father's hair." I loved it.

Dad's hand was resting next to the gold frame picture of Patrick and Andrew and Sean, all behind each other like they're riding a sled or something. Stuffed in the corner of the frame is this beat-up wallet-size school photograph of me, from when I was in second grade.

Leaning against the picture was a stack of mail, and I lifted it quietly. I thumbed through it, thinking maybe something had come from Hellman House. And as soon as I thought those words my mind flashed to where Mom really was and I remembered having the beach dream last night. It's been a long time since I've had that one, and technically it's not a dream I guess because it's mostly memory.

That was the day they took Mom away, the story everybody wanted me to tell over and over. But after I fell asleep on her warm belly, I woke up in the lifeguard house — that's all I remember. The only one who ever believed me was Patrick. Everybody else figures I'm keeping some kind of secret.

Patrick told me he believed me in one of the letters he sent me from Philadelphia. When he first ran away, he drove around America for a while and sent me postcards from the road. But then he settled back in Philly and sent this big, long letter, trying to explain why he had to leave and all. He said that when I turned eighteen I could maybe come live with him. I think he was just saying that because he felt sorry for leaving. But I don't blame him.

I keep Patrick's letter and his postcards in a brown paper bag buried in my locker at school; back in September I caught Sean snooping around my bedroom. Even though it's been a couple years, I still keep checking the mail, thinking maybe he'll send me something. And whenever the Phillies or the Eagles come on TV, I squint into the crowd thinking maybe Patrick might be there. You never know.

The phone rang on Dad's desk. I dropped the bundle of mail and snapped the phone up quick. I turned away with the receiver and listened, then whispered, "No, he's not here."

I set the phone down softly and though my father's body hadn't moved, his face had turned from the ceiling and his eyes were fixed on me. "Good morning," I said.

"Morning," he replied.

"Want some coffee?"

"No," he said. He didn't ask who'd called.

"I could make you some. Maybe scramble a few eggs?" After Mom went to Hellman House, Patrick and Dad burned a lot of food trying to learn how to cook. But they figured out scrambled eggs right away, so we had those a lot. It used to be our little joke. But this morning, Dad didn't laugh.

"I'm not hungry, Keegan."

It was very quiet in the study, and Dad looked at me without saying anything.

"Your radio was on," I explained.

He looked at it. "Thanks."

He noticed the ashes on his shirt, sat up, and in the same

motion wiped them onto the floor. Then he put his glasses on, focused his eyes on me.

Standing across the desk from him, this is what I wanted to say — "I'm afraid something bad is going to happen. Yesterday I heard Michael's voice, and even though that's impossible I'm sure it happened, and Michael thinks I should die before I turn sixteen and if I agree it'll make up for everything that's gone wrong but I don't know what to do."

This is what I said — "How are things at the courthouse?"

And he answered, "Fine. Just fine. Busy."

He undraped his tie and folded it into his pocket.

"Any interesting cases these days?"

He looked at me strangely. "Work is fine. Are you alright?"

I nodded that I was okay, then waited for something else to happen. Dad seemed tired, like if I wasn't there he'd fall right back asleep. Like my presence had somehow interrupted a dream he had been escaping into. In the silence I became aware again of the sound of the sledge connecting with the metal wedge outside the window, and now it made me think of a chain gang and prison.

I remember hiding from the police when I was a kid, afraid Judge Nicholls might not wait for my sixteenth birthday like he'd promised Dad. Sometimes just the cry of sirens would send me scurrying under my bunk bed, trembling and filled with the urge to disappear. Sooner or later Mom would notice I was missing and then she'd tiptoe up to the side of the bed in her tennis shoes. She'd speak in soothing tones, trying to coax me out.

"Keegan," she'd promise, "I won't let them take you."

Every now and then Dad's loafers would appear in the doorway. He never came in my room, just stood in the entrance. And I never heard him say anything, but when the loafers disappeared, Mom's voice would have a more urgent edge. Like she might get in trouble too.

I know it all sounds silly, but back when I was a kid, the threat seemed real to me. The deal with Judge Nicholls was Dad's idea, and, after all, he was the one who'd had me arrested when I was only seven.

The pressure to say something was building with the weight of the silence in his study, so I said, "How's old Judge Nicholls?"

Dad ran his fingers inside his glasses, rubbing sleep from his eyes. "Judge Nicholls? He retired. Maybe four years ago. What makes you ask about him?"

I knew then that I wasn't going to say what I wanted to say about Michael. Somewhere along the line, little by little, my father and I had come to inhabit different worlds. "No reason," I said. "I'm going outside. They're cutting wood."

He nodded. On my way out I closed his door, even though he didn't ask me to, and as I stepped out through the kitchen into the yard, I chucked my burned Pop-Tart onto the cold ground for the robins.

The deal Dad worked out with Judge Nicholls was this — the day I turned sixteen I'd be sent to Rockdale Juvenile Detention Center for stealing a bag of M&M's when I was seven. That's what Dad told me, and I believed it for a long time. It didn't matter to Dad that I wasn't the one who actually did the stealing. It was all Hans Metzger's idea.

We had ridden our bikes to the 7-Eleven on the far side of Muhlenberg Lake and were trying to figure out how to make seventy-five cents buy a Coke, M&M's, and the latest copy of *The Incredible Hulk*. Hans told me to bring the comic up and ask the guy behind the counter how much it cost. Even though it seemed like a dumb idea since it said twenty-five cents right in the corner, I walked over and did as I was told. When I held the comic up, the clerk didn't even look at me — his face was pointing toward the far corner, and I looked there too. Hanging off the ceiling was a round mirror, and in it I saw a fun-house reflection of Hans, all stretched out. He was sliding a bag of M&M's inside his jean jacket.

I looked back at the clerk and he looked at me; I dropped the *Hulk* and ran for the door. We'd never done this kind of thing before, but we had seen *Butch Cassidy and the Sundance Kid.* I felt a rush of energy and for a split second I was someone else. Keegan Flannery: Desperado.

Through the glass I saw my bike, waiting outside like a faithful getaway horse. But as I reached out my hands to knock open the door, something caught a hold of the collar of my jacket, and just like that my feet were in the air and I was trapped.

The clerk forced our names out of us. Phone calls were made. Mothers arrived. Looks exchanged. Bikes loaded into station wagons. When we got home Mom sent me to my room. I heard her downstairs talking to Dad on the phone, but I couldn't tell what she was saying. Patrick came in and sat next to me on my bed. "What'd you do?" he asked.

I sniffled into my sleeve. "Just tell me what happened," he said, rubbing my shoulder. So after I calmed down some, I started in on the story. About the time I was getting to the failed getaway, Mom showed up in the doorway. We both looked at her.

"I'll be honest," she said, "he's pretty upset."

I felt a trembling inside me. Patrick stood up. "It wasn't Keeg's idea, Mom. He didn't even know what was going on."

Mom kept her eyes on me. "You'll have to explain that to your father."

An hour later, the police car pulled up. There were two of them and they knocked politely. Mom let them in and called me downstairs, and they had real guns and shiny handcuffs. They made me put my hands onto the living room wall and they searched me for weapons. Patrick must have heard the commotion and came down in the middle. "What's going on here?"

"Stay out of this, son," one of the cops said.

Patrick stepped in front of me. "Don't you know who our father is?"

"We're here on orders from the district attorney himself. Your dad wants us to bring the boy downtown."

Patrick's eyes dimmed. "No," he stated flatly. The cop squared up with Patrick and raised an eyebrow.

"Enough," Mom said. With a new chill in her voice she commanded, "Sit down." None of us were sure who she was talking to, but all four of us sat down — Patrick into Dad's easy chair, the cops on either side of me on the couch. Mom went into the kitchen and I heard her pick up the phone. The TV wasn't on so the living room seemed really quiet, and I could tell the officers were trying to hear what Mom was saying just as hard as I was. When she slammed the phone down all four of us jerked at once.

It was the only time I ever remember her doing anything in anger.

She came back into the living room and knelt down in front of me, ignoring the officers. She took both my hands into hers. "Keegan," she said, "what you did today was wrong. And your father has decided to teach you a lesson. But I want you to be brave and remember that I love you."

"I'm going with him," Patrick said.

"I'm afraid that's impossible," a cop told him.

Mom said, "Patrick, you'll stay with me."

The policemen led me out of my house. They didn't handcuff me but I had to sit in the backseat with the cage between us and they wouldn't talk to me. I leaned over the back of the seat and saw Patrick waving from the front door as they drove me away.

Down at the station everybody looked at me, and other officers made jokes at the two who brought me in. One cop sat me in a chair and rolled a form into a typewriter and he asked me my name and current address and I told him even though it was clear he already knew. Looking back, I should've made something up, told him my name was Flash

Gordon and I lived on planet Mongo. But I was just a scared kid then, I hadn't figured out a lot of things.

After a while he led me over to a different desk and took my thumb and pushed it onto a black soggy pad and rolled it across a little card, then gave me a tissue to wipe the black smudge off. I had to stand in front of a filmstrip screen and hold up a plate with my name on it while he took a picture. I tried to look innocent.

I decided when they gave me my one phone call I would call Hans and warn him. I knew he couldn't break me out and this was all his fault but it seemed like the kind of thing Butch Cassidy would do. They never offered me a call though. I was brought into the basement where there were four or five empty cells. I should have been scared, I guess, but when that guard nudged me into the cell and I heard the clank of the barred door behind me, I had a sudden sense of being home. For directly in front of me was the one piece of furniture in the cell — a bunk bed. And as the guard's footsteps disappeared up the stairs, I had the strongest sensation that he'd locked me in with Michael.

I lay on the thin gray mattress that didn't have any sheets and tucked the scratchy green blanket up to my chin and tried to think of something else — of Mom telling me to be brave, of Patrick's hand on my shoulder. But try as I might I couldn't keep my eyes off the mattress above me. I couldn't help listening for some sound of Michael, and knowing the cell door was locked I wondered what would happen if he finally appeared. I'd have no way out.

Then it struck me as strange that Michael would be in jail. After all, he'd never done anything wrong. Ever. He never embarrassed Dad at the church picnic when he couldn't hit even a whiffle ball. He didn't have to get carried down the trail at Hawk Mountain, too tired to hike anymore. He never broke Dad's putter trying to teach himself golf in the sandbox, or got lost at Muhlenberg Lake and made Mom cry, or had his bike stolen because he didn't lock it. Michael was the perfect son. When Dad looked at me, how could he not think of Michael? My real crime, I was beginning to understand, was not being more like my brother.

I tugged my mattress off onto the floor so the top bunk wouldn't be above me, and curled up into a ball with the blanket wrapped around me. All this time I hadn't cried. My eyes had watered up and my throat had gone tight a couple times, but I bit my lip and thought of Butch Cassidy. But down there, picturing myself through Dad's eyes, seeing what a disappointment I was, I finally lost it.

Eventually, I must've fallen asleep because when the guard came back for me he had to wake me up.

I was led upstairs, back through the desks, and left in a room with one of those two-way mirrors. I figured I was going to be interrogated. After a long time, the door opened and my father walked in. He was carrying one of his law books, a folder, and a Bible.

He opened the Bible to a page and put it in front of me and pointed. "Out loud."

I followed his finger. "Thou shall not steal."

He slammed it shut. He opened the law book and pointed again.

I read, "Criminal Code 104 point 5: Robbery. Any person found guilty of attempting to willfully deprive another person of property, goods, or lawful services, or of collaborating with persons for that purpose, shall be found guilty of robbery."

He stopped me and pointed beneath it. "Sentencing recommendation," my voice wavered, cracked, "two years minimum."

"Did you think you could do this because I'm district attorney?"

"No, sir," I said. "I'm sorry."

"Do you think you're different from everybody else?"

"No, sir," I said.

"Do you think you're special?"

"No, sir," I said.

"This is a book of rules. We can't break them whenever it suits us. This book is the way things are, and the way things are going to be."

I nodded.

"How old are you?"

"I'm seven and a half, sir."

"If you were sixteen, I'd have you brought to the prison tonight. You wouldn't see Patrick or your mother or anybody for two years. How would that be?"

I didn't want to cry in front of him, but I couldn't help it. He let me go on for a minute, then his hand came onto my shoulder and I felt its warmth through my shirt. I looked up and his face softened for a moment and I thought of us working the leaf blower.

Then he pulled his hand away. "But you're not sixteen, so we can't put you on trial as an adult. However, we could send you to Rockdale."

Rockdale Juvenile Detention Center was where Mitch Haroldson's brother got sent when he stole his neighbor's pickup truck and wrecked it. They have barbed wire fences and the inmates have to eat in a cafeteria all the time.

Dad reached for the folder. "I've talked to Judge Nicholls and we've come up with an arrangement. You are to stay here tonight until I'm done working. Then you'll come home under my custody. He's suspended your trial until you turn sixteen. At the trial he'll look at how you've acted up to that day. He'll be the one who decides how long you'll be in prison."

I didn't really understand it all then; I just wanted to go home to Mom. Dad pulled a contract from the folder and told me I had to sign it, so I did. It had Judge Nicholls' name across the top, and a little picture of the scales of justice.

That night, as we were leaving, Dad marched me over to a wall of metal drawers that looked like a giant card catalog. He flipped along and pulled out a manila folder. There was the sheet the officer had typed up, a copy of my contract with Judge Nicholls, my fingerprint card, and the photograph of my face. I looked scared.

"They'll keep this on file."

That's why for a long time whenever I thought about my sixteenth birthday, I thought about that file, and barbed wire fences, and the way things were going to be.

Head deep in my sweatshirt hood, I shuffled across the fresh carpet of crisp leaves, finishing my Coke. I smelled cigar smoke, and for one incredible second I thought Dad had somehow gotten outside ahead of me. But when I looked up I saw Andrew pulling a cigar from his mouth. He set it on the woodpile and said, "Morning. How about giving us a hand?"

I stopped and started clapping, but neither of them thought it was funny. "I'm here to help," I said. I pull my own weight, no matter what Sean says.

Andrew selected another log for splitting. "Great," he said, then looked past me into the yard, "How about filling up the tub on the porch with kindling. Can't start a fire without good kindling."

At this, Sean laughed. Though I know it's probably a sin, I've actually prayed that Andrew and Sean were adopted, that I would one day learn they're really not my brothers at all.

I turned my face away from them and shuffled back into the yard. I dropped my empty Coke off on the porch, then started kicking the leaves up and uncovering the small sticks and twigs that fall every year from the oak. I couldn't believe he was giving me instructions. Like I hadn't filled the tub on the porch with kindling every winter since I was three.

The spring on the screen door is set like a bear trap. Every time I dropped off a handful of dead sticks and went back out into the yard, the door snapped shut behind me and the spring hummed. I wondered if a bear trap could kill me, and if it would be quicker than a guillotine.

The branches are mostly leafless now in early winter, and as I worked I could see squirrels perched in the great wooden elbows of the oak. When it has all its leaves, the oak hides the squirrels, and anything else that crawls into its branches. My mind rolled back to a day in first grade. The kids on the school bus made fun of me so bad I didn't even wait until the bus had come to a complete stop before I got out of my seat and went to the front. Mr. McCoy dropped me by the side of the house, and I ran straight to the oak and scrambled up into its branches. I climbed as high as I could, thinking about the top, where Patrick and Andrew had carved their initials. I settled in the crook of a big branch and concocted plans for revenge on Joe Jezzick so I wouldn't cry or anything. Then I heard Mom's voice. From so high up, looking down, I could only see her face. She said what a funny squirrel I made with no tail. I actually laughed and I started down. Then came Dad's voice, "Something in the oven is smoking."

I looked down and now he was waiting for me. I lowered myself branch by branch until I came within reach of his long arms. His big hands lifted me off the branch and for a second I was afraid he was going to carry me like a baby but he set me on the ground. Then he put his hands into his pockets and walked away slowly. I knew he wanted me to follow him and tell him what happened, so I did. I told him all about Joe Jezzick, who said I was a munchkin from *The Wizard of Oz.* Joe had started yelling, "Follow the yellow brick road," and his friends joined in when I got up to go, and by the time I was running off the bus it seemed even Mr. McCoy was chanting it. What made this all even worse of course was that although I was the smallest by far I was also two years older than all the other first graders.

Dad didn't say a word; he just walked real slow and listened. When I got to the end of my story, he stopped. I stopped. We were in the middle of the yard. He turned and faced the oak. I did the same. It was late spring and the tree was flush with thick green leaves, rustling in the wind. I watched Dad look the tree up and down, slowly, and I did too.

"Next time this Joe kid gives you a hard time, invite him out back here. Show him this tree." He pulled his hand from his pocket and held a closed fist in front of my face. His fingers unfolded to reveal a single, perfect acorn in his palm. He rolled it into my hand. I never saw him pick it up, and to this day I wonder about how it came to be in his pocket.

"You tell this kid that this whole oak tree came from just one little nut. And then," Dad said, "you tell him you've got two."

That was the first dirty joke Dad ever told me. It took me a minute to figure out he was being funny, but when I did I laughed till I couldn't breathe.

Andrew's voice startled me: "How's that tub coming along?"

But I didn't say anything as he and Sean walked past me into the house. Because all at once I saw my chance to prove I was more than everybody thought. For a moment, I felt the confidence Dad tried to give me that day, the sense of potential. I headed for the woodpile.

The metal wedge was stuck into a log, and the sledgehammer leaned against the oak. I picked it up and hoisted the head onto my shoulder, like a contestant trying to ring the bell at the Allentown Fair's "Mighty Test of Manhood" game. The sledge was heavier than I expected, and I'd expected it to be pretty heavy. Standing in front of the log, I lifted my hands over my head and felt the weight sliding down my back. I wanted to open that log up, to reveal the fresh heartwood I knew was waiting inside.

I planted my feet and yanked my hands down, feeling the weight arching over my body. I kept my eyes on the top of the metal wedge, and waited for the sound of the strike. The red flash of the hammerhead streaked past and there was a strange low sound and the sledge went light in my hands and all at once I was stumbling backward. I fell back on my rear, with my hands behind me. I had no idea what happened.

There was a hammerhead over by the log pile, with half a broken handle sticking out of it. I thought, *Where did that come from?* Then I saw the other half of the handle, next to me on the ground, one end splintered. I picked it up and got to my feet and looked down at the spike, unmoved in the log. There was a smudge of pine in one corner, with tiny splinters sticking out. The sharp snap of the porch door startled me, and I turned toward it. Andrew and Sean stared at me across the yard, their hands locked on their hips. But I didn't look at them for long, because a stirring along the house caught my eye.

A slice came open in the curtains of my bedroom window, just a little one, as if a wind had come by, and I thought I saw a dark shape inside, looking out. And I stood in the yard, exposed under the oak, gripping half of a broken handle, and watched that slice sweep closed before I even had a chance to explain or plead my case. I looked at the splintered wood and I knew I couldn't change, and I wondered why I'd even tried.

SUNDAY · MONDAY · TUESDAY

~~7~~

12

Sᴜᴛᴛɪɴɢ ɪɴ ʙɪᴏʟᴏɢʏ ᴄʟᴀss, my back a little stiff from a night sleeping on the couch, I was trying my best to listen to Father Jim, but I couldn't stop staring at the sterile needle and thinking about death row. The other night on TV, these two guys were arguing about some states out west that want to start putting condemned criminals to death by pumping them with chemicals instead of just electrocuting them. They call it "lethal injection." I wonder if the chemicals would put you to sleep first, or if you'd be wide awake when the sting pierces your heart.

"No one has the exact same blood as you," Father Jim said when he got done handing out the supplies, "just like with fingerprints. In His divine wisdom, God created every individual with a singularly unique DNA pattern, a blueprint that makes you different from everyone else."

Father Jim is new at Our Lady. He shoots baskets down in Rocker sometimes and when Father Halderman is around you should call him Father Montgomery. "However," Father Jim continued, "we all have one of several common blood types."

That was the whole point of today's experiment. We were each supposed to type our own blood. Of course the first step was getting a sample, and that's where the sterile needles came in. Father Jim made a big deal saying the word "sterile" so I figured they must have cost a lot of money. *Baked Goods for Biology*, I thought, imagining a future fund-raiser.

Father Jim had us all crowd around the table in the front of the room. He showed us how to clean a spot on our pointer finger using an alcohol-soaked cotton ball. Then we were supposed to prick ourselves with the needle and drip some blood in a test tube. Most kids started gently pushing the needle into their skin, like they were afraid of bursting a balloon. But Sally Dean wasn't even doing that. She had snuck over real quiet and was trying to hide behind Frankenstein. That's what everybody calls our anatomical dummy. Both his arms end at the elbow and he's got no legs at all and you can take him all apart. The skin snaps off in little sections so you can see the stringy muscles in his shoulders, or pull out all his organs to see how they fit to-gether. The skin things that cover his face are broken, so the muscles of Frankenstein's one cheek and that side's eyeball are always showing. It's kind of cool and usually grosses the girls out. But Sally Dean didn't seem to mind, and as she hid behind him on the card table he stands on, Frankenstein seemed happy to be protecting her, almost proud, like he was finally doing something more than just being stared at.

Meanwhile, Mitch Haroldson had jabbed a hole in his finger and squirted the blood into a test tube, mostly. When he noticed Sally Dean, he asked Father Jim if he should "help" the kids who didn't know what to do. Mitch went to public school until this year. His dad has a tattoo of a pig's head on his forearm.

"Be still, Mr. Haroldson," Father Jim said when he no-ticed. "I have every confidence that Ms. Dean will find the inner strength she needs."

By now the whole class was watching, and Father Jim moved carefully toward Sally. His voice went all soft like a cop's when he's trying to talk somebody away from the edge of a roof.

Sally Dean caved in and oofed and aahed and came huff-ing out from behind Frankenstein, mumbling under her breath that her father was going to sue the school, a threat she makes about once a week. Father Jim handed her a fresh needle, and she looked at it for a second as if it were full of poison. As she eased it close to her finger, the hand holding the needle started trembling. Her legs wobbled and her face went paper-white and she swayed to one side and fell straight back. Right into Frankenstein's table.

Frankenstein crashed to the ground just before Sally, and the top of his head popped off and his brain jumped out, somebody screamed, and his plastic organs came tumbling across the tile floor like spilled vegetables at the A & P.

Sally was passed out in a heap on the floor and Mitch Haroldson said, "Faker, faker," and started for her, leading with his needle, which was nowhere near sterile by now.

But Father Jim got a hold of Mitch by the back of the neck and yanked him out of the way. He knelt by Sally and sat her up as the class crowded around; then he cupped her shoulders and started shaking her. Shaking is pretty big when it comes to first aid at Our Lady. Sally blinked her eyes open and Father Jim told Tony Dickert to run to the nurse's office and get some smelling salts and a glass of water. Tony spun on one heel and bolted, but when he did he kicked one of the organs. Frankenstein's heart slid across the floor and stopped at my feet. I bent to pick it up and held it in my hands.

A real heart doesn't look at all like those valentine things. They've got it all wrong. And the heart's got absolutely nothing to do with emotions. Nothing. The doctor guy from the disaster drill explained all this stuff back when he donated Frankenstein to our biology class. I guess they got a new, improved model and didn't need this beat-up one anymore. Amanda Jennings, who writes in pink ink and dots her I's with little hearts, didn't like what the doctor said. She asked what organ emotions do come from if they don't come from the heart. She asked which one love comes from. The doctor smiled and opened Frankenstein's head and I'm sure he was about to say the brain when Father Jim stood up. "Love comes from the true source of all life, the Lord God, who instills love in us through our immortal soul."

The doctor grinned and said, "Well, that's one thing Frankenstein here doesn't have," and snapped the top of the head back on. Then he told a dumb story about how they started calling it Frankenstein and everybody in the class laughed. Except for me. Because the doctor had it all wrong. He kept calling the model Frankenstein. But I read this Classics Illustrated comic version of the story, and Frankenstein was the doctor's name. The monster never got a name of his own; he just got called Frankenstein's monster. Even though he was a monster, he was kind of sad, and I felt sorry for him. Bad enough he had no name of his own and no soul, but on top of that every single part of him was really somebody else's. Dr. Frankenstein dug up dead bodies and sewed all the rotting pieces together and made one body. So the monster's arms were one guy's and his legs were another's and his brain and his face and his blood belonged to all different dead people and not one part of him was just his.

I figure he was doomed from day one.

Suddenly, I wanted to know more about how my DNA was different from everybody else's. I wanted to know what I had that nobody else did. On a table by the window, there are three microscopes. I wondered what I would see if I looked at my blood under one of those revealing lenses. Our textbook, *Your Body, Your Friend,* says blood is full of platelets and white blood cells, but this morning for some reason I got a very different picture in my head of what I'd see in mine: faces. Flannery faces floating in my blood. Dad's face and Patrick's face and Michael's face, all versions of the same model.

By the time Tony came back from the nurse's office, things had calmed down some. Sally's face was the right color again and Father Jim counted thirteen organs on his desk including the heart and was going through his top desk drawer looking for Frankenstein's instruction manual.

He announced that anybody who didn't want to participate in today's experiment didn't have to, and Sally Dean and her friends put down the test tubes and the sterile needles and went back to their desks. But I'm no chicken so I jabbed away. It felt like a little bee sting, no big deal. I dripped the blood into the tube and mixed it with some stuff that smelled funny. The next step was putting a few drops from my test tube into each one of these tiny puddles Father Jim had set up on glass slides. The puddles were clear and had special chemicals in them. He told us if you saw "clumping" in puddle A, you had Type A blood. Puddle B meant Type B blood. And if you saw "clumping" in both, your blood type was AB. So I carried my glass slides back to my desk, held a cotton ball over the cut on my finger, and waited for clumping, figuring I'd know it when I saw it, whatever it was.

After two minutes, which is how long it was supposed to take, nothing had happened. So I started looking around to see if any of the other kids were having trouble with their blood. And that's when I noticed it wasn't only Sally Dean's gang who had backed out of the experiment.

Nathan Looby, who's got a fake arm and wears this huge hearing aid, sits a few seats up in the row next to mine. And on the corner of his desk rested his needle, still wrapped in its sterile package. Nathan's about the only kid in school who talks less than I do. If it weren't for that shiny hook that sticks out of his sleeve and the fact that he always wears a turtleneck, he could probably do the disappearing act like me.

Turtleneck sweaters are against the OLPH dress code. Sister Regina, who's in charge of girls' softball and discipline, can't tell if you're wearing a tie if you're wearing a turtleneck, and ties are a major big deal.

There's no way Nathan's wearing a tie under there, but good for him.

Right after school started, he was out for three weeks, and when he came back, it was turtlenecks every day. His sister Marsha, a senior, said he had some operation on his throat and the doctors told him he had to keep it covered so it wouldn't get infected. Whatever it is, it must be serious because I noticed whenever the priests give Nathan communion at the fake masses down in Rocker, they bless him on the forehead, like they do with old ladies and little babies at regular mass on Sundays.

Nathan and me are kind of friends. Our lockers stand side by side, and he asks me about homework in the hallways sometimes. We sit at the same table at lunch. He takes off his hearing aid when he eats, and kids make fun of him up close because they know he can't hear. Sometimes I give Nathan one of my Yodels — he's on this special diet and his mom only packs him celery sticks with peanut butter for a snack. We sit down at the far end of the room past the jock tables and the cheerleader table and the nerd table and all the other ones. I guess it's kind of a leftover table. Keegan Flannery: Leftover.

Other than in the cafeteria, I don't talk with Nathan a lot, but I still speak to him more than anybody else. And sitting there staring at the sterile needle on his desk, I began to feel like I should do something. By this time a few of the guys were pointing at him, and I guess they had decided Nathan was a chicken like Sally Dean, afraid to draw blood. But I had figured out the truth. One time I saw Nathan leaning over the side of his desk, stretching for a pencil with the metal curves of his hook. When he pinched at the pencil, it skittered away across the floor. And if he can't handle a pencil, how could he hold a needle?

I wanted to help Nathan. I imagined myself marching over to him and seeing if he wanted to type my blood or something. This was a strange urge for me because I knew that taking action like that would make quite a scene. At the same time, I had this feeling that it was something I should do. But I didn't. I just sat there.

"Mr. Flannery," Father Jim said from behind me. "What's all this then?"

We both looked down at the puddles on my desk. There were no clumps, but both my puddles had turned ivory white.

"What did you do?" Father Jim asked.

I told him I did everything just like I was supposed to.

"That's impossible," he said, looking a little confused, but not really mad.

Luckily, just then the bell sounded, and everybody started scattering. Father Jim shouted and told us to be sure to clean up our supplies before we left. As everybody threw things away, I saw Mitch Haroldson pocket his needle. Sally Dean bolted for her next class.

When I'd cleaned up and as I headed out the door and into the busy hallway, Father Jim came over and looked down at me. "I just don't understand, Keegan. There must have been some kind of contamination in the materials."

I think he really figured I'd screwed up somehow but didn't want to say so. But I didn't screw up, I'm sure. And if there had been something wrong with the materials, why was I the only one who ended up with milky white puddles? Still, I guess he must have been right. After all, what other explanation could there be?

"A SAINT," Sister Teresita wrote on the blackboard at the beginning of theology class, "IS A HOLY PERSON WHO TAKES AC-TION IN THE NAME OF THE LORD. A SAINT IS ONE CHOSEN BY GOD FROM BIRTH TO DO HIS WORK ON EARTH AND ENJOY HIS REWARDS IN HEAVEN." As I copied her definition into my notebook, I found myself wondering how God decided which babies to pick to be saints. It didn't seem fair to me that somebody who tries hard and lives a holy life isn't allowed to be a saint just because of how or when they were born. I wondered for a second if sainthood is connected to DNA.

Sister Teresita always starts off class writing something on the board, then we fold our hands on our desks and she gives a long talk about whatever she wrote. We don't have to take notes on what she says, just listen. I think she wishes she could be a priest.

She leaned against the blackboard as she was describing the special nature of saints' souls, and when she came away everybody saw white chalk dusting the back of her habit. There were some little chuckles but Dicky Pudliner let out a shot of laughter loud enough to make Sister Teresita stop talking. Back in grade school, Pudliner was a paste eater. He sits a few seats in front of me and a row over, so when Sister Teresita turned her head and stared at him like an owl, I was right in her line of vision, and it was scary. Two years ago Sister Teresita broke an umbrella over Chuck Germano's head after he asked her on a dare if nuns had to wear bras. I figured Pudliner was in for it.

Just then Nicky Carpelli, the wrestler who brought me

back from the dead on Saturday, opened the door and walked in. The clock over the crucifix read 1:06. He wasn't carrying a late slip. If Nicky noticed there was trouble, he didn't show it. He just strolled through the silence with his fists in his pockets, all the way over to the last aisle, and took his seat behind me in the back. I heard this is the same desk he had last year, when he took this class the first time.

Everybody was facing Sister Teresita. Dicky Pudliner sat perfectly still. Sister Teresita stepped to her podium and gripped the sides like Father Halderman does with the pulpit. She glared into my corner of the room and said slowly, "As I was explaining . . . God knows from the beginning . . . which of His disciples will be saints . . . and which individuals are destined to be failures."

After she finished her sermon, Sister Teresita handed out packs of paper to the person at the front of each row. "These notes," she told us, "contain information from which I will compile an examination on the lives and deaths of the saints. The examination will be administered Wednesday next, during this same period."

She always talks like that.

The sheets came to me and I took one of each and handed the last ones to Nicky.

Across the top of the first page it read, FIFTY SAINTS TO WHOM YOU CAN PRAY. Sister Teresita told us the list was important because if you forget a saint's name and pray to the wrong one, it doesn't count. I guess it's like dialing a wrong number.

Sister Teresita settled in behind her desk and told Jason Blevins, who sits right inside the door, to begin. "Two each, Mr. Blevins," she said, "if you please."

He read, "Patron saint of juvenile delinquents, St. Dominic Savio. Patron saint of young people, St. Stanislaus Kostka."

And Amanda Jennings behind Jason read, "Patron saint of students, St. Albertus Magnus. Patron saint of children and especially unmarried girls, St. Nicholas."

Then Frank Murphy read, "Patron saint of Catholic youth, St. Aloysius Gonzaga. Patron saint of grandmothers, St. Ann."

I'd never heard of most of these saints, and they all had special duties like that. The list had saints to watch over librarians (Jerome), baby-sitters (Lambert — who covers dentists too), schoolgirls and teachers (Ursula), and family problems (Baldus, also in charge of cattle). This got me wondering if there might not be a saint for everything. Was there a patron saint of kids getting bugged by bullies who might take out Mitch Haroldson? Or a patron saint of little brothers who might tell Andrew and Sean to lay off? Was there a saint I could bring my problem to, one who specialized in kids-who-shouldn't-have-been-born-in-the-first-place-who-screwed-everything-up?

When it was Nathan Looby's turn to read, I got nervous 'cause I knew what was coming. Just like always, Nathan read real quietly, hardly more than a whisper.

"Loudly enough so that we might hear you, Mr. Looby," Sister Teresita shouted. "I do hope you don't pray so timidly." Some of the kids laughed.

Nathan scratched at the outside of his turtleneck and raised his voice. "Patron saint of backward children, St. Hilary. Patron saint of the sick and patron saint of battle, St. Michael."

That was one that I knew.

I always imagined St. Michael watching over a battle, then waiting around for all the wounded people afterward. I knew about St. Michael because of the report I did on him back in second grade. Everybody in class had to pick a saint to take as their confirmation name, and then write a report on him or her. Since I got confirmed at birth, I didn't have to get confirmed again. But they still made me and Peter Zincenko go to the classes and take the tests and attend the rehearsals. Peter is from Russia where they confirm all the babies as soon as they're born. Even though I wasn't going to really get a confirmation name, Mom said I should pick Michael for my project. She said it would be nice to learn about St. Michael, and maybe he was looking out for my brother in Heaven because they had the same name.

I spent all kinds of time looking through library books and wrote a three-page report on St. Michael. Patrick helped me draw a great picture of him on the cover, with a flaming sword and big wings. He's called Michael the Archangel because he was in the biggest fight ever, the war with Lucifer, the Devil. But St. Michael won, so even the Devil is afraid of him. Because of that, St. Michael has the special power of going into Hell and rescuing souls from damnation. One time he fought with the Devil for Moses' soul and won. I remember a painting of him standing at the gate to Heaven, holding the golden scales he has that help him judge people's lives, weigh the very worth of their souls. Lately, I've been thinking about those scales.

Just before confirmation day, everybody had to dress up as their patron saint, which wasn't so bad because I got to carry a sword, even though it wasn't a real one. Jason Blevins picked St. Patrick, so he got a shepherd's staff and a giant three-leaf clover. And Adam Marshall picked St. Francis, so he had a bunch of stuffed animals. He said they were his little sister's.

Jason and Adam and most of the guys made a big fuss because they had to wear big white robes that looked like dresses. But I didn't mind. I liked the idea of pretending I was St. Michael. I remember getting ready that morning, with my white robe and wings. That was a big deal too, because not all saints are angels and not all saints get to have wings. Andrew and Sean came in and started making fun of how I looked, but Patrick chased them off. "You look great," he said. "I'll bet you're the best-looking saint in the whole class." Then he had to get to school.

After the boys left, Mom gave me the sword and told me to give it to Mr. Guyon at recess for safekeeping, and then she pulled out a banner I hadn't seen before. It was like the ones they put on beauty pageant winners, and she draped it across my chest and I looked down and read the name, SAINT MICHAEL.

She marched me upstairs to show Dad. He was busy shaving in the bathroom, but he smiled when I came in. He stood me up on the sink counter and I saw myself in the mirror with Michael's name spelled backward across my chest. Then I saw Mom's face, her eyes red and a little wet around the edges.

Looking back, it was almost like my parents knew which one of us was supposed to have lived, and were trying to correct the error themselves. I know that's not true, that they couldn't possibly have thought those things, but crazy ideas like that are filling my head now and I can't seem to stop them. I wonder if Mom ever felt this way. I wonder if there's a patron saint for kids afraid they might be going insane.

Today in theology class, these thoughts made me read

ahead on Sister Teresita's list and look for a St. Keegan. There's no such person.

I was glad when Sally Dean finally read the last two names off the list. She sits two seats in front of me, and I was worried I might have to read. But then Sister Teresita handed out another stack of papers. Across the top of the first page it said, GREAT MARTYRS OF THE FAITH. Christian Taylor, who sits right in front of me, read the first one. "On order of the Emperor Diocletian, St. Sebastian was shot with one hundred arrows and left for dead. When the emperor learned St. Sebastian was still alive, he sent his guards and they beat him to death with cudgels."

Christian had a hard time with the last word. Sister Teresita said, "Clubs."

"Clubbed to death?" I heard Mitch Haroldson whisper. *"Cool."*

Then it was my turn. I read, "Because she refused to renounce her Christian faith, St. Margaret Clitherow was sentenced to death by pressing. A stone block weighing eight hundred pounds was lowered onto her, but she did not die immediately. Witnesses report she clung to life for fifteen minutes, trapped beneath the awesome rock."

I looked up at the clock on the wall and thought about how long fifteen minutes would be. I decided pressing would be worse than fire or sharks or lethal injection and remembered the top bunk bed closing down on me Saturday night. I tried to imagine being crushed to death and in a heartbeat found myself strapped to a wooden table, the descending boulder above me blocking out the sun as it came close. When it reached my body I heard my ribs crack all at once. As the weight forced my broken bones into me, the shock of pain made me imagine my organs being mashed like rotten vegetables. My skin stretched, threatening to burst with the pressure.

Nicky Carpelli's voice snapped me back. He was reading about Joan of Arc. How she was bound to a stake in a crowded marketplace. "French soldiers stacked wood around her and then ignited it. Even as the flames scorched her, Joan refused to confess to being a heretic." And I was struggling against the ropes that bound me to the flagpole outside school. My hands were tied behind the pole, and a rope crisscrossed my chest and held me straight. The faculty parking lot was filling with students and teachers, and above me I heard the whipping of the flag. Sean and Andrew were coming across the lawn, each pushing a wheelbarrow loaded with quartered logs. They tilted their wheelbarrows and the wood tumbled out, then Andrew took out a can of lighter fluid and aimed it at my knees. I could smell it. A stream squirted out and splashed onto the logs and soaked my pants to the skin. I heard a match flare to life and looked up in time to see Sean flicking it into the air, where it cartwheeled in a slow arc toward the waiting wood.

I jerked against the ropes and felt my chest hit my desk and my eyes came open. I had my hands behind my back, behind my chair, the fingers locked into each other. I tugged and they came loose. My eyes snapped down to the fabric of my pants. There was no lighter fluid. Dicky Pudliner was staring at me. I turned away.

And so for fifteen minutes I died one death after the next alongside the all-time greatest martyrs of the faith, and even though each one seemed more real and more gruesome and more frightening, with each heroic death I felt something growing inside me. A purpose.

Jason Blevins read about the last martyr on the list. "At the young age of eighteen, St. Catherine of Alexandria publicly denounced Maxentius the Emperor's persecution of Christians. He ordered her to be tortured to death on a great spiked wheel, but the wheel miraculously burst into a thousand splinters. When the emperor beheaded Catherine, it was not blood that ran from her veins, but milk, a sign of her purity and righteousness." My headless body strolled calmly down the halls of Our Lady, wearing a tie and holding books and everything. Students and teachers cleared out of my way, parting to make way for me like I was somebody special. And from out of my neck came a great fountain of my blood, white as milk.

The bell rang out and my hands shot to the sides of my head, and it was there. Comforted, I must have sighed with relief because the whole class looked my way, Sister Teresita included. I lowered my hands slowly back onto my desk as if nothing had happened. I thought about St. Catherine's pure white blood. What happened with my experiment in biology had nothing to do with contamination.

After a long silence, Sister Teresita told us to copy the lists into our notebooks for tomorrow. She ended class by saying, "Understand that although their deaths were horrible, these great saints did not try to escape their appointed ends. Rather, they embraced their destinies and underwent divine and sacred transformations."

I remembered my vision from Saturday night, and my body with wings rising from my grave. And I knew then that Sister Teresita was wrong about one thing: Some saints may be chosen, but some can be made. I may have been doomed by my birth, but Michael is giving me a chance to redeem myself, and if I take it my reward is clear.

Keegan Flannery, I thought, *patron saint of second chances.*

I closed my eyes and saw Michael on a cloud, standing side by side with St. Michael and his golden scales; they were waiting for my answer, something to tip the balance toward either redemption or damnation. In my mind I genuflected in front of them with my head bowed and though I knew it meant my death I said, "Amen."

As Sister Teresita's class filed out into the hallway, I reached one hand up onto my shoulder and rubbed the muscle there, wondering what it will be like to really fly.

By about 7:00 tonight, when Dad still wasn't home, I figured I was on my own for dinner. He works late a lot of nights, though sometimes I think he just uses new cases and paperwork as an excuse to stay away from things he doesn't want to think about. I pulled the leftover pork chop from the refrigerator and decided to eat it cold. I put it on a plate with a pile of potato chips and some applesauce, then carried my gourmet meal into the living room and watched TV while I ate.

I couldn't find much worth watching — I'm not really into game shows — but even after I finished my meal I stayed on the couch for a while because I'd done half my homework, and couldn't think of any really good reasons for doing the other half. What finally got me going was a commercial that came on for *Monday Night Football.* The Philadelphia Eagles versus the Washington Redskins. From the edges of my memory came the betting game Dad would play with me and my brothers when we used to watch sports. He'd pick a team and give points, bet us a thousand dollars that the Dolphins would win by eleven points, or Sugar Ray Leonard would score a knockout by the third round, or Reggie Jackson would hit two homers that day. Even during the game, he'd smile suddenly and say something like, "I'll bet a hundred bucks they'll hand off to Csonka." All the while me and my brothers would either shout that we were in or shake our heads and say, "No way." Dad swore he kept track of all our bets in his head, and after the final whistle blew or the last bell rang, he'd announce our new totals: "Patrick owes me 20,000 dollars. Andrew is about even. Sean owes me almost a million. And I owe Keegan a hundred thousand."

Sometimes Dad still watches football, at least I've seen him glancing over the scores in the paper now and then. I started forming a strange plan: If I set things up like they used to be, when he came home tonight he might sit and enjoy the game with me, and maybe we'd get to talking. Thinking in saintly ways must have inspired me.

The best nights were ones like this, in the winter. We always had a fire on those nights, so the first thing I did was clean out the fireplace since we haven't had any yet this year. Lifting the metal tools from their stand next to the fireplace, I scooped out the old ashes and cleared away a few chunks of wood too stubborn to burn from last winter. Then, just like Dad taught Patrick and Patrick taught me, I rolled up a few pieces of newspaper and put them under the grill that cradles the wood. I went out onto the side porch and selected a few handfuls of kindling from the tub, brought the pieces in and snapped them into even smaller pieces, then scattered them on top of the grill, where they'd catch fire easily once the newspapers were lit. I carried in a few loads of logs. Carefully, I picked three medium-size ones that seemed dry and set them on top of the kindling. I looked at the structure and rearranged the logs a couple times, making space for air and flame to pass through so everything would burn evenly. Finally, I reached my hand up into the chimney and pulled down the metal bar that opened the flue.

Dad was the only one allowed to actually light the fire. So tonight I simply prepared the wood, set a book of matches on the mantlepiece, then settled back onto the couch to wait.

The Redskins kicked off to start the game, and the first quarter came and went without any sign of Dad. Now and then, when the camera scanned the crowd, I found myself staring hard at faces that might be Patrick's. It's sad, but I'm not even sure I'd recognize him. Maybe he's grown a beard or cut his hair. Whatever he looks like, I wish I could talk to him.

Midway through the second quarter, the sound of Dad's

car in the driveway shocked me from the cozy cushions. I heard him coming around the side, so I went to meet him at the kitchen door, and when I opened it there he stood — a brown A & P paper bag in either hand. He looked at me evenly and explained, "Andrew and Sean cleaned us out. Figured I'd restock."

"I'll get the other packages," I said, stepping past him into the cold without putting on a coat.

Dad's kind of a mess when it comes to shopping, and I always tell him I'll go with him. I used to go with Mom and I know where everything is at the A & P. See, Dad never uses a list or coupons — he just wanders from aisle to aisle buying whatever looks good. I've put lists on the fridge, but that's where they stay. In the six years since Mom's been at Hellman House, we've never even had the same kind of toothpaste twice. So unpacking groceries is kind of like opening Christmas presents from aunts who always buy you clothes you don't really like but know you'll have to wear.

I came in with the last two bags and set them on the counter then started helping Dad unpack, a little afraid of the treasures he'd brought home from this week's expedition. Putting some eggs in the fridge, I noticed the new milk was some weird low-fat stuff that I'm just sure will taste wonderful with my Cheerios, and hamburger meat that expires tomorrow.

"Should I try meat loaf tomorrow night?" I asked hopefully.

Dad didn't turn from the cabinet where he was stacking cans of soup. "If you want," he said. "I'm supposed to go to some dinner for work."

I emptied the rest of my bag: butter, orange juice, weird-looking cheese.

"Here," Dad said a minute later, when we were almost finished. He was holding a white box from the last bag. "I know you like these." He handed me the Ring-Dings and half smiled. The truth is, Mom was always the one who loved Ring-Dings. I like Yodels. I lifted the box from his hand and nodded my head. "Thanks," I said, plastering a false smile across my face.

"And for your lunch," he added, pulling out a package of deli meat.

Please God, I whispered in my head. *No bologna.* Last time he bought bologna, I had to take a few slices a day and throw them away until it was all gone, even though I know it's a sin. Is there a patron saint of bad luncheon meat?

I read the label on the bag, "Honey-baked ham."

"Bet you thought I'd forget," he said.

Grinning for real, I put the ham in the fridge drawer and together we folded up the paper bags.

"Did you eat dinner?" I asked him.

He shook his head. "I had a late lunch. You eat that pork chop?"

"Yeah," I said. "It was good."

"A bit stiff. Sean overcooks everything."

With nothing left to do, we stared at each other for a moment. Together, we heard the sound of the TV in the other room. "*Monday Night Football*," I said. "Eagles and the Redskins."

He studied my face. "Head in. I'll be right behind you."

Once I'd returned to the couch, I heard the familiar tinkling of ice bouncing around a glass, then followed his footsteps into his study where he fixes his drinks at his liquor cabinet. I don't know why he doesn't just do it in the kitchen. It's not like it's a secret.

When he came in, he set his glass on the table next to his easy chair and asked the score.

I leaned off the couch and looked back at him. "It's halftime," I reported. "Eagles are up 14–10."

I waited for a bet. He lifted the glass and took a sip of the tan liquid, smacked his lips, and watched the McDonald's commercial.

I settled back on the couch. "I made a fire," I offered. Looking at the logs I'd carefully placed, I waited for him to get up and ignite the blaze.

"A little warm, don't you think?" he said from behind me.

"Sure," I answered. "Better to save it for some other night."

Over halftime, Howard Cosell showed highlights of yesterday's games. Once, I said, "Nice catch," when a Steeler wide receiver gracefully pulled a ball from the sky with one hand. Once, Dad disagreed with a controversial touchdown call in the Rams game. "Looked to me like his knee was down, don't you think?" I agreed. Other than that, we just stared at the TV and watched.

I tried not to think about Michael or Frankenstein or Mom or the Great Martyrs of the Faith. I just wanted to be a son watching *Monday Night Football* with his dad. But the images in my head, and all the things I wasn't talking about, kept building up inside me, like air being pumped into a balloon that can't take much more. Maybe it was all this pressure that made me say what I did.

"Sometimes I look for Patrick," I said. The words startled me even as I spoke them. "In the stands."

Dad was quiet. I can't remember the last time I said Patrick's name to him. Philadelphia kicked off and we watched together. After the tackle, Dad said, "He always liked the Eagles."

"I'll bet he still does."

Dad exhaled. A minute later when they cut to a commercial, he stood and walked over to the fireplace. He took the matches down from the mantlepiece, then knelt. With one hand, he reached inside the chimney and touched the flue, more out of habit than real concern. Then he struck one match to life and brought the flame down to the edges of the crumpled newspapers. As they caught, he tossed the dying match into the fireplace and moved back toward his easy chair. Before sitting he flipped off the light switch, so the blue glow of the TV played with the dancing shine of the fire in the darkness.

Now THAT I KNOW WHAT MY FUTURE HOLDS FOR ME, I feel free in a way that's hard to describe. Usually the career posters in Dr. Connors' office, up on the third floor of Our Lady, get me upset. But sitting there this morning, waiting for him to show up for our twice-a-month Tuesday session, the posters seemed almost funny. The smiling man in glasses with his stethoscope hung around his neck: WILL YOU BE A DOCTOR? Or the nerd with the hard hat studying plans at the foot of a building under construction: WILL YOU BE AN ARCHITECT? Posters like those used to put a lot of pressure on me because I've never known what I wanted to be. I've always had the idea that I was going to screw up some important decision and wind up being an accountant instead of an astronaut. But now that I know I'm going to be a saint, everything's different. I don't have to worry about making straight A's or joining the right clubs. All I have to do is wait for next Saturday, when Michael will give me the chance to redeem myself. No matter what I do until then, my future is set, so I can do whatever I want.

For example, on the geometry quiz during second period, when I couldn't even guess at how to prove that the circumference of circle A was twice the circumference of circle B, I wrote, "It just is."

And when I was one more messenger in the Pony Express from Amy Chiavetta to Christine Melchamp in social studies, I did what I've always wanted to do and unfolded the note on my lap and read all about Amy wanting Christine to ask Ricky Smith if he was smiling at her in study hall yesterday or not.

And sitting there waiting for Dr. Connors, I was filling with the urge to do one more thing I've always wanted to do — break into that file cabinet and sneak a peek at my private file. I wanted to know if, after all these years, Dr. Connors had come to any conclusions.

Connors' first visitation was in third grade back at St. Joseph's, not long after Mom got sick. Over lunchtime Father O'Donnell pulled me out of the playground and walked me to a room where this strange man with suspenders was waiting. Father O'Donnell explained that Dr.

Connors worked for the diocese down at the high school where Patrick went and his job was to listen to kids if they wanted to talk, but I knew right away it was really about Mom and the beach. Everybody'd been asking me over and over about what happened. I told them about the yellow raft and falling asleep on her warm belly and waking up in the lifeguard station. But when I finished, they always said things like, "Think hard, it's very important that you tell us everything."

That first day Dr. Connors didn't bring up the beach though. He sat in one of the tiny kid desks and asked me weird questions like did I prefer being called Keegan or Mr. Flannery. I said everybody called me Little K. He said it sounded like a ranch. He wanted to know if I felt funny being ten years old when everybody else in my class was closer to eight. I told him nobody really noticed, on account of my being kind of small. I remember being afraid he'd tell my secret.

We talked for a while about I don't know what else and at the end he told me that since we were friends now I should call him Mark, something I never did.

That afternoon, I was waiting for Patrick when he pulled in the driveway. I went out to meet him and told him about Dr. Connors. He knelt down on the macadam and looked me in the eye. "Did you tell him about your nightmares?"

"No," I said.

"Good. He loves stuff like that. I'll tell him to leave you alone when I see him tomorrow."

I nodded my head, but I knew even then that adults and kids are in two different worlds, and no matter what Patrick wanted, Dr. Connors would come for me again if he wanted to. Patrick knew too. As we walked inside together, he said, "But if he comes by to talk to you again, just tell him you're feeling fine. Tell him everything is okay."

And that's just what I did. Seeing Dr. Connors was like seeing the dentist: About twice a year he'd come by St. Joseph's and me and Jerry Marple would get pulled out of class to talk with him one-on-one. After Jerry's dad died in a car crash, he spent a lot of time chewing his fingernails, and sometimes he'd cry for no reason at all in the middle of class.

I looked up at the wall clock in Dr. Connors' office; he was fifteen minutes late. Not that I cared, it just meant more time out of study hall. But if he wasn't coming, I was taking advantage of it. I walked over and stood in front of the file cabinet. The top drawer was labeled A–F. That's where my file would be, with five years of "talks."

I tugged on the metal handle but it didn't give. There was a keyhole in the upper corner of the drawer. Driven by that strange feeling of freedom, I scanned his desk, wondering where the key was. But when I heard footsteps coming down the hallway, old instincts took over.

I was in my chair when he came in.

"Sorry to keep you waiting," Dr. Connors said.

I said, "Don't sweat it, Mark."

That stopped him. Then he moved to his side of his desk. "I got held up in the cafeteria. Started talking with Coach Morgan. He says you did him a mighty big favor on Saturday."

I shrugged.

"Did you like being a part of the wrestling team?"

"I got pinned," I said. "Twenty-six seconds."

He smiled that fake smile. "But that's not really the point. The point is you got out there and participated. You competed. Coach Morgan wants to say thanks. He asked if I'd send you his way when we're through here. Sound okay?"

I told him I only had study hall. Down there, kids mostly just pass notes and chew gum when the monitors aren't looking. Me, I don't get many notes.

Connors reached into the top drawer of his desk and pulled out my folder. It had been right there all along, which means he must have been looking at it before. "According to this, your sixteenth birthday is just around the corner. Any plans?"

I thought about the plans that were coming around the corner, wondered what exactly Michael had in store for next Saturday, and imagined myself standing at the intersection of Sixth and Hamilton staring into the crosswalk. The

Beiber bus barrels out from behind the Ambassador Hotel and turns down Sixth Street, bouncing off parked cars. The driver's hat presses into the windshield. In the road before me, a woman with long black hair like Angela's holds a baby to her chest and screams. My legs jolt, my hands flash out to push her to safety, then I turn to the grille of the bus, like a huge mouth bearing down on me. And even though I know the pain that will come, I smile because I'm a hero and Mom will be coming home and my soul will float straight to Heaven.

I hid my grin from Dr. Connors and said, "No plans. Nothing major."

"That's a shame," he said. "You should do something special."

He put the folder down, sat back, crossed his legs, and propped a legal pad onto his lap. All standard operating procedure. Up with the pencil, out with the questions.

"How are classes going?"

"Fine."

"Getting along with your teachers?"

"Fine."

"How's Sister Teresita?"

"Fine."

"You know, she was my theology teacher when I was a student here."

He tells me that every session.

"How are things at home?" He looked up at me here.

"Fine," I said. "Everything's fine. How are things at your home?"

"My home?" he asked, squinting at me like he wasn't sure I was really Keegan. "Well, um . . . fine. Thank you. Thank you for asking." He pulled out a copy of my schedule. For the third time in three sessions he asked if I had given any thought to joining the Spanish Club.

For the third time I told him I hadn't.

For the third time he said I should.

"Why?" I asked.

"Excuse me?"

I said it again. "Why?"

He hesitated, then went into some bit about expanding my understanding of other cultures.

The first day in Spanish class, Señora Schmidt told us all our new Spanish names. John Tyler became Juan. Ed Calla-han became Eduardo. Tony Dickert became Antonio. Know how you say Keegan in Spanish? Keegan. But Dr. Connors didn't ask that.

Out of the blue I announced, "Me gusta comer panque-ques en la selva."

"That's great," he said, nodding his appreciation. "Really impressive. What's it mean?"

"I like to eat pancakes in the jungle. It's the first sentence I ever wrote in Spanish."

"Ummm," he rubbed his lip with the eraser of his pencil. "That's terrific." Then he was writing like crazy, probably trying to decide if my Spanish sentence means that I'm depressed, or that I yearn for adventure, or that it's a desperate cry for help, or if maybe I just don't eat a balanced breakfast. But when he finished writing, he looked up at me and his eyes seemed different than usual. "Keegan, are you feeling alright today?"

"I feel great. Things couldn't be better."

He put the yellow pad down and just stared at me for a time. Then he stood up and I thought our session was over, but when he came around the desk, he settled into the chair next to me.

"Look, I know you don't like talking to me. I know you think this is a monumental waste of time. But I'm worried about you. I want you to get involved with some things here at Our Lady so you can feel like part of the family. You could make a lot of friends this year."

I've seen him watching me and Nathan Looby in the cafeteria.

"It's understandable that you're having a hard time adjusting. High school is enough trouble for kids without having to worry about — without having extra complications."

That word stood out. Complications.

"If you don't want to talk to me, you should talk to somebody else about what's going on inside you. You can't keep it all bottled up."

I felt bad then for my crack about the pancakes, for trying to be funny. Because I realized that even if he doesn't know how to help me, Dr. Connors cares, at least a little bit.

On the way down to Coach Morgan's office, I got to thinking about what Dr. Connors said about doing something special for my birthday. Even before all Dad's stuff about Judge Nicholls coming to take me away, I never liked birthdays. Even though Mom always threw me a big party. Because after she forced the boys to sing "Happy Birthday" and after the ice-cream cake from Carvel was put in the freezer, after I opened my presents but before I got to play with them, she'd load me in the station wagon and we'd drive out to the Consolata Garden Cemetery, out to Michael's grave.

On the drive down 309, I'd hold the present I'd picked to give to my brother. I had to choose one of my new gifts for him every year. And it had to be a toy. I couldn't try to give him socks or underwear. I remember the sound of Legos in a box I'd never open. Shaking it in my hands.

When we'd get to the same strip mall, we'd walk into the

same flower shop, and she'd pick something out and show it to me and ask me how I liked it. What she really wanted to know was if Michael would like it, but I was the best she could do.

Then we'd be on our knees, in front of his headstone like some altar, Mom's lips alive with silent prayer. I would pray too, the Our Father or a few Hail Marys. And when I got to the part where you ask for things, my request was always the same. The same wish that rode my breath across all those boyhood birthday candles, the same wish that was filling my mind as I drifted to sleep on Mom's warm belly at the beach — I'd wish Michael alive, so I could stand up to him, face-to-face.

Morgan stood up when I knocked on the open door. "I didn't hear you sneaking up on me," he said. He shook my hand and I sat down. Morgan reached into a drawer and his hand came back up with a blue grade book. He opened it and slid it across the desk without saying anything.

I picked it up. It had MEREDITH STRUBEK across the top of the page, and beneath the name were the words, FRESHMAN HEALTH, FRIDAY 11:00. My name was halfway down the page. The only score I paid any attention to was the last one. My quiz on human sexuality, one of the reasons I was blackmailed into participating in the disaster drill. But somebody had penned over the three in my thirty-five. They'd made it into an eight. Somehow I was passing.

Morgan grinned. "How's Doc Connors?"

I didn't say anything. I couldn't tell if the correction was Strubek's or Morgan's, if this was thanks for playing dead or payback for wrestling on Saturday.

"Shrinks make me nervous," Morgan said.

I put the book down on the desk and said, "He wants me to join the Spanish Club."

"What for?"

I said, "Who knows?"

He dropped Strubek's grade book back in the drawer.

"Thanks," I said. Even though it didn't matter. It felt like a million years since I was worried about flunking health. I'll never even have another report card. No more comments like, "Student is not fulfilling his potential." But Morgan couldn't know that.

"Yeah," he said, "keep it to yourself. Did you see your name in the paper Sunday morning?"

I told him I hadn't.

"I should've told you. They write up all the matches in real tiny print inside the sports page. Right by the horse-racing results."

I shrugged.

"You know," he said, "some guys like to see their names in the paper."

"Sure," I answered.

Morgan got up and walked around the desk. "I guess you noticed Miscio wasn't in school yesterday. He's out today again."

I nodded.

"Mrs. Miscio called this morning with some bad news from the doctor. Turns out Miscio's got the damn chicken pox. Can you believe that? Well, of course he's not coming back to school anytime soon. Two weeks at the earliest. In those two weeks, we've got four matches, starting with one the day after tomorrow — Thursday night at six-thirty."

Somebody came pounding down the bleachers overhead, two steps at a time. The sound rattled like fake thunder.

"Now understand that this is no mandatory draft. I'm asking you to sign up on a strictly volunteer basis. The decision is yours. Bugalski should make weight from now on, so we won't be in the same jam as we were in on Saturday. That reminds me, I need to talk to Van Fowler today. Anyway, the team shouldn't forfeit any matches if you say no. It'll just look a whole lot better for me. And the school."

He was quiet for a moment then, and I wondered if Dr. Connors had put him up to this. "We practice after school for about two hours, and I'd be happy to give you rides home. Don't let that first match bother you. First time in a combat situation is always rough. But you can't hide in a fox-hole your whole life now, can you?"

It's a shame I can't die in a war. Morgan served in Viet-nam. Dad fought Hitler in World War Two. I pictured my-self in camouflage, charging across a field with explosions all around me. I come across a group of wounded allies, men with missing legs and bloody stumps for arms. A grenade lands on the ground. Without thinking, I throw myself onto it, hoping my body will somehow contain the explosion, sacrificing my life so they can live. It would be glorious.

I looked over the desk at Morgan and asked, "Were you ever shot?"

"What?"

"When you were in the army," I said. "Did you get shot?"

Morgan leaned back and crossed his arms. "I was a Ma-rine," he corrected. "I took one in the leg. Why?"

"No reason," I said. But suddenly, I had the urge to tell Morgan about Michael. I wanted to explain that I already had a mission and it didn't have anything to do with wrestling. I wanted somebody who understood about duty and honor to know about my courage and slap me on the shoulder and say, "Good job."

"If this works out right, you'll wrestle four more matches.

With the one from Saturday, that's five. Five matches earns you a varsity jacket. So what do you say, are you my new ninety-eight-pounder?"

I got up and put my hand out for Morgan to shake. "Thanks, Coach," I said, "I'll think it over." But that was a lie, and I knew it.

TELLING LIES, I wrote in my notebook, knowing that Sister Teresita was watching to make sure everyone was working. Christian Taylor was writing like a madman, and I couldn't figure out how many sins a guy like that could have — I've seen him in the cafeteria saying grace over a stale square of pizza.

Every other Tuesday we spend the second half of theology class going up to the chapel on the fourth floor and giving our confessions. Before we go up, Sister Teresita asks the class questions to help us remember all our sins. We're supposed to listen and meditate on the answers and write down all our sins so we don't forget any in the confessional. I was kind of excited today since this would be my last confession. I want to go to Heaven with a clean soul.

Standing at her podium, Sister Teresita said, "Who can name the Seven Deadly Sins?"

In my head, I thought, *Grumpy, Doc, Sneezy, Blitzen, Rudolph . . .*

But Sister called on Sally Dean. She answered, "Pride, greed, lust, gluttony, anger, envy . . ."

Sister Teresita let the silence get louder for a bit, then she said, "Mr. Looby, can you assist Ms. Dean?"

"Sloth," Nathan said. He didn't even pick up his head. When I said hi this morning at our lockers, he barely even nodded. I figure the infection under his turtleneck is making him sick.

I thought about his answer and penciled in on my list, BEING LAZY. NOT DOING ALL MY HOMEWORK.

Writing down my sins is nothing new for me. I've done it ever since I had Sister Anita for fourth grade back at St. Joseph's. She warned us about forgotten sins. They happen when someone commits so many sins he can't remember them all. The thing is, God doesn't forget. He keeps track. So if you repent, but forget one of your sins, it isn't forgiven and it stays on your soul and you'll end up going to Hell.

I believe in Hell. I see some holes in what the priests and nuns tell us, but Hell is one part I've always known is real. And that's why back in fourth grade, after Sister Anita explained about forgotten sins, I used to stay up late in my bed the night before confession and work on my list, putting down every little thing I could think of. I wrote down sins like burning toast and sneezing during mass and playing Patrick's drums when he wasn't home without asking permission. Anything that God might be upset about. But every time I've ever made a sin list, from fourth grade on, I've always had the awful feeling that there was something more. And after what I saw during my big wrestling match on Saturday, that made sense.

Sister Teresita said, "Mr. Dickert, define venial sin."

Dickert answered, "A venial sin is one committed without reflection . . ."

"And therefore," Sister Teresita prompted.

"And therefore . . . is considered more easily forgivable in the eyes of the Lord."

Venial sins are the good kind to have. I wrote, DAY-DREAMING IN CLASS.

Then Sister Teresita pointed a bony finger at Nicky Carpelli, who made it to class today on time for once. "Define mortal sin."

I didn't hear anything from Nicky, and I turned around to make sure he heard her. Nicky was back there, staring straight over my shoulder. The paper in front of him was blank. No sins. Sister Teresita said, "Read it to me from your notes if you must, Mr. Carpelli."

Nicky turned a few pages of his notebook this way and that, then finally he recited, "A mortal sin is a great transgression that deprives the soul of sanctifying life and deserves eternal punishment."

"Grave," Sister Teresita corrected. "A grave transgression."

I saw the headstone from my vision, and my family gathered around the mound of fresh earth. I thought about what I'd done to Michael.

The tip of my pencil, hanging over my list of sins, started to tremble. Murder is a mortal sin.

I wondered what the penance would be for a sin so terrible. I tried to imagine what would happen if I confessed such a thing upstairs in the chapel. I saw my lips moving, close to the tiny screen between the two sides of the confessional. I pictured the door of the confessional flying open and Father Fitzpatrick yanking me out by one arm. Then Dr. Connors was shaking his head, and before I could explain a thing I was strapped into a straitjacket.

And that would be the end.

But then another picture came into my mind. I saw the spires of St. Mary's, up past Muhlenberg Lake. I saw myself pedaling over there next Saturday, the day before my birthday, and confessing to a priest who couldn't possibly recognize my voice. One who wouldn't know all about me and who would be shocked and assign me a stern penance. It was a good plan.

My pencil had stopped shaking, but instead of writing anything about Michael, I wrote down, BEING WASTEFUL

WITH FOOD. I was thinking about the bologna from last week.

By now, Sister Teresita was out of questions, but we still had a few minutes before heading for the chapel. She told us to open our *The Saints and You* books. While the class flipped pages, she said, "Being human, even the saints sinned. But like you, they suffered penance and great hardships to scrub the stain of sin from their souls and safeguard their own holiness."

I found the right page. There was a cartoony picture of a giant man with thick muscles, standing waist deep in a river with a baby on his shoulders. The baby was Jesus; you could tell by the halo and the funny peace sign he's always giving.

Amanda Jennings volunteered to read. "St. Christopher searched the world for a king worthy of his might, but he found none. For a time, he concluded that Satan's power was supreme and worshiped him. But God entered St. Christopher's heart and showed him the error of his way. To demonstrate his new humility and repent for his sins, St. Christopher took up the lowly job of carrying travelers across an impassable river. At night the frigid waters chilled his skin, and during the day, crocodiles ripped chunks from his very flesh, but still he persevered. One day, a child needing passage revealed Himself to be Jesus, come to reward the saint for his dedication. This tale explains the name of this saint, which means 'Christ-bearer'."

Looking at the picture of Christopher, I wondered how he knew. When the muscles in his legs grew numb under the moon, or when the sun brought crocodiles circling under the surface, how was he sure that this was what God wanted?

We turned the page and Christian Taylor read about St. Rose of Lima. "Cursed by legendary beauty, St. Rose battled with the evil sin of pride. Rubbing pepper into her cheeks and lime into her lips, she disfigured her own face. Furthermore, she wore a crown of thorns and used a pile of broken bricks as a bed. Thus did she resist temptation."

There was no picture of St. Rose, which upset me. I wanted to see just how beautiful she was. And like with St. Christopher, I wanted to know how she knew. I began wondering what penance Michael would give me if it were up to him. That's when this creepy feeling came over me, like he was watching me from close by. I looked out the window almost expecting to see him over the buildings, staring at me from on top of a cloud.

And I started worrying about next Saturday — what if the priest at St. Mary's gives me some penance that will take more than a day to complete?

You can't die with a sin on your soul and still go to heaven.

Sister Teresita's words pulled me back to the class. "Think of what these saints endured! Weigh the depths of your sins against the pettiness of theirs! Consider what they subjected themselves to. What are you willing to do? For the sake of your soul, how far will you go?"

I thought about my holy mission. I thought about the chance that Michael was giving me and how much I didn't want to screw it up. How I wanted to do just this one last thing right. I didn't want to wait for next Saturday at St. Mary's. I hungered now for a penance of my own, something once and for all to make me pure.

I picked up my pencil and wrote down, I KILLED MY BROTHER, then added, BUT I DIDN'T MEAN TO.

In silence and with our hands at our sides, the class filed into the chapel. It's only as big as a regular classroom, but it's dark like a church.

Next to the second row where I was kneeling is a giant stained-glass window of Heaven and Hell. When I took my place I made sure not to look at it. Kids say that it's haunted, that Mr. Dan, the janitor, hears voices coming from it at night.

Nathan Looby, down at the end of my pew, was kneeling and waiting his turn like everybody else. Nathan can't pray the right way — he just holds his real hand over the hook. But he was squeezing the hook so hard that his knuckles were white, and his eyes were shut tight. I wondered if everything was okay. Suddenly Nathan looked up and I turned away so he wouldn't see me watching him, and I found myself staring straight into the red pit of Hell.

Hell is the bottom half of the stained-glass window and Heaven is the top half. All the angels are smiling and praying, or playing harps. Their faces shine white, and a few blow into trumpets. In the center of Heaven, a divine golden light floats above the clouds, but you can't make out anything inside it. That's God.

A river of blood runs right through the middle of Hell, and parts of it are on fire. Sharp mountains rise on either side, and some of the people are trying to climb up. In one corner a demon sticks a nail through a man's tongue. Tall spears line the riverbanks, human heads spiked on top. But their eyes are open, so you get the feeling those heads are somehow still alive. Some men rot in cages, some hang upside down off tree branches at the foot of the mountain, some boil in pots of bubbling oil. The damned have red faces, just like all the demons.

While I was looking at the stained glass, the sun must have shifted behind it because all at once the picture changed. The red color in the flames and in the blood shimmered. The eyes of the demons and the angels all twinkled with life. Red faces and white faces. And for some reason I expected to see Michael in the stained glass, staring back at me from Heaven. He was nearby now, I felt certain. In my pocket my fingers tightened around the list I'd made. My face felt warm, then hot.

I thought, *What if there's another forgotten sin? Other than Michael? What if I die with some scab on my soul?*

The stained-glass window grew larger, like a movie screen coming toward me, and I got dizzy. I looked at the river of blood and thought I heard the rushing of rapids. But when I closed my eyes and listened carefully, the bubbling water started whispering. Whispers coming from the stained glass.

I shook my head and the sound was gone, but when I looked up again the sinner with the nail through his tongue screamed at me, a cry so crisp it stood me up.

Everyone in my pew was looking at me. I thought to ask to go to the bathroom, just to escape, and turned around to find Sister Teresita. But she was right behind me and I almost spun into her. "Mr. Flannery," she said, "it's your time."

I took slow steps toward the confessional, trying to remember all of Sister Teresita's notes on sins, searching for some clue to the one I was forgetting. It would ruin everything if I couldn't think of what it was. I kept seeing the faces in the stained glass. The red skin and the white skin.

The golden doorknob of the confessional felt cool on my hand, and when I pulled the door closed behind me, all the sounds and smells of the chapel were completely cut off.

I knelt down on the cushion and looked up at the screen between the two sides of the confessional. Father Jim was sitting back, but on the screen was a shadow profile of his face with its short, fat nose. The profile came to life and I heard the words, "You may begin."

I said, "Bless me Father for I have sinned. It has been fourteen days since my last confession."

"Go ahead," Father Jim said.

I got nervous. "I told some lies, I didn't do my homework, I was daydreaming in class, and I was wasteful with food."

"Whoa," Father Jim said, "slow down. When were you wasteful with food?"

"At home. I don't like bologna, so I threw away the sandwich I'd made."

"Next time, don't make a bologna sandwich."

There was a silence. I'd wasted my sins too quickly. I pulled out my list and unfolded it. Just a sliver of light sliced through the screen, so I could hardly read the words. Only the sin at the bottom of my list, the sin about Michael, was left, but I was certain there was one more. I needed a chance to think, so I used an old sin to buy some time.

"I was disrespectful . . . to my father."

"Would you like to tell me about that?" Father Jim asked.

"What for?"

"Well, do you love your father?"

All kids love their dads, I thought, so I said, "Of course I do."

"Then I'll bet you didn't mean to be disrespectful at all."

I was silent. From the stained glass just on the other side of the door, the voices whispered.

Father Jim said, "Is there anything else?"

I couldn't think. I needed more time.

Father Jim took a deep breath. "Are you finished confessing, my son?"

I crushed the paper into my folded hands and tried to pray for help.

"Are those all your sins?"

I had the sin about Michael left, but I couldn't make myself say the words. I felt his presence in the air, heavy heat all around me, and I knew he was getting impatient.

And then came the voice. "Are those," it said, "all your sins?" But the voice wasn't Father Jim's.

My eyes opened to the screen. The silhouette had changed. I whispered my brother's name, and found myself spinning inside the darkness of the booth, tumbling end over end. I closed my eyes and felt myself falling, dropping as if a great pit had opened up below me. My hands jerked out to catch hold of something and I felt the corner of the kneeler. The world came still again, but the darkness swirled around me. I got halfway up and turned to the door, my fingers scrambling along the wall for the doorknob, but it was gone.

"Kneel down," the voice commanded, and I did.

"Now calm yourself. Finish your confession."

I closed my eyes again, so hard they hurt.

The voice said, "Finish your confession."

And I heard myself say faintly, "I didn't mean to."

"Didn't mean to do what? You must confess it."

"When I hurt you," I whispered, ". . . when I hurt my brother."

"That's better," the voice said. "There was a fight?"

"Yes."

"And what would make you fight with your own flesh and blood?"

"I don't remember. We were just fighting."

"I see. Have you ever told him you're sorry?"

"Yes. I've tried."

"And you think he's still angry?"

"Yes. I know it."

"Have you ever wondered if he's angry with you for more than the fight?"

A crowd of red-faced demons stared at me in my mind, accusing me. Among them, I saw my own face. Half red — sunburned. The beach. My birthday wish.

And just as I was being sucked back to that summer afternoon, I heard myself saying, "Oh no. Oh God. No." *Mom's hand is tussling my hair and I don't want to wake up, don't want to lift my head from the warmest warmth I've ever known. But then I feel the hot sting on my face and when I look up her cheeks are pink and raw. "Uh-oh," she says, but she's smiling.*

She stands and says something about Solarcaine, then picks me up and starts toward the boardwalk, toward the bathhouse we got changed in, where they have outside showers and giant mirrors.

On the boardwalk, Mom steps in front of our reflections and I see her holding me and there's my face, half pale white and half sunned-red. A borderline splits my forehead and my nose and my lips, cutting right down through my chin.

Mom says, "I guess we're having too much fun."

She sets me down, ready to lead us into the rest of our special day. That's when I hear a sound like she's spilled something hot on herself, and with it her hand grips mine tight, then goes limp. I turn to the mirror and see a white shape on the skin of her stomach, surrounded by the burn, and in the shape I can make out the curve of a nose and the cup of a chin. It's a cloudy silhouette of my face, the shadow I left behind.

I say, "Mom?"

Her fingers are shaking, and I say, "Momma?"

Her face snaps to mine and her eyes are locked open, but she doesn't recognize me.

"It's me," I say.

She whispers the headstone name from Consolata Garden, the name no one in my house ever, ever says. Then she steps away from me, into the passing crowd, and it's like she's floating. Down the steps without touching the wood and onto the beach without touching the sand. I look through the boardwalk railing, clutching the middle bar. Something holds me in place, unable to follow any farther or call for help.

She walks straight at the ocean, tracking sand across blankets and stepping over sunbathers. She wades in up to her waist, then dives into a wave. A second wave rises and falls and I spot her thin arms, arching over her head. She's kicking hard now, facedown, allowing each wave to swallow her whole. The lifeguard, standing in the wet sand, blasts his whistle. People are crowding around him.

Once Mom passes the other swimmers, still aimed at the edge of the world, the lifeguard charges in after her. She looks peaceful out there all by herself, swimming a steady pace, and a part of me doesn't want the lifeguard to disturb her. I want her to reach the calm waters of the open ocean. But she's not rushing and the lifeguard is fast, so he closes in on her pretty quick.

Mom's scream freezes the beach. A splinter from the wooden rail digs into my hand. When I look up white foam is exploding

105

around the two of them, and I can just make out her arms swinging at the man trying to save her.

All at once the splashing stops. The lifeguard tows her back to shore. She seems dead in his arms. I look away. But when I turn back she's sitting in the wet sand, her head tucked into her bent knees and her hands grabbing her ankles. Two lifeguards are kneeling next to her. A man steps up and wraps his dark beach towel around her shoulders, and from somewhere down the boardwalk an ambulance siren starts wailing. As the crowd surrounds my mother, she curls the towel over her head, like a hood.

I should be with her. But when my hands release the railing, I find myself drawn back to the beach-house mirror.

I'm standing in front of my other self, his face evenly split — half red and half white. My twin stares at me, urging me closer, and I lean in. Our two faces are almost touching now and he's angry, breathing through his nose. I'm watching his lips when they start moving, and I try to block his voice — try to trap those words inside him — though they sneak out just the same. Michael says, "Look what you've done."

I lock my eyes and drop to my knees and pray harder than I ever prayed before. I pray to God to make me forget the words my brother said because instantly I know they're the truth and I know what I've done is horrible and I know it's all my fault.

From down the boardwalk I hear Father Jim's voice in the darkness, "Are those all your sins?"

And in the confessional this afternoon I lifted my head and opened my eyes and for the first time ever was sure. "Yes," I said. "That's all of them."

Knowing exactly what I did to Mom, how I failed her, made me sad, but it wasn't a new feeling. Just like with Michael, I'd always known that I was to blame, it was only a question of how. But along with that sadness came a strange new sensation, a lightness. At last I knew all my sins, so my holy mission could go on.

And as Father Jim explained the prayers I should say to absolve the sins I'd told him about, I realized that like St. Christopher and St. Rose, part of my punishment was that I had to find my own penance for what I'd done to Mom. And I knew that fate, or maybe Michael, had given me the perfect opportunity. I would suffer before I was martyred, and it would be my own choice, and that made me happy in a way that's hard to explain.

I opened the door and stepped out into the cooler air of the chapel. The sun had moved and the stained glass was dull and lifeless. Nicky Carpelli, the only one who hadn't confessed yet, stood up and headed toward the confessional, just as I was moving toward the pew. But as we neared, I put one hand up to stop him. I leaned in close and said, "Tell Coach Morgan I'll start tomorrow."

WHEN LAST BELL RANG TODAY, it sounded like an alarm blast, warning me that time had run out. Yesterday accepting my penance seemed perfect — a noble act in my holy mission — the kind of thing I should charge into without hesitation. But when the hour came, instead of rushing down into Rocker, I wandered the hallways for a good fifteen minutes. Finally, I made my way to the locker room. Everybody was already gone. I dressed alone, in silence. The gym was empty too, so only the Wrong-Hearted Jesus watched me cross the basketball court, only He witnessed my slow descent down the stairs that lead to the wrestling room. Through the battered wooden doors, I heard strange factory sounds — the crash of metal on metal and the hush of escaping steam. And I froze then, as still as I'd been on the boardwalk, and I tried to imagine the punishment I deserve for letting Mom go.

My hand gripped one of the rough handles and when I pulled back, the door came open and a breath of heat flashed across my face. I stepped inside, half expecting to see flames.

Instead, my eyes fixed on the muscles of a barebacked wrestler, his arms stretched above his head and held apart by ropes. The ropes went up and out through two pulleys, then down to weights resting on the concrete floor. The wrestler faced a jagged piece of mirror, duct-taped to a black door. His head shivered as he brought his hands slowly together, raising the weights from the floor. At the instant his fingers touched he relaxed and his hands were yanked up and away again. The weights clashed back to the concrete floor.

I wondered what sins he was atoning for.

"McMillen!" Morgan yelled. His back was to me. "Get your ass back on this mat before I kick it to next Tuesday." The wrestler jumped back onto the edge of the mat.

I heard the rumbling machine sound and realized it was coming from behind the strange black door with the mirror on it. It was low and steady but strong, the kind of sound you hear in your bones.

All the wrestlers were paired off, jerking and tugging their opponents, rolling and tumbling. Their muscles were bright with sweat and quick snorts of breath made the whole room seem alive.

Morgan saw me. "Three-Quarters. We were about to declare you AWOL." He motioned me over to him, and I moved along under the slanted belly of the away team bleachers. Over my head, the angled girders had names spray painted on them: FIFTH AVENUE, 42ND STREET, SUNSET STRIP. Just before I reached the mat, I crossed beneath BROADWAY.

I stepped onto the mat beside Morgan and somebody yelled, "Wipe your freakin' feet!" I moved back and found a dirty square of carpet. I wiped my sneakers.

"Welcome to the doghouse," Morgan said. "What do you think?"

The wrestling area is a little smaller than a basketball court; the cinder-block walls have old pieces of mat nailed to them. It made me think of a giant padded cell.

"It's great," I told Morgan.

Above the mats along the wall, someone had spray painted graffiti on the cinder blocks. I read: OLPH 24, EASTON 22; WRESTLING — THE ONLY SPORT IN THE BIBLE; JESUS SUFFERED, WHY SHOULDN'T YOU?; and, WOOF-WOOF. BE A BULLDOG.

Two wrestlers crashed to the mat behind Morgan, who

spun and shouted, "Flynn! Did your mother have any sons? You've got twenty pounds on him."

Past them, in the far corner was the heavyweight, a senior named Van Fowler, lying on top of someone. All I could see of the guy underneath Van Fowler was one arm and one leg. It was like on a cartoon when an anvil drops out of nowhere and squishes somebody.

Morgan called out, "Carpelli!" and I turned to see Nicky coming from the other corner, wading through the rolling sea of wrestlers. His black wool cap came down over his eyebrows.

Motioning to me, Morgan said to Nicky, "Just the basics, right?"

Nicky mumbled something that made Morgan frown. "It ain't baby-sitting. This is important."

Without responding, Nicky walked past me toward an empty corner of the mat. "Over here," he said. I followed.

He stopped, leaned against a wall, and said, "Are you sugar foot or square?"

I didn't know what that meant.

"Your stance. Get ready to wrestle."

I crouched a bit, put my hands in front of me.

Nicky kicked away from the wall and shook his head. "Sweet Jesus."

He tapped my feet apart so they were directly beneath my shoulders, bent my knees more, tilted my back some, moved my arms in so my elbows were over my hips, and turned my hands so my thumbs were facing up.

Then he stood in front of me and got into his stance. He grabbed both my hands with his and that felt kind of funny. I've never even held hands with a girl. He shuffled to the right and pulled me along. "Don't cross your feet," he corrected, "glide side to side. Watch me."

We moved to the left and Nicky's sneakers slid side to side as if he were on ice.

After a few minutes of that, he locked up with me, putting one hand on the back of my neck and cupping my elbow with his other. I did the same to him and we kind of leaned into each other. Then, tugging with the hand on my neck, Nicky moved us left and right, back and forth, around in circles this way and that.

Without warning Nicky dropped from my grip, scooped his hands behind my knees, and drove his head into my stomach, sending me flailing backward. As my shoulders hit the mat, Nicky scrambled up my body and vined his arms around my head. In the sudden stillness that followed his attack, he said, "Takedown." Then he stood up and commanded, "Grab my leg."

I got on one knee, and Nicky reached down and put his

hands on mine and arranged them in the proper positions. I put my head tight against his leg as if I were listening to his muscles, which were hard and sweaty. No sooner had he let go of my hands than he eased both his legs back, and his weight settled into me. My arms burned but I held on as Nicky explained, "Sprawl."

Then he said the word, "Crossface," and jammed one hand into the exposed part of my face, digging his palm in so it cupped my nose. He shoved hard, and the jolt turned my head until I was almost looking behind me. But still I held his leg.

Nicky relaxed for a second and the burning in my arms dimmed. Then he said, "Crossface and sprawl," and his weight crashed over me at the same time his hand rammed hard into my nose. My arms stretched and snapped and I crunched belly-down, flat on the mat with Nicky lying on top of me. My arms ached, my face throbbed, and I was glad. I pictured a drawing of me and Nicky in some future edition of *The Saints and You.*

"Get up," Nicky said. "Again."

I positioned myself again on his leg. Nicky said, "Cross-face and sprawl," and flattened me once more.

"Again," Nicky said and the exact same thing happened. He said, "Again," and "Again," and "Again."

Time after time I got onto his leg, and time after time he

squashed me. I wanted more of this good penance pain, and one time decided to hold on no matter how bad it hurt. Nicky leaned his body into mine, and went knuckle hard into my nose, grinding like a madman. I promised myself I wouldn't let go of that leg and the pain crackled through my body so hot I thought that at any second I might scream. Then somebody else did. One of the other wrestlers.

Nicky stopped and we both looked in the direction of the cry. The team was in a huddle. The heavyweight, Van Fowler, was on the outside, his hands out, palms up. "It's not my fault. I didn't do anything."

Through the legs of the team, I saw the crucified wrestler from the weight machine balled up on the mat clutching one knee. Morgan was kneeling at his side. "McMillen," he said. "Mac."

"I heard it pop," Kook said. He's a senior too, real name Kuchralitz, but everybody calls him Kook, even the teachers.

Van Fowler pushed into the circle and said again, "I didn't do anything."

McMillen rocked on the ground. His face was clenched shut and he was ignoring Morgan. The older Grieber brother smacked one hand to his forehead. "That's great. That's brilliant."

"Grieber junior," Morgan said, "go get Kenny."

The younger one took off up the stairs and the team watched Morgan try to get McMillen to let go of his knee.

Bugalski, the skinny 112-pounder just above Nicky on the roster, spoke up. "I'll bet it's broken."

"That's the season then," Kook said.

Morgan picked up his head but did not turn. "Look," he said. "Shut up."

Nicky paced along the wall with his hands on his hips, bouncing on his toes like a boxer trying to stay warm.

Over his head, I noticed some graffiti that was different from the rest. It was stenciled neatly, some kind of list. I squinted and could make out the top line, THE OTHER TEN COMMANDMENTS. I moved closer and read the rest:

10. THOU SHALL HONOR THY COACH.

9. THOU SHALL WIPE THY FEET.

8. THOU SHALL NOT MAKE EXCUSES.

7. THOU SHALL NEVER SAY "IT HURTS."

6. THOU SHALL NEVER LAY ON YOUR BACK ON THE MAT.

5. THOU SHALL MOVE OFF THE WHISTLE.

4. THOU SHALL STRETCH OUT.

3. THOU SHALL MAKE WEIGHT.

2. THOU SHALL NEVER QUIT.

1. THOU SHALL LOVE PAIN.

If Father Halderman knew about this, I figure he'd give birth. It's probably sacrilegious, and at the very least it's a bad idea. Still, whoever did it is safe. Nobody comes down here but the wrestlers.

I looked back to McMillen, still rocking and squeezing his knee. I wondered how much it hurt. The whole team turned when Grieber junior came back, but he hadn't brought Kenny. Behind him, carrying what looked like a white toolbox, was Angela Martinez.

She was dressed in sweats and shiny white sneakers that reminded me of the disaster drill. I looked at her and smiled, but she was all business and her eyes rolled right over me. Nobody reacted as she stopped at the edge of the mat and wiped her feet. But by the time she got to Morgan and McMillen, looks were jumping back and forth on the team, mostly to Van Fowler. Angela just broke up with him.

She knelt next to Morgan. "Stop rolling around like that," she told McMillen. He did.

Van Fowler asked, "Hey, where's Kenny?"

"On the bus with the basketball team," she said. "Halfway to Easton. Let go of your leg, Mac."

She laid her hands on either side of the knee and eased it out straight. McMillen let go reluctantly, as if it were a baby he was handing over. She slowly straightened his leg flat on the mat, then asked what happened.

McMillen said, "Fowler fell on me."

Angela threw him a look. "Brilliant, Bobby."

"Bobby?" the older Grieber said under his breath.

But Angela didn't pay anybody any more attention, and everything focused then on her hands. Her fingers spread out, massaging the flesh around his knee, barely moving, feeling for something only trained fingers would know, and I thought of Angela's mother, the nurse. Angela wasn't looking at her hands, wasn't looking at anything really. Her face was blank with concentration, and it struck me that she looked like a safecracker, itching for the right combination. Suddenly, she found it.

She frowned and shook her head, but it wasn't a badnews frown. She let go and stood. "Get up. Ice tonight. Heat tomorrow. We probably won't need to amputate."

Kook looked at Bugalski. "I told you he was fine."

Morgan said, "Thanks, Angie. Can he wrestle tomorrow night?"

"Sure," she said, "but he won't be a hundred percent."

"What else is new?" Grieber asked.

Van Fowler said, "We better talk to Kenny. Get a second opinion."

"Lay off, Bobby," Angela said, and picked up her white box. She walked out without looking back. I'd been hoping for some reason that she might recognize me, see that I wasn't completely dead anymore like the last time she saw me. But that didn't happen.

"Who said they heard a pop?" Morgan demanded.

"Really," Van Fowler said. "What if she's wrong and wants Mac crippled? She could be out for revenge."

"Stop it," Morgan said. "She knows more than Kenny anyway."

McMillen backed himself against a wall, and Grieber junior got him an ice pack.

Nicky wandered back to our corner and I followed him. But when I went to get down and grab his leg, he stopped me. "Your turn," he said, and I confess I smiled a bit. My nose was sore from being shoved around, and now I'd get a chance to dish out what I'd been taking.

Nicky got down, wrapped his arms around my leg, and laid his face snug along the outside of my thigh. "Okay," he said, "crossface and sprawl."

I kicked back as hard as I could and tried to wedge my hand in between my leg and his face. He pushed harder into my thigh, so hard I could feel his cheekbone digging into my muscle. Then suddenly my hand slid down into place, but not because I had pushed hard enough. Nicky had eased up. He was letting me do it. That got me mad, and as soon as I had his nose cupped in my palm I jammed it stiff and tight. His face twisted sideways, and I grew warm with the thought that any second he would give up and release my leg like I'd released his.

"Harder," Nicky said.

"Harder," he said again.

His head was still tucked in tight to my thigh, his arms still hugged my leg.

"Ten seconds," he said.

I pushed my weight onto him, stepping in with my free leg. I raked my hand back and forth on his face, pounding his nose.

Pain flashed in my leg, and I tumbled backward. I glimpsed the BROADWAY beam and the back of my head bounced on the mat, then Nicky covered my face.

"Takedown," he declared. "Two points."

He let me up, then knelt and motioned for me to give him my leg again. I did.

The next time he did that "One-two-three" thing before he dropped me. And the time after that he said, "Ready or not, here I come." After that he stopped talking. He didn't tell me what I was doing right or wrong or anything. He just knocked me over and stood me up, time and again. The skin on my face burned, my skull felt like a marching band was practicing inside it, and I could sense the ham sandwich I'd had for lunch threatening to make an unscheduled return. I'd had enough penance for one day.

"Enough," I said. "No more."

Nicky's eyes filled with disgust. Kneeling, he motioned for me to give him my leg again.

"Forget it."

Nicky stood and stepped into me. He reached for my left hand and lifted it to his chest. Then he grabbed my middle finger, the same way you'd wrap your fingers around a knife, or a rope.

I looked at his face, past the strange knot of hands, and Nicky said without anger, "Kneel down or I'll break this finger."

My eyes flashed to Morgan and the other wrestlers, and just as I started to turn back to Nicky electricity shot from my finger straight to the nerves in my legs and — whammo — I was on my knees. The pain cut off, and I picked my head up. He still held my hand tight to his chest, my finger still in his grip, though he was no longer bending it backward. From my knees, I listened.

"This is what's most important in wrestling," he said. "Not speed or strength or skill. This isn't about those things. It's about pain. It cannot be avoided. The only question is what you do with it when it comes your way."

Nicky let go of my hand and I pulled it down and cradled it inside the other. He walked away and left me kneeling alone.

From behind the strange black door the rumbling seemed to change. Like something back there was asleep but starting to wake up. I wondered where Michael was, if he were witnessing this from close by and approving.

Morgan clapped his hands and the other drilling pairs broke up. I followed Nicky back toward the others as if nothing had happened. I knew enough not to tell Morgan.

Coach led everybody through some cooling down exercises, and the team counted out push-ups and squat-thrusts and sit-ups with one loud voice. But during the last set of fifty sit-ups, I noticed Morgan stand up when the team was around forty. I was somewhere between ten and fifteen. The team kept on counting, and when they stopped at fifty, Morgan was already at the door. He stopped and said to no one in particular, "Good practice. I know you guys wanted to work out a little extra."

Bugalski scrambled to his feet and stared openmouthed at Morgan. "Coach," was all he said. Bugalski is the 112-pounder who didn't make weight on disaster drill Saturday, when Miscio was sick.

Morgan said, "Don't go crazy, guys. We've got a match tomorrow night. Showers in ten minutes." And then he was gone.

The slam of the door as Morgan left silenced everyone in the room. Behind the black door the rumbling noise suddenly cut off. Bugalski turned slowly on the mat, and one by one the other wrestlers stood up facing him. "C'mon guys," he said.

"You know the rules, Bug," somebody answered. The team was huddling now around him, closing in. Even McMillen was up, limping.

I stood just so I wouldn't be the only one sitting down, but I backed into the wall and wished I were a chameleon.

When Van Fowler bear-hugged him from behind, Bugalski didn't resist. He seemed resigned. He did not struggle in Van Fowler's big arms, nor did he cry out as he was forced to the mat. I saw him disappear, and the team surged forward and it looked like a goal line pileup. When some of the guys got off, I inched closer along the wall, curious about the smiles on their faces. Four wrestlers held Bugalski down, stretched spread-eagle on his back. The Grieber brothers each secured a wrist, and each shoved a foot in an armpit. They pulled back on his wrists and his arms rose taut off the mat. He winced but did not speak. Flynn and Kook knelt over his feet, cupping his ankles with both hands and grinning over him like gargoyles.

Van Fowler, kneeling now, took a hold of the bottom of Bugalski's sweaty T-shirt. He yanked it inside out, up over his face, exposing the flat white skin of Bugalski's belly. Without warning, Van Fowler brought one hand up over his head. "Woof-woof," he said, then smacked it down open-faced. Bugalski's body twitched. The team leaned in over Van Fowler and watched as five pink fingers slowly rose on the flesh. There was a nodding and some smiles, then Van Fowler began in earnest. For thirty seconds his blurring hands slapped down on Bugalski's skin, stretched like the top of a drum.

The barking started little by little, one wrestler here and there, but soon they melted into one another, and they all barked louder and louder as the beating went on. They seemed like a pack of dogs. Bulldogs, I suppose.

After Van Fowler stopped, the barking ceased, and I could hear Bugalski under his shirt. He wasn't crying or whimpering; the sound was tight and pressed and constant, like air escaping from a big tire.

Van Fowler sat back as if surveying the body. Still kneeling, he said, "Half a pound, Bug. This is a mess for a half pound."

And with that, he made a fist and drove it knuckles-first into the near leg, in the place where you give somebody a charley horse. The leaking noise squeaked at the shock, and became a low moan. Van Fowler stood and Flynn came over. "Woof-woof," he said and punched Bugalski in the same spot. Then Flynn held the leg that Kook had, and Kook leaned up and repeated the words before pounding the muscle.

McMillen limped in and gave him one. Everybody took a turn.

Except Nicky. After the younger Grieber brother delivered his punch, everybody looked at Nicky. He shook his head side to side, hard to even notice. At that signal the four guys let go of Bugalski's limbs, and he snapped into a tight tuck, his hands flashing to his wounded leg.

I was amazed to see the wrestlers help him up, and Van Fowler actually put his arm around him when they walked off. It's crazy, but I swear I heard Bugalski laughing as they reached the door. As the wrestlers filed out of the room, I leaned against the wall and tried to make sense of what I'd seen. And in a divine burst of understanding it all became clear.

Bugalski had done wrong — broken one of the Other Ten Commandments. But he'd been punished according to the laws, he'd accepted the penance for his sins, and so he'd been forgiven. He was part of the family again and everything was all right.

Smiling, I looked up and saw Nicky, the only other person in the room, standing on the mat in front of me. For a few seconds neither of us moved, and my mind fixed on two things: the dull burn lingering in my finger, and the stillness I had seen in his eyes when he spoke the word "pain." I wondered if he was going to "teach" me more.

But Nicky was through with me for the day. He shuffled to where we'd been drilling together and scooped his wool cap from the mat, then slipped it on over his sweaty hair and moved to the strange black door where the roaring was coming from. He opened the door and closed it behind him, looking as if he were going home for the night.

It's weird, but that made me sad somehow. I felt suddenly satisfied with the way the whole practice had gone, and all the aches and pains in my body felt like blessings. I walked over to the weight machine with the pulley, the one I saw when I first came in. I reached up and wrapped my wrists inside the rough ropes, so high up I had to stretch on my tiptoes. Staring into the jagged mirror hung on the strange black door, I saw the raw skin of my face and the sweat bleeding from it. I tugged on the ropes and imagined Michael coming to assist me with my penance, lashing me with a whip for all I did to Mom, burning that sin from my body with holy pain, making me pure for Heaven.

Morgan dropped me at the curb around 6:30, just about the time it gets dark as winter moves in. There were no lights on in the house, which made what was in the driveway even more surprising: Dad's car. Opening the kitchen door led to another surprise — the greasy smell of pizza. I had plans to try and salvage a meat loaf from that southbound hamburger.

But there on the dining room table sat two take-out boxes from Luigi's, down by Muhlenberg Lake. There was no sign of Dad. I put my hand on the warm cardboard and pretended I was a detective guessing how long ago it was brought home. *Twenty minutes,* I decided. I cracked the lid of the top box and saw the perfect circle, no slice yet taken. And the same with the second box, an undisturbed pepperoni. He'd been waiting for me. This was bizarre.

Figuring he might be working or stealing a quick nap — two more avoiding strategies he's developed — I didn't want to yell out, so I crept around looking for him in the unlit house, first in his study, then in the living room. I headed upstairs planning to check his bedroom. Some of the steps creak, so I moved on tiptoes as if I were in a minefield.

I don't like going in Dad's room 'cause a lot of Mom's things are still there. Her dresser — top covered by little perfume bottles. Her bookcase — full of paperback romances. The exercise bike she used to ride — its handlebars now draped in Dad's ties. I wasn't looking forward to opening that door. But I never had to. The door to Patrick's room, last one on the left, was cracked just a sliver. I rushed ahead, shouldered through, then stopped fast at the sight I saw: There in the shadows was my prodigal brother, returned home at last, sitting behind his drum set. "Paddy!" I shouted out, forgotten joy rising inside me. But when the shadow figure's face turned to me, I saw the glint of glasses in the darkness. It was Dad.

"What," I said. "What are you doing in here?"

He lifted a glass from beside the drum set and tipped it to his mouth. "What was the name of that crazy band your brother was in? The Powder Monkeys?"

"Power Junkies," I said.

"Right, right. Power Junkies. I remember now."

I reached behind me and flipped the light on. Patrick's bed was made. A corner of his Led Zeppelin poster had come away from the wall. Dust hung in the air like dirt in an aquarium that needed a good cleaning. Dad was still in his work clothes, but his tie was loosened. He lifted his chin toward me. "Say. What happened to your face?"

I told him about the wrestling team, about Morgan needing a warm body to make weight.

"Fine," he said. "Do you need some money for it?"

"This won't cost anything."

"Sports are good for a boy. They'll give you confidence. Teach you discipline. Like the army." His speech was slow and deliberate. He sounded like a recording of a father, and he again lifted his drink.

"There's a match," I said, "tomorrow night." But his eyes

had rolled to Patrick's dresser, home to a few trophies topped with faceless, golden statues of runners, their luster robbed of its shine.

"Remember how he'd get up before school and jog in the cold?" I asked. "Even in the winter." Sometimes I'd ride my bike to keep him company, though we never really said much on those mornings. "He sure loved to run."

Dad's head hung now, and he seemed to scan the carpet around his feet. "I can't find his sticks. I could've sworn he left those here, but I can't find them."

My mind flashed to Patrick's drumsticks, under the pillow on my bed. "Why are you in here?"

He shook his head, like he was trying to rattle the reason free. "Craziest thing really. I got done early and decided to come straight home. I bought us some pizza. When you weren't downstairs, I came up here looking for you." He paused while he climbed off the drum seat, came around behind the standing cymbal. His steps were slow and unsteady. "I knocked on your bedroom door, and when you didn't answer, I pushed it open. Only it was the wrong door. I was here. Isn't that crazy? I know which room is which in my own house. What would make me go to the wrong door?"

I wondered if Michael had anything to do with this. *Leave Dad out of this,* I thought.

"I don't know, Dad," I said. "Let's get some of that pizza. Before it gets too cold."

"Yeah," he answered. "Pizza sounds good."

"I can heat it up in the oven," I offered.

But he only repeated himself, "Pizza sounds real good."

While Dad sat at the table, I heated the pies and set out some paper plates. *No sense in making work,* I thought. I poured myself a Coke. I couldn't find the pizza cutter, so after I pulled the boxes from the oven I just sawed into the gooey mess with a steak knife, down into the cardboard. Dad took a slice of pepperoni and a slice of cheese, and even though I wasn't that hungry, I took one of each too. We sat at our seats and sprinkled pepper on our pizza, wiped our mouths with napkins, lifted our glasses to our lips and drank. My soda was flat, but I drank it just the same.

My eyes kept catching on the empty wooden chairs around the table — four of them. I tried to stare down at my plate, because what kept conjuring in my mind was a vision of The-World-That-Should-Have-Been. Instead of just me and Dad sitting here eating reheated pizza, I imagined Andrew and Sean and Patrick and Dad and Mom, even Michael, all six stretching arms over arms, reaching for green salad and steaming rolls, plates piled high with sliced meat, bowls thick with mashed potatoes and white corn. All the while, they talked about their days, laughed and listened.

Neither Dad nor I went in for seconds, and the two opened boxes revealed the pizza that was left.

"Guess I bought too much," Dad said.

"No." I shook my head. "I'll have some cold for lunch tomorrow. It's good cold."

He stood up and walked away from the table without saying anything else, into the darkness of the house toward his study or his bedroom, some sanctuary to which I was uninvited. I studied the empty chairs again, five now surrounding me, and wanted to call out to Dad that he hadn't screwed up. He'd bought just the right amount of food; we just didn't have the family we were supposed to. But I was working on that, I wanted to tell him. And sometime soon, I'll be making everything right.

Munching on cold pizza at our leftover table, I was trying to decide whether or not to tell Nathan Looby about Michael and my mission. After practice went so well yesterday, I had the urge to tell somebody. And lately I've had the feeling Nathan knows something's up. He's been acting weird all week, though I can't say exactly how. Little looks he gives me at our lockers, times when he smiles or laughs for no reason, like he knows a secret he's getting ready to tell. But during lunchtime he was being quiet as usual, sitting next to me with his hearing aid out on the table, concentrating on the fruit salad his mother had packed for him, not saying a word.

At the tables around us rumors were flying about an early dismissal. Some monster snowstorm was supposed to be moving up from Philly. "Six to eight inches by tomorrow morning," Tony Dickert reported.

"Old news," said Adam Marshall. "At least a foot."

I decided to tell Nathan about the blizzard coming our way. And, to be honest, I figured once he had his hearing aid in, the conversation might wander to what else might be in our future. But as I was reaching out to tap Nathan, my eyes fell on Angela Martinez stepping through the double doors and into the lunchroom. Most girls crisscross their arms and hold their books tight over their chests, like a Maxwell Smart security system. But not Angela. She presses her books against her hip with one hand, like guys do. So as she strolled through the cafeteria crowd, on those long legs I've watched take stairs two at a time, there wasn't much of anything between her blouse and my eyes. I knew it was a sin not to avert my eyes and look away, but with the way things are shaping up lately, I figured I'd live a little. I focused on the tiny plastic buttons holding her shirt, curious about how far she went with Van Fowler before they split up. As I wondered, her chest seemed to grow larger and larger as if she were walking over to talk to me, and it wasn't until she spoke that I realized that's exactly what was going on.

"Take a picture kid," she said. "It'll last longer."

Nathan reached for his hearing aid.

"You Three-Quarters?" she asked, looking down at me.

I nodded my head.

"Coach Morgan sent me. You're supposed to be in his office."

"Right," I said. "It slipped my mind." I had no idea what she was talking about.

She tilted her head at the door, spilling black hair from her shoulder. "C'mon," she said. I dropped my pizza and hopped up, taking a few quick steps to catch her.

"Are you going back to the gym?" I asked.

She shook her head and lifted the books a bit from her hips. "Study hall," she said. Behind that tan hand, nails trimmed tight, I saw a drawing of the Eiffel Tower.

Side by side, we walked down a hallway lined with lockers. We were alone. The silence felt huge, like an empty church. Normally, this wouldn't bother me. A week ago, when I was still in zombie mode, I'd never even consider talking to somebody like Angela. But things feel different now, and I wanted to talk with her. I thought hard of something to say. "What you did with McMillen's knee yesterday," I finally came up with, "that was cool."

"Mac's a baby," she said. "Can't cut it."

I said yeah and nodded, like I'd always had reservations about McMillen's toughness. "I hope you don't get in trouble for being late," I said, just to keep the conversation going.

"Father Jim's proctoring," she told me. "No problema." She sounded just like Señora Schmidt.

We took five more steps in silence, before I looked again at her textbook. "Wait a second. Don't you take French?"

"I take French," she said. "Pero hablo español."

It took me a second to translate. *But I speak Spanish.* The recognition showed in my face. "Since I was a kid," she added. "I was born in Puerto Rico."

I nodded my head, thrilled with the secrets Angela was telling me. It's not so much that they were any big deal, just that she was sharing. With me. I wanted more. I got so excited that my tongue took on a life of its own, and before I knew it I'd said, "Me gusta comer panqueques en la selva."

Her legs stopped. "What?"

I turned my face toward the lockers, feeling the blood rushing to my cheeks. Then she started to laugh. "You are one funny little dude," she said.

I laughed too, just to show that I knew she meant funny in the good way. As we neared the steps I had to take down to the gym and she had to take up to the study hall, she paused and said, "So tell me something. How come they call you Three-Quarters?"

I hadn't considered the ways that could be taken, and it looked to me like maybe she was about to giggle. In the bad way. I smiled, as if this nickname were an old joke that had nothing to do with how small I was. "That's my favorite move," I told her. "The three-quarter nelson."

I'd heard somebody shout that at the match last Saturday. I had no idea what it meant. Angela smirked. She knew I'd told a lie, but she knew it was a good one. I thought I'd better get out of there before she asked me how long I'd been wrestling or something, so I turned and pushed open the doors to the stairway. She said after me, "I'll see you at the match tonight, Three-Quarters. You and your favorite move."

I found myself actually looking forward to tonight's match, and I was worried that the snowstorm might cancel it. Even though I knew for sure I'd be beaten, Angela would see me try. Maybe I could use that crossface and sprawl that Nicky taught me. I began to wonder if Michael might not be able to arrange it so when my death comes Angela is there as a witness.

Stepping into the locker room, I heard two voices coming from Morgan's office. One was his, the other sounded familiar.

"Stacy's been on this new diet," the strange voice said. "You should see her. She was sexy before, but now . . ."

I walked right through the tilted doorway and looked at the stranger's back. He turned around and it was the doctor from the disaster drill, the same one who'd given us Frankenstein. If he recognized me as the dead kid from center court, he didn't show it. Morgan stood from his desk. "Three-Quarters, this is Dr. Prescott. He's gonna do us a quick favor."

Morgan explained that every other wrestler had a physical before the season started. He said I needed one too, the same way a car needs an inspection sticker. "Just a technicality," he told me, "but we ran into a little trouble last year. I don't want to give Halderman any excuses. So if you're going to be an official wrestler . . ."

The office fell quiet, and they both just stared at me. I had the urge to ask if I got to make one phone call.

Then the doctor turned and started picking through this little black case he had. "This will just take a minute," he offered. "Please take off your shirt."

I undid my tie and started unbuttoning my shirt. Dr. Prescott pulled out a stethoscope and one of those giant Popsicle sticks. Then he asked, "So how's Jenny doing? It's Jenny, right?"

He was talking to Morgan. Coach's eyes flicked to me and back to the doctor. He was not smiling. "My sister's fine. That cold cleared up nice. I'll tell her you asked."

The doctor placed the plugs in his ears and put that cold disk on my chest. "Oh, yeah," he said. "Jenny, your sister."

I might not be Mr. Sex Education, but I could guess why they were saying "sister" so weird. Last year, Assistant Coach

Fremin got fired because he was living with a woman he wasn't married to.

"Breathe in."

I took a deep breath.

"Hold . . . okay."

We did the open-your-mouth-and-say-ahh thing and he asked me some questions about inoculations and he wrote things down on a form and he weighed me. Eighty-four and three-quarters. The exact same as from Saturday.

He took my height and asked if I knew I had a heart murmur and I nodded my head. I heard voices out in the locker room and wondered if they could hear what Prescott was saying. When he finally started packing up his black case, I thought I was home free. But just as I was reaching for my shirt, the doctor said to Morgan, "Do you want to get that door?"

Morgan looked out at the voices. "Doesn't matter."

Then the doctor said, "Pull down your pants."

I froze, terrified. I figured this was a legitimate part of the examination, but I wasn't so sure how I felt about it. I thought about the day I'd found Andrew and Sean down in the basement, behind the old piano that nobody plays. They were looking at nudie magazines and told me to bug off. I was too little. But I threatened to tell Patrick, who was in charge because Mom and Dad were off playing golf or tennis or something. The pages were shiny and none of the naked ladies looked real happy. And there were strange letters from men about nurses and lady hitchhikers. All the men told how big they were — the exact size of their manhood — and that surprised me. So later that day, I snuck alone into the bathroom with my Lucky Charms glow-in-the-dark ruler, the one with the cut-out shapes of clovers, diamonds, and whatever so you could trace them. I held the ruler in one hand and laid myself out on it with the other. I barely made it to the clover. I was just a kid, so this bothered me. I hadn't figured out that like everything else in those magazines, those letters were fake.

But I still never shook the idea that I didn't quite measure up, so as I lowered my pants to my knees, some childish part of my brain almost wanted to ask the question, "How big do I have to be?"

Dr. Prescott snapped on a rubber glove, then stood real close to me, his chest against my face. He seemed suddenly real serious, and he stared down at the floor. Then he reached down and took a hold of me and said, "Turn your head and cough."

"Which way?" I asked.

"What?"

"Which way should I turn my head?"

He told me it didn't matter, so I looked over at the scale

and gave this big hack, thinking that might make a difference. After a few seconds, he let go and stepped away and said, "You can pull those up."

He reached for the form and scratched down a few more things. I leaned over, wondering just what that last part of the exam was for anyway, but I couldn't get a good look at what he wrote. He signed the bottom and gave it to Morgan and said, "Okeydokey, smokey."

Then he packed up the rest of his things and closed his bag. Morgan stood up and they didn't shake hands, and as the doctor was leaving Morgan smiled at him and said, "Thanks. I owe you one."

So that explained it all. I just wondered what kind of favor Morgan is going to do for Dr. Prescott in return for signing me off as normal.

Since there were still fifteen minutes left in the lunch period, I made my way back to the cafeteria. Nathan's chair was empty, but there was plenty of his fruit salad left. Looked like he hadn't even taken a bite. Even stranger, his hearing aid was still on the table, so he couldn't have gone anywhere. Hoping he was treating himself, I looked over at the vending machines, but he wasn't there either. While I was scanning the room I did see Nicky Carpelli, head resting on crossed arms, off by himself at the end of one of the tables the jocks usually take. In front of him was a metal

Thermos. I've heard he fills that with half a can of chicken broth, that that's all he eats all day. The wrestlers call it sucking weight — eating nothing and working out hard to sweat yourself to death so you can make weight before the match. Nicky wrestles at 105, but before the season he was closer to 115, or so they say.

As for me, I've got fourteen pounds to spare, and I was hungry, so I went back to work on my pizza, unfolding the second piece from the aluminum foil triangle. I was lifting it up and opening my mouth for that first big bite when the fire alarm shattered the air and froze everything.

They have fire drills every few weeks at Our Lady. They plan them in advance, just like the Authentic Disaster Simulation, and run them during homeroom. You can always tell, because it's the only time Mrs. Miller yells to keep the aisle clear of books. Then after she takes roll she looks at her watch and smiles and waits, like the whole class doesn't know.

Once the alarm bell goes crazy, everyone gets into a double file line with hands at their sides and in complete silence. Father Halderman is out back in the faculty parking lot and he's got a clipboard like Mr. Strubek's. He shouts for everybody to hurry, but yells if you run because then you'll fall and get trampled or burned up, or both. He waits till everyone is out, then tells us how the latest time was and how many people would have died "had this been an actual emergency." Last time while he was talking, I saw sweet senile Sister Cecilia Agnes, wiping the windows of the library on the third floor. I wondered if she was included in the body count.

So today, since we weren't in homeroom when the bell sounded, I knew it was no drill. Everybody in the cafeteria stopped talking and turned to the alarm bell hanging on the wall next to the broken clock that always reads five till noon. Then Sally Dean screamed and somebody yelled, "Fire!" and that was the signal for everybody to go nuts.

All the kids shoved their chairs out and started rushing for the door. Mrs. Abercrombie and Sister Francis, the lunch monitors, did the same.

I wasn't afraid, and thought it was kind of neat the way they were yelling and pushing to get out like in one of those disaster movies where all the people scream and die in the last few minutes. The mob at the door looked like a place where I could get hurt, and I didn't smell any smoke, so I decided to stay put till things calmed down. That's when I looked in the other direction, over by the hallway that leads to the bathrooms. Leaning out of the hallway, just showing half of his face, was Nathan Looby. He was smiling. Down that hallway is one of those red BREAK GLASS IN CASE OF boxes.

By this time Sister Francis and Mrs. Abercrombie had stationed themselves on either side of the double doors and were herding everybody through. So nobody was looking at me as I slid off my chair and sat Indian-style under the table. It's pretty gross down there, lots of old gum lining the underside of the table like the stalactites out at Crystal Caves. I got that little rush of not being seen. I could only see people's legs and it reminded me of a cattle stampede. The pack of girls' black-and-white shined shoes and the boys' loafers mixed in with the white stockings and white sneakers of the cafeteria ladies. I wondered for a second if Mrs. Stabler kept her ice-cream/rice/mashed potato scooper with her as she fled.

Then all at once they were gone. The only sound was the alarm bell and it was going full blast, so I didn't hear Nathan come out of the hallway and his shoes seemed to make no sound as they passed in front of the table. Down by the door the shoes stopped, and I inched out and peeked my eyes up and looked over the tables, covered with abandoned brown bags. Nathan was standing at Mrs. Olsen's snack table. He ripped opened a bag of peanut M&M's and popped one in his mouth, then headed out the doors and up the stairwell without even paying.

I gave him a little head start and then followed him. I knew he'd tripped the alarm and I wanted to know why. I figured maybe he was going to go steal something else. From below him on the staircase, I looked up through the middle and watched his hook slowly gliding up the handrail, past the doors on the second floor, then at the third it was gone.

Over the alarm bells, I heard the sirens of the fire engines.

When I got to the third-floor landing, one of the doors was still slowly closing, and through the opening I saw Nathan. He was down at the other end, just past our homeroom. I let the door ease shut and put one eye against the slit between the double doors. Nathan was standing at his locker, right next to mine. I couldn't tell what he was doing. Finally he turned and went through the doors at the other end of the hallway. As soon as those doors closed I ran down the hallway as fast as I could. I didn't want to lose him.

The sirens were right outside now, and for some reason they reminded me of the ambulance I heard standing on the boardwalk, holding that railing. I pushed the thought away.

The other stairway was empty when I got there, but there was no way Nathan could have already gone down three flights. I walked up to the fourth floor and spied through the doors.

Nathan was there, just passing the chapel. He turned into a classroom across the hall, and I went through the doors. Between the sound of the bell and Nathan not having his hearing aid in, I figured there was no way he could know I was following him, so I got brave and snuck a look through the door. I saw him in profile, standing in front of the black-board. He picked an eraser off the chalk shelf and pushed it back and forth on the board, sending little puffs of white dust into the air. Then he lifted a piece of chalk and touched it to the board and held it there, not writing, for what seemed like a very long time. I figured he was going to write some funny graffiti or something, but he just put the chalk down and turned away.

He tilted the bag of M&M's up like a glass and poured the rest into his mouth, then crumbled the wrapper and threw it on the floor. He wandered toward the back of the room and I couldn't see him, so I crept around the door and stood frozen against the wall. Nathan had swung open one of the big windows, and was looking out onto the faculty parking lot. I pictured the whole school out there, standing around in the cold and wondering what the heck was going on.

I glanced over at the board, thinking maybe Nathan had written something before I looked inside, but it was blank. When I turned back, Nathan was facing me, eye to eye. He didn't look mad and he even smiled a little, like maybe he was happy I was there. He crossed his good hand and his hook and got a hold of the bottom of his turtleneck sweater and peeled it over his head.

He had a yellow tie on and the knot was perfect.

I took one step toward him and stopped. He undid the

buttons of his shirt one by one, then shrugged it off his shoulders.

Straps for his fake arm cut across his flat chest and buckled over and under his far shoulder. He reached up with his hand and unhooked one silver buckle, then another, and his arm clanked to the floor. There was a small stump between his shoulder and the place where his elbow was not. Then I noticed his neck — there were no bandages on it, like his sister had told everybody, but there was a scar. Nathan saw what I was looking at, and he walked toward me then, lifting his chin so I could see it, a thick pink necklace rising from the flesh. When he got about three feet away, he stopped. Then he turned slowly, just for me, and the scar went all the way around, like a noose. And just as this hit me, he finished his turn and our eyes came together again. It looked like he was about to say something, but then he turned away and walked toward that open window, his step steady and calm, like Mom's had been as she crossed the hot sand.

Nathan slid up onto the windowsill with one hand and then stood up in the open space, and I didn't do a thing.

Standing in the open window, Nathan spoke to me. I saw his lips opening and closing and I knew the words he was saying were important but the alarm was still blaring away. And then he stopped talking and smiled and right then the bell stopped ringing. The silence brought my face around to the still, red bell and when I turned back to the space where Nathan was, it was empty. There was one scream outside and then a crash of screams. My legs started me forward but I froze. I knew what I'd see outside that window and I didn't want to look at it. I didn't want to think about what Nathan had done and what I'd just stood and watched and what all that meant for me.

And I knew that if my face appeared in the window, with all those people looking up at it, I'd be seen. I had to get out of the room. So I headed for the door, already seeing myself hiding in the bathroom stall with my feet up until the coast was clear. But as I crossed in front of the blackboard, something stopped me. Slowly, I picked up a piece of chalk and I closed my eyes and I pictured Nathan's lips and tried to hear what he'd said through the alarm.

Maybe what took over me then was Nathan's spirit, passing by on its way to Heaven. Or maybe it was Michael, spelling it out for me to be sure I understood. But only when I heard the soft scratch of chalk did I realize my arm was moving, sweeping in low, cursive arcs. When it stopped, I opened my eyes and read the words I'd written: *It has to be this way.*

I turned back to the mouth of the open window. The first snowflakes of the storm were drifting past, and a few lost ones were sprinkling inside, carried by a cold wind that crossed the room and chilled my face.

MAYBE I'VE BEEN KIDDING MYSELF ALL ALONG. I mean, what kind of potential saint watches somebody jump out a window? The same kind, I figure, that lets his mom wander lost into the ocean. I could've saved Nathan. Even my two skinny arms would've been enough to tackle him. And I could've saved Mom, just by holding her hand instead of letting her slip away. But I'm such a good friend, such a good son, that when the moment of truth came, I didn't move to help either one. I simply stood there — frozen.

When I got home from school yesterday I lay on my bottom bunk in the dark, spinning Patrick's drumsticks, replaying moments from the beach and from the fire drill over and over in my head. The phone rang a couple of times during the night but I didn't feel much like talking. I don't even remember falling asleep, but it must've been before Dad got home. Then this morning, when he opened my bedroom door and stuck in his head I heard him just fine, but I pretended to be out cold. Maybe I didn't want him to look in my eyes and see what I'd done wrong. When he whispered, "Keegan?" I didn't move, and after a few moments he eased the door closed and went downstairs. I guess he knew about school being closed today on account of Nathan's accident.

Nathan's accident. That's what they were calling it.

Like Nathan accidentally pulled the fire alarm and accidentally walked up four flights of stairs and accidentally took off his shirt and his hook and stepped out a window. Accidentally.

He landed on the grass by the flagpole. About fifteen feet from where Señora Schmidt's sophomore Spanish class was waiting out the fire drill. She had her back to the school when she saw everyone's eyes flash up. She turned around just as Nathan passed the first floor. Something small and dark splashed against the shoulder of her white shirt.

Father Jim and Sister Teresita took Señora Schmidt across the street to the hospital, along with a group of hysterical kids and Marsha Looby, Nathan's sister.

I found out all this in Rocker Hall, where they herded everybody after it happened. A couple of kids came into the bathroom where I was hiding and I followed them back to

Rocker, which looked like a Red Cross setup after a flood or hurricane. Everything was real quiet, and people seemed in a daze. And to make things worse, the boiler had gone out again. So even though we were inside, you could see everybody's breath.

Some people sat by themselves in the bleachers. Others huddled together in small groups on the basketball court. The sound of crying came from everywhere, as if the walls themselves were weeping.

But me, I never cried.

A stranger in a long overcoat was creeping around asking questions and penciling the answers on a long skinny pad. I heard a couple kids say he was a reporter. But when Father Halderman came over to him, they shook hands and the stranger pulled a badge from his pocket. He was a detective.

Sister Teresita stayed over at the hospital, but Father Jim came back and went from group to group, hugging students and leading quick prayers with his head bowed. He was saying things like "God works in mysterious ways," and "accidents will happen." But of course, most of the kids had seen Nathan jump.

And then there was Cindy Richards.

Cindy is Marsha Looby's best friend. She'd been in the girls' locker room for a while, but when she came out crying it caused quite a commotion. In between deep heaves by the pay phone, she was telling whoever would listen that Nathan had tried to hang himself back in September. For obvious reasons this made a lot of sense to everybody, so even after Father Halderman and the detective yanked Cindy down into the boys' locker room, the truth got loose. By the time they rounded up all the buses an hour later and dismissed us, nobody was saying anything about any accident. The funny thing is that nobody was saying the other word either. Suicide.

As soon as Dad left my room this morning, I slid from the warmth of my bed and pulled my copy of *The Saints and You* from my book bag. While Dad clattered around the kitchen making his breakfast, I was hunting for a saint who committed suicide. Some precedent that would make my plan possible with Michael's new hitch. The nearest I could find was St. Apollonia. She surprised a Roman mob that was about to throw her into a fire by leaping into the flames herself. That probably doesn't even count. Saints don't kill themselves.

I heard Dad step out through the kitchen door, and though I still didn't have much to say, I was suddenly afraid to be left alone with myself. Dad's car rumbled to life outside and I dropped my textbook, ran from my room, and jumped down the steps a few at a time. But when I reached the kitchen door he was already backed halfway down the driveway, looking away from the house and me. I watched him drive off.

Turning around, I discovered two things on the kitchen table. One, an unsigned note that read, KEEGAN. CALL ME AT THE OFFICE. And two, this morning's newspaper. The front page warned of a severe winter storm forecast for late tonight into tomorrow morning. Yesterday's big blizzard that had everybody talking at lunch turned out to be nothing more than a few stray snowflakes, so I wasn't going to panic.

Nathan's article was on page seven, next to an ad for tires. HANDICAPPED BOY FALLS TO HIS DEATH. There was a grainy picture that I knew was from school last year because Nathan looked the same except he wasn't wearing a turtleneck. The pure white skin of his neck seemed impossible.

The article never came right out and said Nathan's death was a suicide. There was a quote from Father Halderman about what a great tragedy it was, and one of the firemen who saw Nathan jump said, "At the time, I thought the boy was fleeing from a fire."

The next sentence read, A THOROUGH INSPECTION OF THE BUILDING REVEALED NO INDICATIONS OF FIRE.

That was about as close as they came.

It made me mad that they wrote "handicapped boy" in the headline. That even at the end they had to give Nathan a label instead of a name. I wondered what the headline would be for me. I wondered if Michael wants me to do it the same way as Nathan, or if he's got something else in mind.

I kept rereading the end of the article, searching for some mention of services, hoping for slim evidence to disprove what I'd been thinking. See, one of the popes declared that people who committed suicide can't be buried in a real cemetery. The way he saw it, if your last act is a sin, you can't be laid to rest in sanctified ground. And your soul can't go to Heaven.

I folded the newspaper up tight so Nathan's story was buried and tried to eat some breakfast, but I wasn't hungry. When I decided I wasn't going to eat, I wiped down the table. Then I swept the floor in the kitchen, even moving the chairs so I could get under the table.

I scrubbed Dad's plate and his coffee mug and my Coke glass and put them all in the drain board. Mom was the only one who ever used the dishwasher. And then I was cleaning off Dad's knife. The one he used to butter his English muffin. It was a regular knife, not a butter knife, so even though it had a round tip it still had those little teeth along one edge. I held it under the hot water and ran the dishcloth back and forth across its surface. There'd be a trail of suds, then I'd wash them away.

I dropped the dishcloth and began running my hands under the rush of hot water. I cranked the water up as hot as it would go, and let it rush over my palms till they stung. I pulled them out and took up the knife. I held it in my right hand and laid it flat against the blue veins on the underside of my other wrist. I stared in close and tilted the knife till I could see my eyes in the blade. I read the words STAINLESS STEEL MADE IN THE USA stamped into the metal.

I rotated the blade so my eyes disappeared and the teeth took hold. I sawed back and forth, very gently, just to feel the bite. I swept the knife all the way over and pulled it all the way back, like I was playing a violin. The teeth tugged at my skin but did not cut. I lifted the knife and saw the faint white line etched in my skin. I put down the knife and shut off the faucet.

Once I was finished in the kitchen, I decided to vacuum some. I vacuumed the living room. I vacuumed the stairs. I thought about the gun in the bottom drawer of Dad's desk. There's a lock on that drawer.

Moving into his study, I straightened the law books on his shelves, dusted the liquor cabinet and the statue of Lady Justice with her broken scales, then cleaned away the cigar ashes from around his desk. I vacuumed his rug.

He keeps the key taped to the bottom of his chair.

In the movies when somebody pulls a gun out, they always say something like, "Don't move or I'll blow your face off!"

I tried to picture myself like that, with a head but no face.

First there was a big wound there, then I imagined it all empty, like someone had erased my face. Then I pictured a clean tunnel through my head, and I liked that one best. It seemed a fitting punishment. But it scared me too.

Still in his study, I sat down in Dad's chair and picked up the phone. I called Information and when the lady asked, "What city? What listing?" I said, "Allentown. L-O-O-B-Y."

There was only one number and I dialed it. A man answered after three rings. He said, "Hello. Looby residence."

I said, "I'd like to speak to Nathan's mother."

There was a pause. "Of course. May I ask who's calling?"

In the long silence I heard crying in the background.

"Who's calling, please?" the man repeated politely.

I hung up.

I reached underneath Dad's chair for the key to the gun drawer. My fingers couldn't find it, and I knelt down and looked. The key was gone.

With no vacuuming left, I decided to tackle the laundry. I headed upstairs for Dad's bathroom, but I had to cut through his bedroom first. When I opened his door my eyes fell to his bed and it was kind of sad — one side all rumbled up and the other untouched. He still sleeps with four pillows, even though the two on Mom's side haven't been used in years. On his nightstand was an empty glass and half a cigar in an ashtray. I stepped into the bathroom, scooped the dirty clothes out of his hamper, and brought them downstairs to the laundry room.

The shirt he wore last night smelled of cigarette smoke, and when I was emptying the pockets of his pants, I found a black box of matches with the words TABBY'S TAVERN printed in red letters. I sorted the clothes, whites and darks, just like Patrick taught me, then stuffed them into the washer, dumped in a cup of Tide. On the side of the container a box read, WARNING! KEEP OUT OF THE REACH OF CHILDREN! AVOID EYE CONTACT! CALL A DOCTOR IMMEDIATELY IF INGESTED. I sat on the closed toilet and tried to imagine the cleaning ingredients coursing through my body, burning away the impurities. But would that be enough? After I died, would I be sent straight down because I hurt my brother and didn't help Mom? Or would I stand in front of St. Michael to be judged? I imagined him reaching into my chest and drawing out my soul, weighing its worth on his holy golden scales.

I opened the cabinet beneath the bathroom sink. I pulled out the scale that Mom used to stand on after the Jack LaLanne exercise show in the morning. I stepped on. The dial spun and steadied and I read my weight: Eighty-four and three-quarters. No change. No chance.

The phone rang in the hallway, but I didn't answer it. I thought about Dad's note, but decided I didn't have much to say.

I took the squirt bottle of Windex and cleaned every mirror in the house. Then I took some oven cleaner and S.O.S. pads and went to town on the grime that had built up along the walls of the stove. While I scrubbed, blue-gray crud got under the nails of my fingers, but I scrubbed harder, until I saw the sheen of clean metal. On my hands and knees like that, with my head stuck in the oven, I pictured those people with gas stoves who suffocate themselves like this. *S.O.S.* I thought. *Save our ship.* It's crazy, but I actually found myself laughing.

I put the clothes in the dryer and started a fresh load.

The phone kept ringing, every hour or so.

I took some Pledge and went around cleaning the mantelpiece and the railing on the staircase and all the tops of the little wooden tables under the windows and next to the chairs. Nearly every one had little circles stained into the surface, left over from when Mom had all those potted plants. When she first went to Hellman House, we all were so confused. Dad seemed really spaced out, and Patrick tried to take over in the house. He did the laundry and tried cooking the meals, assigned little household chores to Andrew and Sean and me. But none of us noticed the plants. And then one day I heard Patrick getting all upset, crying almost, and when I came downstairs he was holding Mom's red watering can, pouring water into a pot with these sad brown leaves hanging out of it. Anybody could see it was dead. I looked around the living room and they all were dead, but Patrick emptied the can and went back to the kitchen and came back in again. That's when Dad showed up. "What are you doing?" he asked Patrick.

"We forgot about her plants," he said, sniffling a little bit.

"Patrick," Dad said, "it's too late. Look at them. They've died already."

"They just need water," Patrick said. "We forgot to give them water."

Patrick tipped the nose of the can into a dead fern, but nothing came out. He went back into the kitchen. Dad and I heard the faucet. Dad walked over to one of the plants and plucked a limp yellowed stem. Then, before Patrick came back, Dad went into his study and closed the door.

But the next day after school, all the plants were gone. All that was left were the empty circles in the wood, stains left by the pots. I followed Patrick as he ran all over, checking the shed, the garage, even the basement. We didn't think to check the garbage cans.

When Dad got home, Patrick, his eyes red with tears, met him at the door. "Where are they?" he demanded.

"You're upset," Dad said.

"Tell me where you put her plants."

"They were making you unreasonable," Dad explained. "I had them disposed of."

"Unreasonable?" Patrick shouted. "You're acting like —"

"I won't be spoken to in that tone," Dad said flatly. Then he turned to me. "Keegan. I think it would be best if you went upstairs. Patrick and I need to have a discussion." I looked at my brother. His eyes were still red, he was breathing hard, and his hands were balled into fists.

From my bedroom, I heard their "discussion," the first in a long series of ugly fights. That first year was the worst. They tried to hold things together. Dad brought us to movies, even a football game or two, and Patrick tried recipes from Mom's cookbook, but anybody could see we were all just pretending life was normal. Little by little, Dad started staying later and later at work, and Patrick jogged like crazy during the day and spent entire nights practicing his drums. Andrew and Sean hung out with each other, got into fixing cars and playing basketball. We all just retreated I guess.

I picked up the phone and for the second time today I dialed Information. "What city?" the voice asked. "What listing?"

"Philadelphia," I said. "Patrick Flannery."

I heard her clicking away on a keypad. "I'm sorry," she finally reported. "We have no listing under that name."

I thanked the operator and hung up. It doesn't mean he's not there. I have his postcards and that last letter safe in my locker. He'd let me know if he left the city. If I wanted to, I could find him. I tried to imagine Patrick's apartment in Philly, a small place but with plenty of windows to let the sunlight in. And on every surface I pictured plants, beautiful bright greens with yellow and white flowers, healthy and strong.

Dad finally pulled in the driveway around 7:00. The kitchen door opened and closed but I stayed on the couch watching the beginning of a *Star Trek* rerun.

"Hey," he said standing over me. "How you doing?"

"I made some meat loaf," I said. That hamburger had just enough life left in it. I rolled from the couch and walked past him toward the kitchen. He followed.

I had to use the dishrag to pull the pan from the oven, since Mom's pot holders wore out and we never bought new ones. I brought the meat loaf and a couple of plates back into the dining room. Dad was standing, looking around. "House looks nice."

"I cleaned it," I said.

We sat at the table and I put the pan down. The meat loaf resembled a meteor that had come down through the atmosphere, but if you drowned it in ketchup it was edible. I was surprised how hungry I was. About halfway through the meal, Dad said, "I tried calling during the day. I heard about the trouble at school."

First *accident.* Now *trouble.* Like somebody's car broke down. Or the boiler finally kicked the bucket.

"Nathan Looby killed himself," I said, jamming my knife down into the Heinz for the last of the ketchup.

"Yes, I heard about it last night. I was worried."

I pictured him at Tabby's Tavern, sitting alone on a stool at the end of the bar, overhearing some waitress or business-man. "Did you hear what happened at Our Lady? Some kid jumped out a window." What, I wondered, did my father hope for in that moment?

"You were asleep when I came home. And I didn't want to wake you this morning."

"Okay," I said. "I get it. You heard about Nathan and you were worried." For the first time I looked my father in the face. His eyes didn't waver.

"So you knew this boy?" he asked.

"Sure," I said, my voice back to calm. "Everybody knew him."

"I understand everyone was outside. Did you see any-thing?"

I pictured Nathan standing in the open window. His lips moving but no words coming out. If I told Dad the truth, what would he do? Those images were filling my mind, mixing in with Michael and Mom, but I couldn't see a way to let them loose. "I saw it all," I said.

From the corner of my vision, I saw Dad nod gravely. "He must have been very disturbed."

I shrugged.

"Father Halderman called us downtown, asked if we'd be discreet with our investigation. I told him it was all standard procedure with a case like this. A simple inquiry. Dougherty's a good man, he'll find out why this Nathan was so upset."

That's when I figured out why he was grilling me. Our friendly little chat was part of the official investigation. He wasn't being a concerned father, just a good district attorney.

I went quiet for a while, and he must have realized I was on to him. Because all of a sudden he tried to act like a dad. "I guess they had to cancel the wrestling match last night," he said. "On account of what happened."

"Postponed," I told him.

"When is your next one?" he asked.

"Tomorrow night," I answered. "St. Francis."

With my last fork of meat loaf, I mopped up a swirl of ketchup. Dad asked if I wanted some more. Like he was going to cut it. Though I was still plenty hungry, I just shook my head. "No," I said. "I've had about all I can take."

WHEN I WOKE UP THIS MORNING I was just able to catch the fading whisper of a dream I had last night, a dream of flying. I remembered dive-bombing the geese at Muhlenberg Lake, sending them scattering over the water. I remembered circling above Our Lady of Perpetual Help, waiting to descend on it. I remembered the roar of wind in my ears and the rush as I shot headlong into a bank of bright clouds. I remembered the thrill of wings.

But once I came to, I knew it was just a joke my mind was playing on me. After all that I've done, I've got as much chance of becoming some winged saint as I do of taking Angela Martinez to the prom.

Outside my bedroom window the snow yesterday's paper predicted had fallen. In the distance, I heard the familiar whine of a snowblower and the angry scrape of shovels. I headed downstairs into the quiet house, peering into the empty study before stepping into the kitchen. At the window, I brushed the curtain aside and saw the tracks Dad's car left in the snow in the driveway earlier this morning. No doubt he braved the storm to get to the courthouse, his home away from home. Beyond the driveway, soft white coated the neighborhood — pine trees and rooftops, bushes and parked cars.

In the before-time, before Patrick left, before Mom got sick, before I screwed everything up, big snowstorms like this meant something special. Dad would crank up the then-brand-new snowblower while we boys reached for our shiny shovels. It was just like with the leaves in the fall. I had this little red plastic job that hardly scooped anything, but Patrick always worked close by me and helped with his metal one. On days like that, even the cold bite on my cheeks felt good. And since there were five of us, our sidewalk and driveway never took us long, even with Andrew and Sean having occasional snowball battles. When we finished though, we never came straight inside. Dad would lead us down the street, first to Mrs. DeLiberto's house, then usually to the Katners'. Sometimes we'd help out the Liebermans, even though they had two teenage boys. Dad used to always say that it was because we had the only snowblower in the neighborhood, but it was more. We were different, I knew. We were the Flannery clan, sons of Keegan Flannery. You could see it in people's faces, how special we were. The way Mrs. DeLiberto pulled back the curtain and smiled at us and waved her wrinkled hand. The way Mr. Lieberman, chest heaving from shoveling, tipped his head and extended his arm when my father approached, pulling off his glove to offer him his open hand.

Afterward, fingers numbed inside mittens and toes frozen inside boots, we'd trudge home feeling sore and good. Mom would be waiting with four mugs of Swiss Miss and a cup of coffee for Dad, maybe some pancakes or French toast. Before Dad went in to work late, he'd build a quick fire, and we would collect around it, sipping the last of our hot chocolate, crafting plans for the snow day with Mom: making snow angels, ice-skating on the pond at Union Terrace, sledding on Flexible Flyers.

I stepped back from the kitchen window, letting the curtain fall on that snowy, peaceful world. I made myself a breakfast of Pop-Tarts and Coke, which I brought into the living room. Morning passed with me on the couch, kept company by bad cartoons and the tattered blanket that's been around since I was a boy. Every now and then I'd think about digging the battered snowblower from the garage and clearing off the walk, but I figured the snow wasn't going anywhere, and Dad wasn't likely to come home anytime soon.

About 12:00 the phone rang. I could just reach it from the couch.

It was Morgan. The St. Francis Assassins had postponed our match with them tonight on account of the storm. It's been rescheduled for Tuesday.

"Bad break," I said. Like I was really looking forward to having somebody beat me up tonight. "Maybe I'm a curse. I join your team and you have two matches called off."

"I don't believe in curses. Besides, we'll make them up," he said. "But, look. It's too late to call a practice today. Half the guys aren't even home. Tomorrow, I think we might have a . . . a gathering at school. We can't go three days without a workout. Now it's not an official practice, because Father Halderman would have a bird if I held an official practice on a Sunday. Catch my drift?"

"Loud and clear," I said. "Roger that."

Morgan said he'd be by about 12:30 tomorrow to pick me up.

I had just hung up the phone when I heard a noise at the door. I figured it was Dad, but then a bundle of envelopes spilled through the mail slot. I guess the old cliché's true about mailmen making it through snow and sleet and all that. I went over and gathered the stack, then retreated to the couch and the warmth of the blanket. Hoping against hope for word from Patrick, I started thumbing through the mail. He'd know what I should do. Maybe he'd tell me to run away like he did, and I could live with him in Philadelphia, if that's where he still is.

Suddenly, I stopped flipping and my heart skipped a beat. The postmark on the last envelope read, Philadelphia. But when my eyes darted to the corner they found only the neat printing of the not-so-unfamiliar return address: Hellman House.

For a long time these bills were the only way I knew for sure Mom was still alive. I've never had the guts to open one. I wonder if they itemized the price of this and that, if they tell all the things they do to her.

I think Dad's going to go see her soon. It's been about four weeks, maybe five, so he's due for a visit. Nights he goes there, I know enough not to wait up for him.

As for myself, I only got to visit Hellman House one time. Dad drove us, Patrick and Sean and Andrew and me, down 309 and out into the country. The first thing I really remember is being surprised as we pulled up to the building — there were no gargoyles. I'd always pictured it with gargoyles.

After we parked, Dad handed Andrew a comb and told Sean to tuck in his shirt. Patrick held my hand as we walked up these stone steps and into the building. A doctor, Carl Becker, met us and shook hands with Dad. I remember not liking him because his name sounded evil to me, like a mad scientist's. We followed him up some stairs and into a hall- way with black and white tiles on the floor. It looked like a chessboard.

I saw a water fountain way down at the end of the hall- way and was really thirsty, but I stayed close to Dad and Patrick. Dr. Becker whispered to Dad and they went through a double door. The rest of us had to sit on wooden chairs with no arms in the hall. While we were waiting, Patrick bent down to my ear and said, "She might look a little dif- ferent."

A few minutes later, Becker came out for Patrick, and then later he came out for both Andrew and Sean. They left me in the hallway with a nurse in a white hat. She asked me silly questions, like what sports did I like to play and what did I want to be when I grew up.

My mouth was really dry, but I didn't want to miss my chance.

Finally the doctor called me in, and when I stepped in- side there was Mom. She was standing up, rising off a red couch with her arms swinging open to me. She was wearing a white robe, and as her arms spread out she looked like a beautiful bird about to take flight. I ran to her and she swooped down and her arms folded around me and she said, "I'm sorry. I missed you. I missed you. I'm sorry."

My head was resting on her shoulder, and I remember looking and seeing the doctor smiling at Dad, who nodded and watched us hugging. Mom sat me on the couch next to her and held my hand on her lap. Patrick and Sean and Andrew all started telling her about how school had been, and Mom listened and smiled as they spoke, but her eyes stayed on me. Up close, I noticed her face seemed thinner — I could see where the bones in her cheeks were, and I wondered if that was what Patrick meant. The doctor said, "Eileen, don't you think it's wonderful that Sean made the junior varsity basketball team?" And Mom didn't take her eyes off me when she said, "Yes, it is. It's so wonderful I can't believe it."

She started rubbing the same spot on the back of my hand, and it began to burn a little, but I didn't say anything. Dr. Becker said to me, "Aren't you happy to see your mother?"

She stopped rubbing my hand and the muscles in her face went tight like the question made her angry, but she didn't turn. I said, "When can she come home?"

Patrick smiled at me and the doctor opened his mouth but it was Mom who said, "Soon. Very soon now."

The boys talked for a long time and Mom listened and

rubbed the same spot raw on my hand and the doctor threw in little questions every now and then.

It was hot in that room with the red couch. And there was a water fountain straight across from the couch, just inside the doors. I looked at it while the boys talked to Mom. After a while Dr. Becker looked at his watch and said it was time for our visit to be over. Mom didn't look sad when he said it; she just stood up and went over to Dad and put her arms around him. He held her. I think he smiled.

Patrick asked the doctor if he could ask him a question and the doctor said, "Of course, young man."

They went off, smiling, to one side of the room by a big window that looked out on pine trees. Dad didn't seem to mind, but he stopped hugging Mom and followed them. With Dad and the doctor occupied, I made a break for the water fountain.

It had a foot pedal, and when I stepped on it I could hear the splash of water up above, but it was too far up for me to see it. I put both my feet on the pedal and leaned forward, up on my tiptoes, and my eyes just got over the top so I could see the arc of water. Suddenly, Mom's hands were under my armpits and she came in close to me and lifted me up to get a drink. The water stopped until she put her foot onto the pedal. As I slurped at the cool water, she kissed the back of my neck and her hands squeezed my ribs and she whispered, "Michael, it was all my fault. Please forgive me."

I didn't understand what that meant then, but I should've. If I knew then what I know now, I could've turned and told her the truth — that she had nothing to do with what happened to Michael. That it was my fault. I know that would've made her feel better and maybe then they would've let her come home with us that same day and Dad would've gone back to the way he was and everything would've been okay.

But of course, none of that happened because I didn't say anything. After she said those words, she put me down and I turned around to hug her because that's what I wanted to do, but I saw Dr. Becker, standing now just behind her, holding his chin in one hand. Dad and Patrick were next to him. They had heard. All the smiles were gone.

On the long drive home there was no music and nobody talked in the car and when I saw Sean and Andrew fall asleep on either side of me in the backseat, I thought it was a good idea so I tilted my head back and pretended. But I stayed awake, which is the only reason I heard the one word Dad said on that return trip. It was dark by then, and we had just come over the 309 hill. Patrick turned and looked at us in the backseat but my face was in the shadows and my eyes were closed enough that I fooled him. He looked out the window, away from Dad, and said, "Mom's not getting better, is she?"

And Dad's head tilted back and his eyes flashed in the rearview mirror and they looked right at my face and he said, "No."

So I've always known how Dad feels about who's to blame. Michael's not the only one who wants me gone.

The envelope from Hellman House was trembling in my hand. I worked my finger inside one edge and was about to rip away, fevered with the thought that some diagnosis inside might prove my innocence to Michael and Dad and everyone. But then I had a terrible thought: *What if the letter says I'm right?* What if it's a report about how Mom can never come home as long as I'm here? After all, Patrick and Andrew and Sean, they all visited Hellman House again over the years, but not me. I was like poison to Mom, deadly. I dropped the letter as if it were hot, then shuffled it back into the bundle. But even after I'd thrown the stack onto Dad's desk, even after I slammed the study door tight, I still felt the letter calling to me. I ran down to the basement, where I fished out my snow boots from behind that ratty old piano, the one with half the keys missing. It looked to me like it was smiling, laughing at me with broken teeth.

I wasted the better part of an hour trying to get the old blower started. I pulled the spark plug and cleaned out the filter, all the little tricks Patrick had shown me. But no matter what, when I yanked the starter cord, the engine would just cough and hack, rattle for a moment then die. Finally I gave up, grabbed one of the metal shovels and headed into the tundra. Once I got into the rhythm of work, I started to feel a little better. From the front steps, I could hear other shovels, grating distant sidewalks, but snow does something to sound, softens it somehow, so the grating was pleasant, and I felt like I could stand there forever, breathing the cold air and feeling my skin tingle with the chill.

During the day, some people had walked along the sidewalk of course, and when I started in there I forced the blade of the shovel in deep to try and get beneath the footprints they'd pressed down. About six inches had fallen altogether, and the snow on the very bottom was heavy, the kind of snow you can pack a good snowball with. It was hard work, but I was glad for it and I concentrated on trying to make a perfectly even path, two shovel-widths wide. I'd scoop one shovel on the right side and lift and dump the load sideways, then step to the left and do the same. I tried to cut out perfect squares, just to have something to keep my mind from all the places I didn't want it to go.

It seemed like a long time until I reached the end of the sidewalk, but when I did I was upset, as if I'd been hoping for it to go on forever. I turned around for the first time, to survey the job I'd done, and that's when I saw the footprints, set out before me like the shoes painted on the floor of dance schools.

There was only one set, left by someone who came along very early in the morning, early enough for the prints to turn to ice so they held tight to the concrete while the others were scraped off.

The footprints led back to the house, and as I walked along with them, I noticed my stride was about the same. I eased my right foot onto one of the prints and it settled into the mold and fit precisely. I leaned my left foot forward and laid it down onto the next footprint. I took another step and another and found walking on the footprints easy, natural. And when the trail led past the front door and left the sidewalk, breaking into the snow of the side yard, I had no choice but to follow.

They brought me into the middle of the yard, and then just before the fingery shadow of the bare oak tree, they stopped. In front of me was a field of white snow, unmarked.

I knew that the wind had probably blown snow into the rest of the footprints, that no one had walked around the house and then flown off into the sky, but I couldn't help wondering what I would've seen if I had looked outside this morning. If Michael had really been there checking up on me, or if my mind was slipping even further.

Beneath that sprawling gray sky, I felt suddenly as if God were watching me, staring down on me with the same accusing eyes my father had flashed in the rearview mirror on the drive home from Hellman House. The eyes of the Wrong-Hearted Jesus. I knew the sins I was being judged for. Failing my friend, failing my mother, failing my brother. All these failures stacked on one side of St. Michael's scales, and now on top of them I could heap failing my father. No matter how hard I tried, I couldn't think of a single good thing I'd done to balance them out.

I turned around and held my arms straight out at my shoulders and let my body fall backward into that perfect patch, breaking a cross into the snow. Then I swung my arms over my head and down to my sides, and opened and closed my legs, plowing crunchy snow. I don't know why I was doing it — I only know that it felt right, and even as cold snow shot into my ears and up onto my face, I heard myself laughing.

I don't remember stopping the motion of my arms and legs, then all at once I was at rest, and the snow blew in over my face and threatened to cover me, but I didn't move. Even though it would be a week ahead of schedule, I wanted to close my eyes and let the snow take me, bury me in the center of the only angel I'll ever be a part of.

~~13~~

6

Instead of going to mass today like a good Christian, I made my pilgrimage to Rocker Hall and Morgan's secret wrestling practice, hoping to receive more of my penance. The honorable Reverend Nicholas Carpelli, leader of the Church of the Stinky Black Hat Drenched in Holy Sweat, was happy to oblige. After warm-ups he preached to me again from the Book of the Killer Takedowns, knocking me to the mat more ways than I could count. Then he blessed me with a hands-on sermon about the importance of hand control when trying to escape from bottom position, and the sacred need for quick explosions of speed. Finally he worked on my conversion from the pagan philosophy of giving up once you're on your back, lecturing me on the bridge — a move from flat on your back where you pop all your weight onto your head and your feet, arching your spine until it feels like it's ready to snap. By the time Morgan blew his whistle to end practice, I was dizzy with exhaustion and death seemed like an easy way out.

But practice wasn't over, and Morgan called the team around him and Kook so he could demonstrate something new, a headlock. I stood close to Morgan as he hugged Kook in a strange way, one arm around his neck and the other under his armpit. Coach locked his hands and turned away, slowly bending and lifting Kook onto his hip. He was doing it in slow motion so Kook just rocked there. In a flash Morgan sprang up from his crouch and ripped Kook's head and shoulder downward, and Kook's legs spun overhead and his body smacked onto the mat with a mighty *whomp!* that echoed across the wrestling room. Coach ended up sideways across Kook's chest, still locking his arm and neck tight.

"Woof-woof, Coach," Bugalski said.

Behind me Grieber junior whispered, "They ought to get a room." Which I guess was funny because I've seen couples in movies like that, lying on a sunny beach or in a grassy field.

After a bit more instruction, Morgan sent us back into our pairs and counted out the steps — One, step in. Two, pull. Three, spin. And all this time Nicky simply held me in the upright position. But when Morgan said, "Four, throw!" Nicky became a blur and suddenly my body snapped forward and cartwheeled through the air. My ankles cracked together and I was on my back, Nicky staring into my face without emotion. "This is when you'd need to try that bridge," he explained.

Nicky let me up and we did it a couple more times. I noticed some of the other pairs weren't ending up on the mat, or were just kind of falling over. Morgan blew his whistle and stopped everybody, then had the team form a half circle around me and Nicky.

"Throw him, Nicky."

Nicky touched my feet with his so I was standing in the right way. Then he got a hold of me, stepped back, twisted a little before moving in, and then *whoosh-whack* — up and over I went. I was flat on my back looking at the girder spray painted 42ND STREET. Nicky was holding my head down and lying across my chest. Morgan came into view above Nicky's black-capped head. He looked down at me and said, "See, that's perfect."

Coach turned to the wrestlers. "You guys give too much resistance to your partners. You'll never learn how to throw in a match unless you can throw down here. And for that, you need a good partner. Like Three-Quarters here."

Keegan Flannery: Model Throwing Dummy.

After that, Nicky threw me till I was on the verge of throwing up. Then Morgan blew his whistle and changed the drill. "Top man," he said, "throw and hold. Bottom man, escape. Sixty seconds."

From the matwork Nicky had already practiced with me, I knew a couple ways to try and wriggle free. And earlier, Nicky had gone half speed, letting me loose if I did the technique close enough to being right.

So once again Nicky headlocked me onto the mat, only this last time he stayed on top of me, tucking his head in tight to my chest and sticking that stinky black hat of his into my nose. I squirmed and kicked and tried to squeeze my head out. When that didn't work I tried to lock my hands around Nicky's waist so I could roll him across my body, but he had my elbow pinched between his shoulder and his head, so my arm was locked straight up into the air. My hand twitched weakly, like a swimmer signaling for help just before going under. I tried hooking one of his legs with mine to help with the roll, but my feet couldn't even find them. Nothing was working, so I just lay there pinned, defeated.

"Time!" Morgan yelled, but Nicky didn't release me. His arm around my neck squeezed tighter, and the weight on my chest doubled, and with his face buried in my chest he said, "Move."

All at once I couldn't breathe and my ribs felt like they were about to crack. He was crushing me.

"Move," he commanded.

Forgetting about techniques, I began to buck back and forth wildly, but I couldn't shake him. My legs flopped about, and I struggled to get my arm free, but it was useless. I needed to breathe. I blinked hard, blackness hazing in around the edges of my vision. I stopped moving and gasped, "I give up."

The pressure on my chest vanished, and I sucked in a great gulp of air. Nicky lifted his face and looked at me. I thought he was about to get off my chest and let me up. But instead he opened his mouth and sank his teeth into my bicep, biting into my flesh.

I screamed with the burning pain, sharp as a dozen bee stings, and tried to yank my arm free, but his head just followed. He jerked his head side to side like a dog shaking a chew toy, and it felt like something was about to rip off and that's when I thought, "He's trying to eat me."

Then two thick hands locked onto Nicky's face from behind. Fingers forced into the corners of Nicky's mouth and peeled back his cheeks, which flared wide enough to give me a full view of all his teeth.

Right when Nicky's teeth came loose, the pain in my arm flashed brighter for an instant.

Morgan, behind Nicky, pulled on his cheeks like he was reining in a horse, and Nicky released me from the headlock.

The other wrestlers circled around us. Nicky put his hand up, like he was signaling for a friendly car to stop, and Morgan let go. "No more, Nicky," Morgan shouted. "You're 112, as of now. We can forfeit 105 with Three-Quarters weighing in. You're over the edge."

Nicky stood up and walked over to his hat. I couldn't remember when it came off. He scooped it off the mat and yanked it down over his ears. "I'm 105," he said. "Or nothing."

Morgan got up and watched Nicky walking over to his jump rope. Coach noticed everyone looking at him. Nicky's too good to kick off the team. Morgan can't afford it. Still eyeing Nicky, he put his hands on his hips and announced, "Showers."

The team, minus Nicky, started shuffling out of the room, and Morgan examined my arm. I'd been branded by a jagged purple ring.

Morgan said, "Let's get this washed up," and led me toward the stairs. I looked over my shoulders at Nicky, skipping now inside the buzz of his jump rope.

"That boy's sucking too much weight," Morgan said. "Ignore him."

But ten minutes later, after Morgan finally let my arm be, when the team was showering, I left the locker room and walked alone across the basketball court. I went through the battered doors, listening for the whir and smack of the rope, but the room was silent except for the low rumble behind the strange black door with the mirror shard. I moved toward my own reflection. The doorknob felt warm, and when I pulled it open, a wave of heat rolled out. Inside was the boiler, a gigantic twelve-foot-tall metal egg that heats the whole school and the convent too, when it's working.

As I stepped in, I heard a blast of steam overhead.

Pipes crisscrossed above the egg, came together in a knot of joints, and connected to the boiler in a single pipe as thick as a cannon. Down by the main pipe, knobs and dials dotted a panel. Above it hung a sign so grimy I could only make out one word: DANGER.

The chamber ran the length of the wrestling room, and above the maze-work of pipes the angled girders broke through the wall. They attached to thick concrete columns on both sides of the boiler, like the stone columns in the heathen temple that Samson brought down.

Steam blasted again from two or three pipes nearby, and I followed them back and down to the cannon one by the danger sign. Everything was connected.

I couldn't figure out where Nicky was. I looked along the back wall for a secret doorway, but there were only more pipes. Some of them were leaking, dripping water into puddles on the floor. The puddles reflected the only source of light, a bare bulb hanging among the pipes. And up next to the light, squeezed in beneath the pipes, was where I found Nicky, lying facedown on top of the egg, arms hugging the side.

"Woof!" he barked, then slid down. He landed in a puddle. Up so close, his face looked like it was bleeding sweat.

I asked, "What are you doing?"

"Burning weight," he answered. He patted the boiler's side. "Me and my girlfriend."

I nodded, pretending to understand. I hung my head and looked down at the floor, where tools were scattered. Nicky explained, "Halderman's too cheap to spring for a new boiler. Poor Mr. Dan's got to nurse this old monster so it don't blow up."

But I didn't care about the janitor. I suddenly wanted to ask Nicky why he was doing all this to himself, starving himself and working so hard it made him crazy. I wanted to know why being 105 was so important to him. Normally I'd never have the guts, but these aren't normal times. So I said, "Hey Nicky, how come you do all this?"

He looked at me for a second, then smiled and nudged past me. He opened the door to the wrestling room and cooler air rolled in. "Trust me, kid," he said. "You wouldn't understand."

And then he left.

Standing there in the heat and the half darkness, I knew Nicky was right.

I stepped up to the large pipe with the sign, then rubbed away the grit and read, DANGER! DO NOT LOCK DOWN RELEASE VALVE WHILE THIS UNIT IS IN OPERATION.

Right where the cannon pipe met the boiler was a steel wheel, like they have on submarine doors. A blast of steam hissed from above, and I felt a strange rising inside. Again I thought of Samson, blinded by betrayal, muscles pumping with righteous rage, tied between those two columns.

The blast of steam lasted about three seconds, and as soon as it ended I began counting. One-Cross-of-Jesus, Two-Cross-of-Jesus, and at thirty-four the steam came again. The next release came after thirty-seven seconds and the one after at thirty-two.

I put both my hands on the steel wheel and turned. I'd expected it to be stuck but it moved easily, and after about ten turns the wheel locked tight. Once it stopped, I started counting. After thirty seconds there was no steam. And none at forty. At one hundred forty-three, the rumbling shifted pitch, and the boiler began to tremble. At two hundred thirty the pipes rattled and a deep growl began to gather inside the machine. Around three hundred, the metal egg quaked like something within was struggling to break free.

I spun the wheel open all the way and a long blast of steam erupted above, like dragon breath.

I backed into the wall across from the egg. Again I studied the concrete columns on either side. In my mind I could picture the egg bursting open, sending metal shrapnel exploding in all directions. I saw its two halves rocketing away from each other, destroying the concrete columns. Looking up, I imagined the first set of bleachers buckling without support, tumbling into the wrestling room. Then the balcony giving way, causing the cafeteria floor to crumble down from street level. And once the cafeteria goes, then the other three floors of Our Lady of Perpetual Help High School will collapse into the newly created Rocker Crater.

Listening to the *chunk-chunk* rumble of the boiler grown regular once more, I thought about the match next Saturday, the night before my sixteenth birthday. I thought about the darkness of the upper bleachers when everyone is leaving. How nobody can see if anyone is up there hiding. By the slim light of the Wrong-Hearted Jesus, I'll slip across the basketball court one last time and creep into the boiler room. I'll crank the steel wheel shut and then crawl on top of that big black egg and wait for it to hatch.

While Morgan was driving me home from practice, I felt good for the first time since my confession because I finally knew how all this is supposed to end. I could sense Michael's pleasure too, and I was so sure he was close by and smiling that I even turned and looked in the backseat once. I got to thinking, though, that with the way the plan is shaping up, I'd better make some kind of peace with Dad. I was kind of a jerk to him on Friday, and last night we mostly just avoided each other. He listened to jazz in his study and I read comics in my room.

So I was figuring on maybe helping him fix the snowblower, the project he had planned for today. He seemed kind of upset when I told him yesterday that it wouldn't start, probably thinks I screwed it up somehow. But this would be my final Sunday on Earth, and I liked the idea of spending it tinkering together on the snowblower with Dad, finding the problem and solving it, then maybe making a fire and catching some late afternoon NFL action.

When Morgan pulled up in front of the house, though, that dream vanished and a stranger one began. There in the driveway, directly behind Dad's car, sat a Volkswagen Bus, painted with green splotchy camouflage like they do with tanks to hide them in the jungle. Only this wouldn't be hard to spot because dead center on the side, right in the middle of all that camouflage was a big, bright American flag. "You got an Uncle Sam?" Morgan asked, chuckling at the bizarre vehicle.

Instead of answering him, I got out and closed the door.

I entered the house through the kitchen and heard someone talking in the living room. The voice was deep and whoever was speaking was laughing a lot. It was a strange sound to hear in the house.

Following the laughter, I found its owner sitting on the couch, across from Dad in his chair. The visitor looked about Dad's age and was about the same size, but he was nothing like him. He had a long silver-and-black beard and wore a jean jacket with an American flag patch over his heart.

When he saw me, the stranger stood up. Dad said, "Ernie, this is my son, Keegan."

Ernie reached for my hand and smiled widely as we shook. Looking at my face he said, "Of course he's yours. Apple don't fall far from the tree."

Dad said to me, "This is Ernie Holmes. We served together."

I nodded. "Glad to meet you, Mr. Holmes."

"Lose that 'Mr. Holmes' nonsense. After what me and your old man went through, you call me Ernie."

The three of us sat down, Dad in his chair, me next to Ernie on the couch. Without my asking, he explained that only an hour ago he was traveling on Route 22, coming in from a collectibles show in Harrisburg and heading for a brother in New Jersey. "All along the highway I kept seeing signs for Allentown, and the name kept tickling the back of my brain, like I should know it. Then just as I'm passing through, it kicks me — Keegan Flannery. I pulled over at a Sunoco and found me a phone book."

He turned to my father and said, "God, Sharky, I must've given you a hell of a shock."

Dad nodded his head. I couldn't quite tell if he was happy to see this man or not.

"Last time I saw your dad was, what Sharky, the last reunion you made? Twenty years?"

"About that," Dad said. I wanted to know how Dad got that nickname, but I figured he'd tell me if he wanted. Instead, I asked Ernie what kind of collectibles show he was at in Harrisburg. I was picturing rows of comic books.

"I deal in military paraphernalia. Guns. Knives. Boots. Even medals. You should see some of the stuff in my van."

Dad tensed. "Ernie, how about some more coffee?"

"Affirmative," Ernie said. Dad forced a smile and left us alone.

Ernie seemed to me part wizard, part warrior, part hippie. I liked him.

"He's told you about me," he said. "I'm sure he has."

"Told me what about you?"

"All the crazy things we used to do, the action we saw, the friends we lost."

At each category, I shook my head.

Ernie seemed surprised. "Well, hell, at least he told you about the night he saved my life."

This stunned me. Ernie saw the shock in my face. "Nah, that's just like Sharky. I should've figured. This was toward the end of things, when the Germans were mostly young kids, younger than you even. We all knew the war would be over soon, but that just made us more afraid. Imagine living through all that and then dying on the last day. That would be a stupid death. Anyway, me and your old man were part of a night patrol, a group of about ten guys sent ahead to scout and recon.

"On patrols like that, we couldn't use radio because the Germans might pick up the transmissions, so we had to carry this spool and run wire back to HQ. When we had to report, we'd clip a phone onto the wire. Follow me?"

"Yes, sir," I said. I was trying to picture my father as a young man. All I saw was Patrick in combat gear.

"So this night, when we clip in to report no activity, the line's dead. The wire's been broken. Somebody's gotta go back and fix it. I drew the short stick. Well, I pick up the wire and start walking back in the direction we came, pinching it between my fingers, hoping for a break sometime soon. See, sometimes it would get snagged and snap on roots; or a truck, even one of ours, might run over it. But if the Germans came across it, they might cut it and wait for somebody like me to come back, then shoot him. Or capture him. Torture him. It was the end of the war, like I said, and we'd heard all kinds of rumors."

Dad came around the corner from the dining room carrying two steaming coffee mugs. Ernie looked up at him. "I'm telling him about the night."

Dad stopped and his eyes fell on me. I couldn't tell what he was thinking. He handed Ernie his coffee. Ernie set it on the table without taking a drink and went on. "Right, so at one point I leave the forest and I'm creeping across all this French farmland, out in the open beneath a half moon that's shining like a spotlight for a sniper, and the wire goes light in my hand. I bend down and find the end and feel the break, only it's not a break. It's a slice — like the wire's been cut."

"We don't know that for sure," Dad interjected.

"Hell we don't," Ernie said. "I felt it. I know a cut wire. And there weren't nothing else out there to snap it. I dropped to my belly and scanned the tree line ahead of me, maybe only a hundred yards off. For all I knew it was full of Germans. God only knows how long I lay there — I didn't even fix the damn wire I was so scared to move. Bugs were crawling on me and a dog walked by, but I didn't twitch. That moon kept breaking through the clouds, and I remember wishing I could shoot it out, shatter it with a bullet. But even if I had some kind of crazy magic gun that could do it, I was too afraid to move. Do you understand that kind of fear, terror that just paralyzes you, keeps you from moving at all?"

I nodded my head. I wanted to tell Ernie just how well I understood.

"Anyway, out of the blue I heard this low whistle — it's 'Take Me Out to the Ball Game.' That was our all-clear sign. I think I'm having a dream until I look back and there's Sharky, belly-crawling my way. He shimmies right past me and fixes the wire, then turns around and starts sliding back toward the forest behind us. I'll never forget what he said. 'Hey, Ern, you can stay here if you want, but I know two French girls who'd like to —'"

"Ernie," my father said, stopping him from finishing. Ernie laughed.

"Well, let's just say your old man got me moving. Like I said, he saved my life."

It was quiet for a few seconds. Ernie was waiting for Dad to say something. Ernie said, "I'd have done the same for you." He looked my way. "That's how it was back then; we all were brothers. Brothers-in-arms."

Dad said, "Seems like a million years ago."

"Yesterday," Ernie said.

We were silent again then, this time for almost a whole minute, all of us just looking down at our shoes. Suddenly Ernie jerked his wristwatch toward his face and said, "I should be going. My brother's expecting me. Say, before I head out, you haven't kept any of your old stuff, have you, Shark?"

Dad stood and said, "Can't say that I have."

"I could pay you a pretty penny. I mean anything. Buttons or pictures even. I'd take it on commission if you want."

"No," Dad said. He moved toward the front door; Ernie followed. "I don't have anything for you."

Dad opened the door and the cold came in. Outside the strange van waited. Ernie fished in his pockets. "Now that I know where you're at, I'll visit again," he said. Dad didn't answer. Ernie pulled out his keys and shook hands with my father. Then he bent down and looked me over. "You tell your brothers the story I told you. Tell them so they'll know." We shook hands and he stepped outside.

At my father's side, I felt proud and eager. I thought that

once Ernie left I could ask Dad more about what he did in the war, his acts of heroism, the bonds he shared with his friends. When Ernie reached the bottom step, he stopped and looked back at me. "I'm awfully sorry about your mom," he said. "But you hang in there. I know how hard it can be — when I was little, my ma died too."

I did not look up at my father. I kept my eyes straight ahead and watched Ernie get into his van. I watched him crank the engine. I watched him back out. I watched him drive away, honking a good-bye as he disappeared down the street. The instant he was gone, I turned and walked away. Dad closed the door and said, "Keegan, I should explain."

I kept walking. Not with anger or meanness. "I have to take a shower," I said as I hit the stairs.

Behind me he said, "There's a reason I said what I did."

But I kept going, up the steps and into the hallway. I didn't want to hear his excuses. I didn't care how he felt about me, but he'd wished Mom dead, and that was something I would not forgive. Safe in my bedroom, I swung onto the bottom bunk and pulled out Patrick's drumsticks, rattled them on one of the wooden slats that holds the top bunk up. I tried to imagine Dad next Sunday morning. Will they call him to identify my body once they pull it from the rubble? Will I be too crushed to recognize? Will he lean into the viewing window at the morgue and break down in tears?

Or will he just nod at the coroner and turn away, drive home, and go on with his day? Will he tell everyone it was an accident?

At the same time I was lying on my bed imagining my own dead body, somewhere Ernie was driving that crazy van. He was up on the highway, playing music as he drove toward the ocean, heading for a brother who was waiting for him to arrive with open arms.

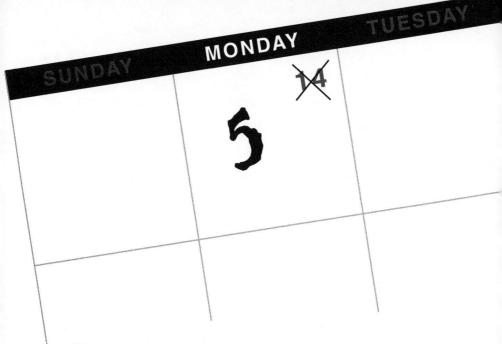

"SOMEBODY PUSHED NATHAN LOOBY," Eileen Giffen whispered from the bleacher behind me, and the shock almost spun my head. It's a good thing I caught myself though, because I'm sure Eileen would've seen the guilt stamped on my face. She'd have seen it and stood up in Rocker, right in the middle of the whole student assembly, and aiming a finger at me she would've cried out, "He's the one!" And then everybody who had gathered together for Nathan's memorial service would have known the truth.

That's what they called it on the P. A. system this morning: a "memorial service." Not a mass. So I'd spent most of the day worrying about what that meant for Nathan's soul, picturing him one instant with wings and two healthy arms, floating on a cloud, the next instant seeing him strapped to a table, demons preparing to ax his real arm and his legs too. In Hell, demons have almost unlimited power, so they could grow his limbs back every night and chop them off every morning if they want to. Forever.

But my mind snapped straight back to Earth when I heard what Eileen said.

Beth Fogel asked who pushed Nathan.

"Mitch Haroldson," Eileen answered. "He was in Sister Helen's English class when the alarm went off, but when she took roll in the parking lot he wasn't there. That's why she was freaking out when the firemen showed up."

Ten to one Mitch was catching a smoke.

"He told Dr. Connors he got separated in the confusion and ran because he almost died in a fire when he was a baby."

That's a good lie for Mitch. I'll bet Dr. Connors wrote that down in his file. He's scheduled appointments with all the kids who had class with Nathan. Eileen must have been in the hallway waiting for her turn and overheard Mitch's "counseling session." It's supposed to be mostly a "How does this make you feel?" thing, but if that detective really thinks somebody pushed Nathan, I'm sure it's an interrogation. I thought of that mirrored room at the police station, how nervous I got waiting for Dad to come in, worrying about Hans.

I'm supposed to see Dr. Connors tomorrow. Fourth period, right after lunch.

"Was the cop with Dr. Connors when you went in?" Beth Fogel asked.

I leaned back and heard Eileen say, "You bet."

I imagined Detective Dougherty standing in front of the blackboard, examining the handwriting I'd left behind with its loopy cursive letters, slanting to one side like a breeze was blowing on them. Everybody's handwriting leans that way, at least everybody who's right-handed. Nathan was an obvious lefty.

"The cop only asked me one question though. He wanted to know who Nathan's best friend was."

"That's weird," Beth said. "What'd you tell him?"

"The truth — that Looby didn't have a best friend."

I'm not sure why hearing that upset me. I mean, it's not like we were tight or anything, but I guess Nathan was my friend. Sort of.

There was some movement down on the basketball court as the seniors took their places in the fold-out metal chairs. In front of them, beneath one basket, was a cafeteria table covered over by a cloth so it could pass as an altar. If I stood on the altar I could probably dunk. Behind the table were nice chairs for the priests, brought down from the teachers' lounge/smoking pit. And in front of the table was a wooden lectern they pretend is a pulpit. It was placed squarely on the foul line.

Above all this, of course, hung the Wrong-Hearted Jesus, waiting to see how the game would come out.

Chubby Terry Fernbacher came shoving down the bleacher row and squeezed in between Eileen and Beth. Terry said she was behind Rose Scott in study hall and read a note over her shoulder. The note was from Lisa Carlson, a library aide.

"Sister Cecilia Agnes saw the killer," Terry said.

My breath caught.

"Lisa heard the detective talking with Sister Cecilia in the periodicals room. After the fire drill she reported two boys running down the hallway during the drill. One after the next. Like one was chasing the other one. That's just what Sister Cecilia said."

I wasn't really "chasing" him.

"Who was it?" Eileen asked.

"Well, that's the thing. Sister Cecilia says it was Jim Butler."

"Who?"

"Somebody checked the old yearbooks. He graduated in 1959."

I smiled. Saved by senility.

Maybe they'd figure she dreamed the whole thing up. But then again, maybe by now somebody had told Dougherty that Nathan and me sat together at lunch. Connors knows that. If they were really looking, it was just a matter of time. With that thought came a rush of some kind. I felt suddenly like a wanted man. A fugitive. I wondered how long it would take them to put the pieces together. And I pictured Detective Dougherty in the crowd during the wrestling match on Saturday, sitting in these very same bleachers, giving me a knowing look. Afterward there'll be a chase through the school. But I know this place too well and I'll escape to the boiler room just before midnight. I realized I was smiling, and that bothered me.

When Mrs. Berry, the bandleader, walked out of the locker room and sat at the piano, the teachers started shushing everybody so the gossip came to a halt. Beside Mrs. Berry sat Sister Shirley, carrying her folk guitar. I heard she knows a lot of Beatles songs, and I always had this secret wish that just once she'd punk out and rip into a version of "Lucy in the Sky with Diamonds" or "Helter Skelter." But today it was business as usual, and everyone stood when Mrs. Berry and Sister Shirley started playing the processional hymn, "Raise You up on Eagles' Wings."

As usual, the only ones singing were a few girls here and there, but then came the loud sound of Father Halderman's voice, rising out of the girls' locker room. The altar boys came out first, then Christian Taylor, the reader, then two people dressed in black who I couldn't quite see. Behind them were Father Jim and Father Fitzpatrick, followed by Father Halderman singing up a storm. As the procession moved through the seniors, heads turned and a wave of whispering rushed through the congregation like a fire across dry grass. I heard the words from someone in front of me, and before they registered, a dozen voices behind me were already whispering them: "Looby's mom!"

Then I recognized the other person in black as Marsha Looby. The two of them took seats in the first row of folding chairs, just about the top of the key, dead center in front of that fake pulpit.

The service began with a few readings from the Bible, then a senior girl I don't know read a poem I didn't understand. Christian Taylor read some petitions like "St. Aloysius Gonzaga, patron saint of Catholic youth, please watch over us in this difficult time."

Then Father Halderman got up and gave a reading from the Gospel according to Luke. When he finished, everyone sat down and crossed their arms, settling in for the long haul. One time he talked so long some of the public school bus drivers came inside to see where everybody was. Nowadays they schedule one class after mass, a cushion in case Father Halderman gets on a roll.

After he closed the Bible, Father Halderman gripped the side of the wooden lecture stand with his old-man fingers and scanned the congregation, most of them already with their eyes half closed with sleep or boredom. "All our hearts are heavy with the loss of Nathaniel Jefferson Looby," he said. "And while his untimely death is sad indeed, we must focus today on the greater tragedy, the loss of his immortal soul."

This opened everybody's eyes. Including mine.

"For God says, 'Thou shall not kill' and this is what Nathaniel has done. Through his transgression, he has sinned directly against the Almighty."

Mrs. Looby stood up. She didn't say anything — she just stood up all by herself, not five feet away from Father Halderman. Everybody in the gym kind of froze for a heartbeat. Marsha grabbed a hold of Mrs. Looby's black sleeve and started tugging on it. But she didn't sit down and Father Halderman didn't let up. He just kept on going.

"God assigns each of His children certain hardships. It is our responsibility to bear these burdens in silence. To obey His will and follow His mysterious plan. To do otherwise, as Nathaniel has done, is to doom one's soul to damnation."

I don't know if it was part of God's mysterious plan or not, but Mrs. Looby had had enough. She said something out loud that I couldn't hear, but everybody close by made a sound like when somebody almost falls off the tightrope. Then she turned and walked away, down the aisle all by herself, like a mad bride dressed in black who'd changed her mind about the whole thing.

Marsha Looby burst into tears and started wailing and Sister Shirley stepped over her folk guitar and rushed over to Mrs. Looby's chair. Father Jim stood up and hurried past Father Halderman and headed down the aisle after Mrs. Looby, even though she was already halfway up the away team bleachers.

Just as she disappeared I wanted to run after her, through that exit and up those stairs and outside into the air of the back alley. Not to talk to her but just to get away. I didn't want to hear what Father Halderman was saying.

Meanwhile, Father Halderman didn't seem to notice anything was out of the ordinary. "For God's laws preserve His plan. And when even one of us disrupts the Divine order of how things are, it pains Him and diminishes us all."

I stopped listening then, and looked down at my shoes. Father Halderman's words seemed to fade away, as if he were on a train moving into the distance. I turned inside myself, and wondered what'll actually happen to my soul if I kill myself. Being a saint is out of the question, I know, but could I still somehow sneak into Heaven?

In Hell, the demons can do more than torture your body. They can make you see things back on Earth. They can make you see things that aren't real. For the first time, I let my mind move with that thought, and wondered what Hell would really be like for me. Everything is dark at first, then a little red light glows up from the edges of my vision and I'm sitting in a movie theater, all alone. When the screen lights up it's a scratchy movie of me, standing next to Mom in front of the mirror at the beach, just standing there. Her fingers lift from mine and I stand there, watching her cross the hot sand. Over and over the film loops back and replays the same scene; every time she disappears into the water and every time I do nothing. There's a quick flash of Dad in his study, then the movie jumps to me watching Nathan climb into the open window. Useless. I can't close my eyes and I can't turn away. And then the film shows Mom in Hellman House, in her locked room, huddling in a corner. She's kneeling and sobbing, praying that Michael had been the one who lived. This part of the film is a lie, a scene the demons make up to hurt me. Mom would never think like that. The image flickers away and again there's Dad in his study. Through the cigar smoke, I see him reaching for the golden framed picture of Patrick and Andrew and Sean sitting one behind the next from just before I was born. As he lifts the picture I see the wallet-size school photo of me, tucked into one corner. Dad holds the frame for a moment, then plucks my picture out, fixing the mistake he made. That one's a lie too. They were all demon lies.

"Here, Keegan," somebody said, "it's okay." I opened my eyes and Terry Fernbacher was pushing a blue tissue in my face. I took it and shook my head to stop the crying. Here and there were other crying sounds, even though Father Halderman had finished his sermon and Mrs. Berry had started playing the recessional hymn. Sister Shirley was still next to Marsha Looby, and they both were crying. The only person who sang the words to the last song was Father Halderman, but his voice was drowned out because little by little more kids were joining in the crying, falling in like the way lonely dogs call back and forth at night.

Some of them were still sniffling half an hour later, after the service let out and we were sitting in Father Jim's biology class. We were fifteen minutes into the period and he still hadn't shown up. He never came back to Rocker after chasing Mrs. Looby. Sally Dean wanted to go down and tell the office that we didn't have a teacher, but Mitch Haroldson talked her out of it.

I lay low in my desk in the back of the room and watched the girls passing tissues across the aisle. The couple of boys who were crying were hiding it, wiping their faces on their sleeves like they just had runny noses. I wondered if any of them had cried right away when they heard the one who jumped was Nathan Looby. I could just imagine kids who couldn't quite place the name until somebody said, "You know, Hook."

Finally Father Jim showed up, huffing from the stairs. I wanted to know if Mrs. Looby was alright but knew I couldn't just ask. He threw a glance out over the weepers and took long steps to his desk, like it was home base in tag and he'd be safe once he got there. He sat down and pulled out the notebook he lectures from and said, still out of breath, "As scheduled, we'll be having a quiz on Friday dealing with . . ." And his voice trailed off like maybe he forgot what he was going to say. But it wasn't that.

Without even lifting his head, Father Jim asked, "Miss Jennings, why are you crying?"

Amanda swallowed some tears, sniffed twice, and said, "I'm crying for Nathan, because he's in Hell."

Father Jim looked at her and folded his notebook shut and said, "We can't be sure of that."

He stood up, crossed the room, and closed the door to the hallway real slow. As he moved back to his desk, his eyes scanned my face, and I looked down at the grain of wood on my desk.

Father Jim said, "Listen everyone. What Nathan did was wrong. There can be no doubt about that. But what we also have to consider is that in the eyes of God, Nathan was only a child. More important, he was in many ways a very sick child, and therefore —"

Father Halderman's voice was suddenly everywhere in the room, like the air itself was speaking. "Father Montgomery, a moment if you please."

My head snapped up, expecting to see Halderman somehow in front of the class. But there was no one there, and everyone was looking up at the P. A. box, hanging over the chalkboard.

The P. A. system works both ways.

The voice from the box said, "At your earliest convenience."

After another hesitation, Father Jim told us to read chapter five and answer the questions at the back. Then he headed out the door, his face down.

I opened my textbook and tried to get the work done but couldn't get past the first sentence of the chapter. "The cycle of life can best be viewed as a series of dynamic changes."

I put the tip of my pen on the desk and pushed it in and felt the wood giving way. I made a small, straight line, then added a leg to make a corner, and that quickly became the top of a block letter S. Before I knew it, I'd carved the words, SICK CHILD.

I know that what Father Jim really meant was that Nathan was insane. Used to be that suiciders couldn't get buried with the full mass. They had to be laid to rest in unsanctified ground. But I think it's okay now if you're crazy. And more important, being crazy gets you off the hook with God, that's what Father Jim was going to say, I'm sure of it. Crazy people don't go to Hell.

Little kids don't go to Hell.

In five days, I'll be sixteen.

Holding the pen like a knife, I carved the words again, SICK CHILD. Bigger, then smaller, then as deep as I could, uncertain of whether or not I qualified. And I whispered a prayer to the Wrong-Hearted Jesus, or Michael, or Nathan, or whoever might hear my pleas, whoever might tell me I won't have to be sentenced to snapping flames and acid pits.

After school, I went through practice like a zombie. Nicky spent most of the time running stairs because he's still two pounds overweight for tomorrow's match. So mostly I worked out with Bugalski, who went pretty easy on me. Really, I think he's just lazy. None of the wrestlers talked about Nathan or what happened at the memorial service, which was just fine with me.

By the time Morgan dropped me off at home it was already dark, almost seven. I was surprised to find Dad's car in the driveway, and even more shocked when I saw him in the garage, door up, lights on, hunched over the snowblower.

Next to him was a dirty blanket with the mechanical guts of the blower laid out in even rows.

"I think I almost got this figured out," he said as I approached.

"What seems to be the problem?" I asked.

Kneeling, he pointed the screwdriver at the snowblower's engine. "These fuel intake tubes are all gunked up. Sean and Andrew didn't empty out the gas like I told them to back in the spring."

I wanted to say, "See, it wasn't my fault."

Oil blackened Dad's fingertips. He said, "I'm cleaning them out one at a time. Next snow you won't have to kill your back shoveling."

"I don't mind the shoveling," I said. "I can do it."

He wiped his wrist across his forehead and looked at the ground. "I know that, Keegan."

Then we stood there for a minute, both of us releasing misty breath into the cold air, waiting. Finally his eyes rose to my gym bag. "So do you need to get washed up?" he asked.

This was his way of telling me I should go. I wondered if he knew anything about the questions Dougherty was asking about Nathan. And we still hadn't talked about the lie he told Ernie. "Yeah," I said. "I should probably hit the shower."

He leaned into the snowblower with the screwdriver, and I turned and left him there, working in the cold.

*   *   *

After a long, steaming shower, I retreated to my bedroom
and huddled again on my bunk bed. Beyond my window,
the tinkling sounds of metal told me Dad was still trying to
work a miracle. I couldn't keep my mind from folding back
to the before-time — when I would've belonged outside
with him, with Patrick and all of us fixing the snowblower as
a team. Those days felt irretrievable now, like a really good
dream you'd woken up from but couldn't get back into.

Patrick left us one August, after a hot Saturday that
started off with big plans. Dad had announced that we all
were going to the Great Allentown Fair, a once-a-year carni-
val that sets up for a week to end the summer. Mostly it's just
cheap rides and games for kids, but Mom had always loved
it for some reason. Each July, when the bright posters would
appear stapled to phone poles as if by magic, she'd start getting excited. She liked to go and pay twenty-five cents to see
the Man with the Mile-long Moustache or to touch the
World's Only Genuine Unicorn Skeleton. She liked seeing
things like that. And she loved to visit the All-seeing Gypsy
Eye, this wisecracking man with bad skin. He'd try to suck
people over to his crystal ball by shouting out small fortunes
as they passed. "Don't you want to know about the money?"
or "Hey, pal, do you know about the baby?" or "I know
what your boss thinks," things like that. Anyway, since

Mom was at Hellman House we'd stopped going to the Fair, missed it, like, three years in a row. So it came as kind of a surprise that Saturday morning when Dad suddenly wanted to do this, though looking back on it now it was probably just part of his "Let's Pretend We're a Normal Family" plan.

The Fair hadn't changed much from what I remembered. Patrick held my hand through the Hall of Horrors and we all got to sit in a tank from the National Guard and Andrew threw up after eating two candy apples and riding the Tilt-A-Whirl. Dad wiped sweat from his forehead with a white handkerchief. In the heat of the afternoon sun, we all sat on wooden bleachers and watched a monkey named Lewis ride a donkey named Clark as it jumped off a fifty-foot platform into a pool full of water. I whispered to Patrick that Mom really would've liked that. Dad wasn't liking the Fair so much, I could tell. He wasn't being mad or anything, he just had this far-off look the whole day, like he really would've rather been elsewhere.

On Arcade Alley, we pitched pennies onto a rotating table full of mugs and glass dishes. I was trying to aim for a green ashtray I thought Dad might like, but my penny kept bouncing away. It was harder than it looked. Sean spent three dollars trying to break balloons with a dart, and Andrew scored a "Not Too Wimpy" on Hercules' Arm-wrestling Challenge. Dad peeled out the money we asked for, but stayed away from the games, looking in on us from the back of the crowd. As we neared the end of Arcade Alley, we could all tell that Dad was getting ready to call it a day. And then Andrew and Sean, who were always running ahead, stopped at a booth and looked back. "Hey, Dad!" Andrew shouted. "Here's one for you."

We approached, and I read the words on the side of the canvas stand: BIG GAME HUNTER! Around the words were jungle trees dripping with snakes, and a hero kneeling in the dirt, calmly aiming his rifle at a charging lion. "Test your skill!" the man tending the stand yelled out. He was wearing a safari hat.

Dad stepped up to the counter, and we all looked inside. Just in front of us was a rifle, an air gun really, connected by wires to the stand. Down at the far end, about fifteen feet away, a 3-D model jungle hung on the wall — trees and mountains and rivers, painted metal dented by stray BB's. Without looking at any of us, Dad handed the man some money and lifted the rifle, settling the butt easily into his shoulder. He tilted his face into the rifle and nodded slightly at the man with the safari hat, who stepped off to the side.

Suddenly, the jungle burst to life: A growling ape dropped from a patch of leaves, but only for an instant. A *bang-ping* BB rocked it back up into its hiding place. On the left, a crocodile's head emerged from the river, but Dad jerked left and pulled the trigger. *Bang-ping!* The crocodile swung back. Complete with a roar, a lion leaped from its cave, tromping across a track. The tip of Dad's rifle trailed slowly right to left with the lion, then the gun spit again, and the lion went down. Sean and Andrew whooped. I grinned over at Patrick. Along the top of the scene, a vulture swooped in. It was smaller than all the other ones, and was darting across the fake sky real fast, back the way the lion came. Dad pulled the trigger and the BB rocketed past. Dad adjusted and fired again, but the bird kept flying. It was almost off the edge when Dad pulled the trigger the third time, but no BB came out. The music stopped. The lights died down.

"Out of ammo, bwana," the safari leader said, stepping back up to the counter. "But you got three out of four. Care to try again?"

Dad shook his head and put down the gun. The man reached over to the prize shelf. Dad looked down at me and Patrick. "I had that buzzard in my sights," he said, smiling just a little.

"These games are all rigged," Patrick said.

"Hail the mighty hunter," said the man, handing a blue elephant over the counter.

My father held his hands up and shook his head. "That's okay."

"Take it," the man said. "Three hits wins an elephant."

"Give it to the next player," Dad said with certainty. "One of the kids."

"For your sweetheart," the man insisted, pushing the elephant forward. "Every Tarzan's got to have a Jane."

Dad stood there, silent.

The man looked over at Patrick and offered him the toy. "Here, junior. Tell your momma that Daddy done good."

Dad grabbed the elephant, two hands around its throat as if he were going to strangle it. "We said," he lifted it from the man and jammed it onto the counter, "we don't want any prize."

He turned and took long steps into the crowd, and the four of us had to dodge around people to catch up to him. Patrick shouted out, "Dad! Dad!" but he kept on moving, like he was late to get somewhere important.

We just caught up to him at the intersection of Arcade Alley and the Mystery Mile. Patrick got to him first and grabbed his arm, anchoring him for a moment. "That guy didn't mean anything," Patrick said. Dad's face was like stone, or ice. For a moment we all hung around him in this terrible atmosphere. The air felt like it does when the wind brings in the scent of rain on a clear day, promising a storm.

"I foresee great struggles in this man's future!" I turned and saw the All-seeing Gypsy Eye, standing over his table just inside his tent, leaning over his crystal ball and staring our way. "Oh, yes," he hollered. "Great struggles indeed."

Some people passing by giggled. Some stopped. Four boys around an angry father: They must have thought we were whining for more cotton candy, or complaining that we didn't want to leave. The gypsy ran his hands over his crystal ball and went on. "It's all quite clear. I see a woman at home with dinner waiting." His voice pitched high. "*Where's that husband of mine? Late again? Where is he?*"

A small crowd had gathered now, and most were chuckling. Dad turned toward the gypsy. Patrick got in front of him and said, "Dad. No. They don't understand. They don't —" Dad swept Patrick aside, pushing him hard enough that Patrick went down on a knee. Everybody stopped laughing. Dad stepped into the tent of the gypsy, who was suddenly in retreat. "Calm down, Mac," he shouted. But Dad kept coming.

When Dad reached the gypsy's table, he grabbed one end and flipped it over, sending the crystal ball cannonballing into the air. This sounds weird, I know, but that's the one image I remember most about the whole day — that crystal ball in the air. Because it's like slow motion the way it hangs there in my mind, and I can see it so clearly and I know what's going to happen, but for that instant it seems like a miracle, a magic ball floating in the air.

213

But of course, at the Fair it came crashing down and shattered. The splintering shriek froze everybody, and somehow it snapped Dad out of whatever state of mind he was in. Because he reached into his pocket and dropped a wad of money on the ground, then straightened up and walked over to where we all were watching. "Come on, boys," he said. "We're going home." Like nothing happened. I went over to help Patrick, but he got up by himself.

The next morning when we got up for church, Patrick was gone. Dad made a couple of phone calls, but Patrick had a big head start. Besides, Patrick was a legal adult by then. He wasn't breaking any laws.

I found his note inside my sneaker that afternoon, scribbled on a yellow piece of paper from one of Dad's legal pads: *"Keeg, I'm torn up that I have to run away like this. But I can't stay here. Once I'm making enough money, I'll come back for you if I can. Until then, you hang in there."*

In the weeks and months that followed, that phrase — *run away* — always made me picture Patrick jogging along the side of the highway, not with any destination in mind, just occupied completely by the act of running. Of course, I knew that wasn't true. From the postcards he sent me, I knew that he drove his car to New York (the Brooklyn Bridge) first and then down to Florida (an alligator lying on a golf course). There was a long gap, then I got a few from out West, then another long gap. The last couple I got were from Philly (one of the Liberty Bell and one of those steps that Rocky ran up). They're all in a paper bag at school in my locker, safe from the prying eyes of Sean and Andrew. Most have short, quick messages, like telegrams: DOING GOOD. NEW BAND. NEW APARTMENT. CUTE GIRLFRIEND WHO YOU'D REALLY LIKE. STUDY HARD IN SCHOOL. LISTEN TO DAD. LOVE, PATRICK. Some of them have a P.S. that reads SOON, BUDDY. Mostly though, these are from early on. The last thing I got from him was that letter where he tried to explain how he had no choice leaving and how he'd hoped I could forgive him. One more Flannery confession.

Outside my window, Dad had apparently finished reassembling the snowblower. He cranked the starter cord and sent the sputtering engine rising and falling as it struggled to spark to life. The first attempt sounded promising, but then the engine fell to silence. There was a pause, then another ripping pull, another series of sputters, and the heavy weight of silence. I waited for another attempt, and thought he'd given up. But after almost a whole minute he yanked the cord again, this time getting only a hacking cough from the engine. He yanked again and it hacked again. Yank and hack. Yank and hack. Each one sounding more sickly and desperate than the last. Dad just couldn't admit the obvious: The snowblower was dead, beyond resurrection.

215

THERE WAS NO WAY OUT. Trapped, I searched for an escape route in case things went sour, but Detective Dougherty blocked the only window, and when Dr. Connors came through his office door, he locked it behind him. I swear I heard the click. I had no chance to avoid the coming interrogation.

Dr. Connors settled in behind his desk, flipped open a file, and tried to smile. "Well, Keegan, this must have been very hard for you."

"Sure," I said.

"After all, you and Nathan were pretty close, weren't you?"

"Not that close," I said. A muscle in my stomach twinged.

"Didn't you two always eat lunch together?" Dougherty asked.

"We sat at the same table. But Nathan didn't talk much."

Dougherty asked, "How about other than that, you know, like at your lockers?"

"They're right next to each other," I said. "Sometimes he'd ask about homework. He didn't always hear teachers so good."

Dr. Connors cut in. "Did you notice any changes in Nathan's behavior in the last few weeks?"

"He was quiet," I answered. "But he was always quiet."

"Did Nathan ever say that he was depressed about anything?"

I remembered Nathan's white knuckles when he was praying before confession. "Not that I know of."

They fell silent for a moment. I wanted to know how much they knew. "Why do you think somebody pushed him?"

Both their heads snapped and they looked at each other. They said nothing, then Dr. Connors asked, "What makes you think that?"

"Look, everybody knows."

"You shouldn't pay attention to rumors," Dougherty said.

"All we want to know is what led to this tragedy," Dr.

Connors said. "As you've probably heard through the grapevine, Nathan tried this before. But last time he left a suicide note and this time he didn't, which is very unusual. It would help everyone to heal faster if we had a better idea why this happened."

They were only saying that to make me drop my guard and slip up. All the time Dr. Connors was talking, Dougherty's eyes pressed in on me. He wanted me to crack. Instead I played my ace.

"I was there when he jumped," I said. "I watched him."

Dr. Connors' head cocked and he almost grinned and he said, "I think we should talk about this, don't you?"

"Absolutely," I said.

Dougherty took over. "Why don't we start with what you were doing there in the first place?"

"Everybody was there," I said.

Dr. Connors looked at me. Dougherty looked at me.

"We thought there was a fire. Everybody ran into the parking lot like we're supposed to. I was right behind Señora Schmidt."

She won't remember who was where when that body came down.

Dr. Connors rocked back on the heels of his chair and brought the eraser of his pencil to his mouth. "So you were outside?"

"Of course," I said. "Where else would I have been?"

It wasn't great, but it was the best I could do. They both looked confused, so I know I threw them off balance.

We talked for a couple minutes more, about whether or not I felt guilty for having watched Nathan fall and hit the ground and how everybody watched and it was a natural reaction. But Dr. Connors was just going through the motions. Dougherty didn't say anything after my little stunt. He just watched me and scribbled things in his notebook. He knows. And I'm running out of time.

I went back down to study hall and handed Mr. Stevenson my excuse and wandered back to my seat. There was a quiz scheduled for social studies today and even though I couldn't care less about grades, I wanted something to concentrate on, so out came my notes on Egypt. I felt bad for what I'd said about Nathan. I'd basically told them that he wasn't my friend at all, and that was a pretty crappy thing to do. Like Peter denying Jesus.

Being Nathan Looby's friend wasn't much, but it was one of the few good things I had and now I miss it. I wish I had it back.

I wish I had anything. Something worthwhile I could offer St. Michael to balance against being a bad brother and a bad son.

I turned away from my notes and my eyes lifted to Angela Martinez's face. She was staring over her shoulder at me from her chair near the front of study hall. She spun back around as soon as our eyes met, but I kept mine on her. So a few seconds later, when she reached across the aisle and dropped a note on Steve Fulcon's lap, I saw her do it. I followed the note over four rows and back ten chairs until it arrived at Angela's best friend, Lori Pesto.

Lori's in this special English class, and when she began reading the note I could detect the slightest movement of her lips as she mouthed the words. I saw a lip-reader once on TV. He was deaf but he could tell what someone was saying as long as he could see their lips.

As Lori moved down the page, her lips worked the words more and more quickly and her eyes grew larger. Suddenly she slapped the note to her lap with both hands and shot an open-mouthed look over to Angela. I couldn't see Angela's reaction, but Lori's face turned and all at once she was staring straight at me. That's when I knew for sure the note was about me, and I had the craziest thought. Keegan Flannery: Boyfriend.

I knew that idea was impossible, though insane may be a better word. Angela barely knows my name. But with all that's been going on lately, I can't keep my mind from taking off in directions that don't always make sense. If Angela wanted to be my girlfriend, that would be something to have. Maybe even enough to tip those golden scales. Angela was the one, after all, who declared me dead last Saturday. Perhaps she has the power to declare me alive.

Then maybe I could abort my mission and take my chances with Michael. Or follow the plan and somehow still be allowed into heaven.

So as soon as the bell rang, I edged my way toward Lori and Angela. They had moved together quickly, feeding into the crush by the double doors. I got to about five feet behind them, so I could hear their voices but not what they were saying. Right after they crossed through the doors, they stepped out of the stream of traffic, off to the side by the water fountain. As the flow of the crowd pushed me past them, toward the stairs, I heard three quick rips of *vffft-vffft-vffft*. I rounded the first flight and turned, risking a glance back. Angela and Lori hunched into each other, and between them I saw the dome on top of the garbage can. The little swing door was rocking gently.

I spent the whole time during the quiz on Egypt figuring out a way to get back to that can before Mr. Dan emptied it.

I had to wait until just after last bell, when study hall was empty, before I could return. I unscrewed the lid of the garbage can. On top was a scrunched-up orange drink carton, resting in a soggy copy of the periodic table. I pinched it out and continued my excavation. There was a balled-up English essay belonging to somebody named Taylor. C-minus. AVOID INFLATED LANGUAGE the teacher had written. Then a *Helping Hands*, the official school paper of OLPH. Somebody had drawn wings on the picture of Father Halderman. The headline read: POPCORN TRANSFORMED INTO BASKETBALLS: FUND DRIVE A MIRACULOUS SUCCESS!! But a marker had crossed out some words and written new ones: POPCORN TASTES LIKE BASKETBALLS: FUND DRIVE A JOKE!! Everything I touched was sticky with orange drink, and I began to fear that Angela's note would be soaked and unreadable. But then a ragged edge of white paper peeked out from beneath a crumpled bag of Ruffles. I took the slip between my fingers, and even as I unfolded it, I somehow knew the clear, blocky handwriting was Angela's. The paper was about half the size of a business card, but the only words I could read were WEEKEND on one line and LIKE ALWAYS on the other. Part of one word was definitely FOWLER and another looked like LOOBY, but I couldn't be sure. Down in the garbage, larger remnants with full words waited. As I reached in for them, familiar voices echoed down the stairwell — Kook and Van Fowler, cutting through study hall on their way to wrestling practice. I began snapping up the scraps of paper and stuffing them into my shirt pocket. When I heard their footsteps, I scooped all the gooey junk back into the can. I screwed the lid on and stepped to the water fountain just as they turned the last flight of stairs.

We all smiled like meeting here was nothing out of the ordinary, and I fell in step behind them.

I dropped off my book bag in the locker room and headed straight for the bathroom. The stall at the end has a door on it. I bent and looked underneath to make sure it was empty. Upside down, I saw the door to the locker room swing open back behind me. And through it were coming wrestlers, tiptoeing on black sneakers. Just as I straightened, Van Fowler bear-hugged me, his arms like steel clamps. Kook held my feet together, and they lifted me sideways and charged forward with me like a battering ram. Maybe I yelled. My head bounced open the stall door, and I was plunged face-first into the toilet.

When they pulled me out of the water, I sucked in a quick shot of air. Voices bounced off the walls and hands and arms were all over me, holding me upside down in midair. I tried to kick my legs but all I could do was squirm like a fish. Van Fowler had my arms pinned to my side at the elbows. My tie hung over my face. There was laughter, and someone shouted, "Bring him over here, somebody didn't flush."

Then a second voice, calm, that shut everyone up. "No. That's not how this is done."

It was suddenly quiet, almost like somebody was about to say a prayer. A tennis ball was put in my right hand and the voice said, "Let go when you can't take it." After a pause the voice said, "Do it," and I dropped into the toilet again.

Underwater, I had this nightmare image of Michael standing there in the bathroom, directing the wrestlers in this strange attack. The water wasn't warm or cold, but my one cheek must have been resting against the side because it felt cool. The blood started to run to my head, and I felt the need for air almost immediately. Though my ears were just under the waterline, I could hear a rhythmic sound coming from above. They were counting, chanting numbers out loud.

I gripped the ball in my hand and thought about drowning right there, in that toilet in the last stall. I imagined the tennis ball slipping from my dead fingers and rolling away on the slanted floor, forgotten in the commotion, coming to rest in the drain at the center of the room, and all the wrestlers running past it. And Michael bending over to pick it up, smiling at a job well done.

My ears exploded as the water shocked to life, swirled around and flooded up my nose and I scrunched my eyes tight and something sucked at the skin on my face. Air rushed into my lungs and water gurgled down the drain. I opened my eyes as they lifted me, still upside down, out of the toilet. Snowflakes of paper drifted past me down into the newly rising water. Tumbling from my shirt pocket.

Van Fowler stood me upright as the room emptied out. I caught a glimpse of Nicky's black hat in the crowd. "Woof-woof," Van Fowler said. "Consider yourself one baptized Bulldog."

Bugalski took the tennis ball from me and handed me a towel. "Get cleaned up quick. Bus for St. Frank's leaves in half an hour. Coach will kill everybody if he finds out we did this again."

I rubbed the towel over my hair and stared down at the slips of Angela's note, taking on water and going under. Van Fowler followed my stare. "What was that?"

"Nothing," I said. "Nothing important."

When we stepped into St. Francis' state-of-the-art auditorium, we all gazed in awe at the shiny wrestling mat and the gleaming gymnastic equipment stored neatly in the corners, like this place was secretly hoping to host the next Olympics. Benedict the Bulldog barked twice, and the cheerleader holding his leash had to hush him up. "I guess he don't like the smell of money," Kook said.

As we moved in, I wondered how many fund-raisers this

place held, how much peanut brittle and Christian greeting cards these students had to peddle. Probably none. St. Francis serves the rich families on the far west side.

"Give me a freakin' break," I heard Morgan say, and I looked up and saw a camera. Not a picture-taking camera, but a movie-taking camera, on a tripod by the scorer's table. We walked behind it and lingered, checking out the polished lens. Morgan exhaled hard. "We can't afford new headgear and these yahoos are takin' home movies."

Benedict sniffed at one of the legs of the tripod, considering it for a pee break. "Woof-woof," Bugalski told him. "Hose it down."

The head cheerleader yanked on the leash and said, "Bad dog," then shot Bug a look. The girls stepped up into the bleachers. The wrestling cheerleaders are the ones who didn't make the varsity squad or the j.v. squad. The fact is, they're a bit bitter about the whole thing.

We filed down into the Assassins' locker room to meet the enemy. As soon as we came through the door, eyes flashed back and forth as each wrestler tried to pick out his opponent by size. Their lockers were huge, and we saw a sauna off to the side of their showers. The Assassins' coach came out of an office with a straight doorway and shook hands with Morgan. The referee followed and Morgan handed him a piece of paper. Then all three stepped over to the scale and started checking it out.

"Make sure it's accurate," Nicky whispered to himself. He skipped last class today to work out and shed the final quarter pound. On the bus ride over, he chewed gum and spit into a Styrofoam cup. He looked kind of white.

Both teams formed two loose lines of undressing or semi-naked guys along opposite walls, so the smallest guy on their team stood straight across from me. When he swung his varsity jacket off, there was a flash of metal, and after he hung the jacket on a hook, I saw thin rows of straight silver along one sleeve. They were safety pins, the biggest ones I've ever seen, big as penny nails, in the same place as sergeant's stripes.

The referee held up a little notebook and said, "Assassins, 98, Larry Fuller." And my opponent stepped forward, pulling off his shirt and revealing a hand-size patch of hair on his chest. Pausing in front of the scale, he peeled off his underwear. He took a long, deep breath and then picked up one naked foot and set it down on the scale like it was a land mine. The metal arm rose and tapped the top bar, dropped and rose again, hanging just shy. The referee squinted and saw light in between. "Dead on," he said, and penciled a mark in his notebook. Then he called my name and I walked over, shoes and all, and when I got on, the metal arm didn't budge, like the scale didn't even notice I was on it.

"Under," the referee said.

Nicky's opponent stepped up to get weighed, and my eyes fell back to Larry Fuller, sliding back into his clothes and his varsity jacket with the shiny metal sleeve.

Nicky leaned into my ear. "Those are pins."

I looked at him like he thought I was stupid. But he just nodded real slow and I realized he didn't mean safety pins. He meant pin pins. Those were people on Larry Fuller's sleeve, like painted silhouettes on the Red Baron's plane.

"Our Lady. Carpelli. 105."

Nicky stepped up gingerly onto the scale, and the metal arm rose, tapped the top and settled in the middle. "Even," the ref shouted.

Nicky turned with a smile and said, "No sweat."

After everybody weighed in, the team made its way to St. Francis' girls' locker room, and all the guys started eating. Bugalski spooned honey from a glass jar, explaining, "It's supposed to give you energy."

"You look like Winnie the Pooh," said McMillen. He was walking around testing the wrap job on his knee and eating an orange.

Nicky ate a bowl of cold spaghetti noodles with his hands. Even Van Fowler, whom I'd seen eat two hot dogs at lunch, pulled a Snickers bar from his gym bag and tore off the wrapper. I was the only one who didn't have something to eat, and it made me hungry.

But I didn't have anything and I wasn't going to mooch. So I settled onto the floor against a wall in a corner of the room, and toyed with the dial on a lock, wondering how long it would take to try every possible combination. I was up to 1–1–25 when I heard a voice behind me.

"Move with the whistle."

Over my shoulder I saw Nicky, scooping noodles out of the bowl with his fingers, sitting on the edge of the bench. He wasn't even looking at me so the only way I knew for sure it was he who had spoken was that nobody else was around.

"Picture a move in your head. Know it. Forget everything else. That's the important thing. The forgetting."

That was all he said, but it lit a tiny fire in my mind, and I began thinking about the moves I knew. I felt pretty good about my single leg and I'd practiced a high crotch enough times that I knew how my feet were supposed to be. I also kind of knew a double leg and a headlock and an ankle pick. But how was I supposed to know which move would be right?

All during warm-ups and the national anthem, my mind flipped from one move to the next, but the images of the single legs and high crotches shuffled too quickly. So when Larry Fuller shook my hand and the referee blew his whistle, I had no move at all.

Fuller stepped into me and one hand gripped my arm at the elbow and the other slapped onto the side of my neck. I put my hands on him in the same places, a reaction from being a good throwing dummy no doubt. He tugged on my arm and pushed on my neck, and scooted the two of us in a tight circle. I thought about pushing on his neck, trying to turn our dance in a new direction. But before I took action, he dropped out of my hands, a blur swinging low and rising again. Only when he stood again, he had my right leg wrapped inside the knot of his arms. He sucked my leg tight to his chest and pulled. I hopped once and kept my balance, but then one of his feet shot out and swept the foot I was standing on, and the earth gave way beneath me. I fell flat on my back and his weight dropped down upon me.

The next thing I knew he was on top of me, his chest pressing on mine. His one arm snaked around my neck and pinched it, and his legs wrapped inside mine like vines. He arched his back and split his legs, flaring mine open. The muscles in my thighs burned as they stretched.

He wrenched at my neck like he was trying to pop open a bottle.

While he had me there, stretched out and trapped, my

whole world was only the sharpness of pain. My eyes must have been closed because I saw nothing. And when the pain dulled, I was glad it was over, happy that I'd been pinned. But he did not release me, and I saw the referee on all fours, whistle in his mouth, face turned and close to the mat, shaking his head slightly side to side. I realized that somehow, in all that eternity, my shoulders had not both touched the mat. I knew right away too that my opponent was only pausing, that he was taking a break before casting me back into the pain and the dark. And in that moment, my ears brought me the only sound I heard during the whole match. Who knows how, but my ears screened out the crowd and the coaches and the cheerleaders, and brought me instead the steady clicking of the film, passing frame by frame before the lens of that camera.

My mind flashed on the hundreds of frozen pictures, of the images of me helpless like this being burned onto the film. I looked up at the kid running the camera.

It was Michael.

Right there in the flesh, not fifteen feet away, grinning. My brother aimed the lens at me, cranking a handle on the side like on a meat grinder, recording my actions to be used as evidence against me.

I felt my opponent's muscles tense like a trap about to spring, and I didn't want more of that pain and couldn't stand the thought of more humiliation in front of Michael. I found the referee's face and said, "I'm pinned."

The whistle almost fell out of his mouth, but then his surprise became disgust and he raised one hand high over his head as if he were about to strike me, but smacked the mat instead.

I got up and looked at the camera. Michael was gone. A red light on top told me it was running automatically. There was no crank handle. The referee took me by the wrist and held my hand out to Larry Fuller, who shook it and whispered to me, "Thanks, you're my new record."

He was gone before what he'd said registered. All at once I was left alone at the middle of the mat, my hand still out in front of me. I turned to the red numbers on the fancy electronic timer: 1:36. I'd lasted twenty-four seconds. That was Larry Fuller's new record. I was his new record. That was what I had, my new claim to fame, the great achievement I could set on my side of St. Michael's scales.

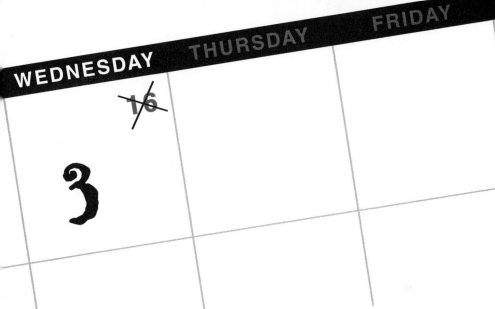

"YOU JUST ABOUT GOT KILLED LAST NIGHT!" Morgan was saying at practice after school. "And you didn't even fight."

The team sat Indian-style on the mat, watching him pace beneath a freshly spray-painted message on the cinder blocks: BULLDOGS 3, ASASSINS 52. I figured it best not to tell him about the misspelling.

Our only victory came, of course, from Nicky, who recovered from his starvation diet fast enough to win 8–2 and score us three team points. After the match he celebrated by spending twelve dollars at McDonald's.

Morgan stopped pacing. "I'm not upset that we lost. Hell, I knew we were gonna lose. But you guys surrendered before you even took the field. I could see it in your faces. You looked more like puppies than dogs! Maybe we should change our name — Our Lady of Perpetually Helpless Puppies."

Behind me, Grieber junior giggled and somebody punched him.

Morgan started moving again, hands behind his back. "My old drill sergeant used to say, 'Never let your enemy know what you're feeling, except that you hate his guts!' It's part of good sportsmanship to want to kill somebody. Tomorrow night when the Crusaders step in here, I want them to know they're in for a fight. Somebody challenges you — the gauntlet's been thrown! It's you or him."

That last line really stuck with me. It's me or him. I pictured Michael's face last night, from my vision or hallucination or whatever. What matters is that I saw him at mat-side and he was smiling, just like Larry Fuller did when he checked me out at weigh-ins, like he knew for sure he was going to stomp me.

Morgan told us his drill sergeant used to make them fight one-on-one to "get that fire burning inside." We were going to try the same thing. He had us match up with our usual partners and I scooted over next to Nicky, then each pair was split up. I went to one wall and Nicky to the other, Grieber to one side and Grieber junior to the other, down the row until there were two teams of seven wrestlers. Morgan stood between us. "Consider this a combat simulation. One period. Two minutes. Other than that, all the normal rules. All the normal points. Winning team goes home. Losing team runs stairs for an hour."

Looks leaped from team to team, sizing up the pairings. I couldn't tell for sure, but judging from the reactions, the team I was on seemed to be the underdog, even though we had Van Fowler and they had McMillen, who was limping around complaining that his knee was reinjured last night. Standing down from me, Van Fowler said something under his breath that Morgan heard better than I did. "Problem with the arrangement, Herr Fowler?"

Van Fowler sat down with a huff, then said, "Whatever."

"Yeah," Morgan said. "That was about your attitude last night. It got you into the second period, but not the third, right?"

Morgan pulled out his stopwatch. I was ready to go out and get creamed by Nicky when Morgan said, "Van Fowler. Mac. Front and center."

Everybody looked around. But Morgan paid no attention, only waited for his orders to be obeyed. He was running the matches in opposite order, starting with the heavyweights, just to get at Van Fowler, who took his time getting up as some kind of protest. As he lumbered toward the center of the mat, McMillen got ready in his stance. Out of nowhere, Morgan blew the whistle and McMillen lunged forward, tackling Van Fowler and scoring a takedown.

Of course Morgan's dirty trick just made Van Fowler angry. He escaped in about three seconds and bear-hugged McMillen until his eyes looked ready to pop. By the time he smacked him onto the mat and pinned him, McMillen was happy just to have it be over.

After that most of the matches were close, and as I added up the points in my head, I began to see the inevitable taking shape. My match might actually matter. Grieber beat his little brother by eight points, then Flynn and Bugalski tied. Going into my match, my team led by four. A pin is worth six. A win is worth three. All I had to do was stay off my back for two minutes. Flynn made sure to explain all this to me when he came off the mat. "Just don't get stuck," was the last thing he said.

At the whistle, Nicky locked up with me, my forehead forced onto his shoulder, his resting on mine. I was holding on, trying to figure out why he hadn't just shot in on me. Then he lifted his head and brought his mouth close to my ear and whispered, "Ankle pick."

His head snapped back and he dropped down. The hand he had on my neck pulled my head down, and his other arm stretched across my legs, reaching for the far ankle. He cupped my ankle and shoved on the side of my neck, tumbling me over that foot. I landed on my hipbone and bounced once, then Nicky scrambled up my body. He started looping his arms around my head in some hold, but stopped suddenly. Morgan had blown the whistle.

"No takedown," he said. "Neutral."

Morgan held his hands up, palm to palm, indicating we should stand up again. I didn't understand, and even when Nicky's team grumbled for some explanation, he didn't question Morgan's call. I thought maybe he'd done something illegal that only Coach saw.

At the whistle we locked up. Again Nicky brought his mouth to my ear. This time he whispered, "Jap wizer."

He spun inside my right shoulder and crouched down quick, faced away from me, holding my arm tight to his chest over his shoulder, like he was Santa Claus and I was his sack. He snapped down and yanked on my arm and my legs spun over my head while my shoulder stayed tight to his chest. My legs whacked together when they hit the mat, and a twisting pain shot up my shoulder, which Nicky still had a hold of. And then again came the whistle.

"No takedown. Neutral."

Kook said, "Coach, what?"

Morgan snapped, "Never talk to the ref." He turned back to us and said out loud, "One minute left." He put his hand between us and said under his breath, "You're on your own."

Morgan wasn't talking to Nicky, who was likely to go berserk any second. He seemed to be calm on the outside but I knew better. The steam was building inside him.

When we locked up for the third time, I kept a little distance. I looked down at Nicky's legs. Taking a deep breath, I broke the hold and dropped. The redness of his kneecap was straight ahead of me as I launched forward, open hands just ahead of my face, waiting for the leg to vanish as Nicky sprawled back from my grasp. But it seemed to zoom toward me, and only too late did I see Nicky's sneaker rising off the mat. Too fast to catch, his knee burst through my open hands and cracked me squarely in the nose.

There was a flash of black, then Nicky's face, the smack of the mat on the back of my head, and the BROADWAY girder above me, spinning like a slow ceiling-fan blade. I closed my eyes because it felt like I was going to fall, even though I was already flat on my back.

Voices passed over me.

"Do you think it's broken?"

"Coach, Nicky's disqualified right? We win. He kneed him on purpose."

"I can't run stairs. My leg."

"Give it a rest, Mac."

I opened my eyes and saw the heads circled above me, like doctors leaning over a patient on the operating table, or a bunch of morticians. Morgan knelt next to me. "Blood stops time. Referee's time-out."

He reached down and pulled my hands away from my face. I hadn't known they were there. My palms were bloody, and I remembered the word "stigmata" from Sister Teresita's class. But then I tasted the blood coming over my lips and realized it was my nose that was bleeding, not my palms. I didn't know enough to fight the urge to sneeze, and when it came a knife spiked back into my brain. My fingernails dug into the mat. When my eyes opened, a splattered cone of blood stained my shirt.

Morgan frowned and pulled back. He turned to Grieber junior and what I heard him say was, "Get Angie. Tell her to bring the mast."

I had no idea what a "mast" could be, and I pictured Angela dragging a long wooden board across the court, like Jesus in the stations of the cross. I didn't want her to see me like this, so I tried to sit up. Morgan put a hand on my shoulder and said, "Just sit still. Don't try to move."

And I thought, *What else is new?*

Morgan cradled one hand under my neck and tilted my head back. I lay there with the taste of my blood sliding

239

down my throat, with all the wrestlers looking down at my wounded face, and the idea of being dead sounded just fine. Because in all those faces circled above me, each and every expression said the same thing: Loser.

I was barely surprised when the others leaned in, joining the wrestlers in judgment over me. Dad peered over Van Fowler's shoulder, staring down on me with that hopeless look. Next to McMillen, Mom shook her head, and even sad dead Nathan Looby couldn't hide his disappointment. And beyond them, up through the ceiling and through the school, I could feel Michael in Heaven, peeking over a cloud and knowing his revenge was working just right. Angela, the only vague hope I had left, was about to come see me all broken up. As I lay there waiting for her, I wondered why it is that you can't just will yourself to die, why if the heart is a muscle you can't just send it a signal that says, "Hey. Stop."

When Angela walked into the room, I turned my head and saw her through the legs of the wrestlers. She didn't have a mast, but she was carrying a human head. In her other hand she had her Red Cross box. The wrestlers parted for her, and she moved to my side, throwing the head onto the mat. It landed next to me, and it was just a wrestling headgear, with a mask attached to the front, kind of like the ones hockey goaltenders wear. The tan material looked like foam rubber, or something soft. There were two big sideways teardrops for the eyes, and a hole for the mouth. It was hollow inside.

Angela said, "Does that hurt as bad as it looks?"

"I'm not sure," I said. "How bad does it look?"

I don't know where that came from, but it was probably the most clever thing I've ever said to a girl. Angela didn't notice.

She pulled some white towels out of her box and dabbed softly at my face, and I remembered how gently Mom used to clean skinned knees. Then Angela settled her fingers on either side of my tender nose, though her touch didn't hurt. Her face got that safecracker look and she leaned in so close I could see the little specks in the wetness of her eyes, like a field of stars.

"Not so bad," she said. "Sit up."

The guys on the team I was on smiled for a moment, then I think the reality of the situation sunk in. Yes, I could go back on the mat and finish the match, but Nicky hadn't even broken a sweat yet, and my boat was on choppy waters. They couldn't tell, but even though the world had stopped spinning for me, it was still tilted.

Angela stuffed bunched-up toilet paper into my nostrils and tugged the wads out. The blood was darker than red, almost black, but that didn't gross her out. She did it a couple of times, till the paper came out mostly clean, and then she asked me, "Do you want the mask?"

I wasn't sure exactly why I would or wouldn't want the mask. But I didn't want her to leave me yet. I wished for the hundredth time for the contents of that study hall note, and almost asked her about it. I wanted her to stay with me there on the mat and tell me that she saw something in me that no one else could see. I wanted her to look at me and see more than Keegan Flannery: Boy Victim.

So I said, "Absolutely."

We stood up and she got in front of me with the masked headgear in her hand, and I leaned my head down and forward like a king about to be crowned. Something sharp snagged for a second on my forehead, then I felt the guards covering my ears and the strap being pulled tight under my chin. I heard Angela say, "Okay, amigo, you're ready to go."

And when I lifted my head and opened my eyes, the world had changed.

I had this strange dizzy feeling that something was missing, that some film had been lifted from my eyes. Even though I could see less because of the mask, it seemed that what I could see was clearer, more focused. All that was there at first was Angela, squinting through the eyeholes. Her head was tilted, and her black hair hung straight down like a veil. The professional smile was gone from her face; her lips were pressed together, and her eyes were searching for something familiar. It was like she wasn't sure whom she was looking at.

Morgan's voice came from behind Angie. "How's the fit?"

She turned to him and the black veil swung back and I saw Morgan. His face went blank. Since I could only see what was directly in front of me through the mask, I had to turn my head to take in the wrestlers on either side. Most of them looked away, which surprised me, but those who did stare had weird glassy eyes. They looked at me like they'd paid a quarter to slip inside one of those freak tents at the Great Allentown Fair, like I was suddenly the Amazing Faceless Boy.

Morgan stepped in front of me. Without peering inside the mask, he put his hands on either side of the headgear and tugged on it. "Looks good," he announced. He took a small step back, enough so I could see his whole face and he said, "Do you want to finish the match?"

As I nodded, his face disappeared then reappeared in my view. He turned and stepped back into the center of the mat and I followed. Nicky was pacing along the wall beneath the Other Ten Commandments. His hands were on his hips and when he saw me and Morgan ready, he straight-lined it for the mat.

"Shake," Morgan said, and Nicky threw his hand out. I reached for it and he slapped at my palm. I hadn't expected an apology, but that slap got me going. Here he was acting like he hadn't kneed me in the face and nearly broken my nose. Like nothing had changed and I didn't have this weird mask covering my face and we were going to go right back to the way things were. And for just a second, I thought maybe he was right.

But as I pulled my hand back, I knew I didn't want things to go back to the way they'd been, and when Morgan blew that whistle, my body bolted into action. My left leg planted down and my right foot came tearing from behind me and drove upward, kicking Nicky right in the crotch. My toes cracked bone, and I saw Nicky's shoes lift slightly off the mat. His hands crossed and his knees came together, and as he crumpled sideways I envisioned a football soaring through the goalposts for the winning field goal. I even imagined the referee thrusting his hands over his head, but there was no whistle. Instead there was a cough, a single one loud and close. I looked down at the mat and there was Nicky, curled in a tight tuck like babies are inside their mothers.

I thought of Michael. Not the Michael that was with me inside Mom. The Michael that's been around lately. I knew he wouldn't pass up such a great opportunity to lay into me. He'd want to take away even this tiny victory.

Yet when my eyes slowly pressed shut and folded inside myself to touch Michael's mind, he was gone. There was no gloating or anger; there was nothing, and instantly I knew that he wasn't with me. He wasn't even watching. He couldn't. Something about the mask camouflaged me from his sight.

Thrilled by the sensation, I was rushed with the urge to shout out, "Alleluia," like they do in some churches. I felt a quickening inside me, as if I were about to somehow burst free of my body. But then I heard Morgan's voice say, "Jesus H. Christ on a Popsicle stick" and whatever glorious bubble I was in for that moment popped.

I turned just in time to see Kook charging at me from behind Morgan. He double stiff-armed my chest and I fell backward. As I landed, Van Fowler stepped over me and clotheslined Kook. Then Kook's whole team charged out and my whole team charged out and I found myself in the middle of a fierce stampede of wrestling sneakers. The feet paired up here and there, and I saw a few guys drop to the mat. Just as I was getting up onto my hands and knees, I heard a loud grunt behind me; Van Fowler had Kook completely in the air, and they were tilting toward me like falling oaks. I spun and scrambled to the edge of the mat. Once outside the pileups, I stood and looked across at Morgan, hands on his hips, grinning over the chaos; this is exactly what he wanted. A hand touched my shoulder and I spun around, expecting to get punched. But it was Angela.

She looked at my eyes through the mask and said, "What did you do that for?"

For some reason it didn't feel right to talk with the mask on, so I reached up and undid the strap and pulled the headgear free. Angela smiled at my face. I said, "I did it because I wanted to."

She nodded her head like she understood and said, "I'd ice that nose tonight." Then she spun on one sneakered heel and walked out, maneuvering with amazing grace through the mounds of swarming wrestlers.

Later, after Morgan had broken up the fight and run everybody through a short practice, when I was leaving the wrestling room, I picked up the special headgear and carried it with me to the locker room. I stuffed it through the mouth of my gym bag, and even though a lot of the guys saw me do it, nobody said a word.

I'm not sure why I brought the mask home. I'm not sure what exactly I was thinking when I came in and snuck past Dad's study, only the soft light beneath the doors and the faint smell of tobacco letting me know he was even home. But something drove me to my room where I closed the door and stretched out on my bunk, holding the strange headgear on my chest. With it staring at me close range, I decided it didn't look much at all like a hockey mask. It reminded me more of one of those sketches of alien creatures that people always make. Big round head, large eyes, no nose, a tiny mouth. Like in *Close Encounters*. A completely different species.

And after a while, those empty eyes definitely seemed to be looking at me, and I was convinced the mask could somehow speak. Even though it was early, I drifted into an easy sleep, dreaming of the secrets the mask might reveal, and of the wonders capable of a boy with no face.

ALL DAY LONG, AS I SHUFFLED FROM GEOMETRY TO ENGLISH to theology, I felt the weight of Michael's eyes on me, thickening like a coat of guilt. He's cranking it up to make sure I don't back out, and I think the mask made him nervous yesterday. After school let out this afternoon, I wanted to try it on right away. But I was afraid that nothing would happen. That yesterday was a fluke. So all through weigh-ins and warm-ups for tonight's match against the Most Precious Blood Crusaders down in Rocker Hall, I waited. During the national anthem, maskless, I didn't risk looking into the crowd for fear that I might see Michael in the flesh. Plus there would be all those dads again, all those proud fathers who'd braved the cold to cheer on their sons. That was something I didn't need to see. Just before I was to go on the mat,

I handed Angela the mask, bent my head, and held my breath. Again came the snagging on my forehead, and again the strap being tightened under my chin. And when I picked up my head, that glorious rising returned. All my doubts and fears disappeared with Michael's weight, and I stood before the mat as light as air, bouncing like a boxer. The team crowded around me, slapping at my arms. Then the wrestlers parted and through the eyeholes of the mask I could see the mat in front of me, and my opponent already waiting, but looking away.

I was about to start forward when Nicky stepped in front of me, filling my field of vision. He put his hands on either side of the headgear and held me steady. Our eyes connected through the eyeholes of the mask. "It can happen," he declared without explanation.

But those words didn't need explaining, and as I jogged through the gauntlet of teammates and onto the mat, I knew the rightness of his prophecy.

When I reached the center of the mat, my opponent turned and looked at me and I could tell he was confused. He had been expecting the pale-faced boy from weigh-ins, Keegan Flannery. Not this other something, this faceless warrior.

At the whistle I leaned forward as if to lock up with him, and he leaned into me to do the same. But just before we touched, I snapped down and shot in, wrapping my arms around his right leg and jamming my shoulder into it, toppling him to the mat. The ref cried out, "Takedown, two!" From the Bulldog bench, barking broke out, "Woof-woof!"

He tried to escape from beneath me, shifting one way then the other, but he wasn't nearly as fast as Nicky, and I stayed on top of him, though I never had a chance to try and break him down. The whistle ending the first period sounded and I couldn't believe two minutes had passed.

At the break, I stood and my face burned with sweat. I locked my hands onto my hips and struggled to keep air coming in. The deep heaves of my breath echoed off the inside of the mask, and the heat came back onto my lips. But I saw Nicky and Morgan nodding at me from the bench, and our cheerleaders were actually hopping on the edge of the mat doing kicks for me, and even Benedict the Bulldog was wagging his stubby tail. The score was 2–0. I felt on the verge of exploding.

Even though I felt so good, my body was aching. I won the coin toss and chose the top position, not wanting to risk bottom until I had to. My opponent got on all fours, and at the ref's signal, I knelt beside him, wrapping one arm around his belly and placing one on his elbow. At the whistle, I chopped the elbow and bucked his body in that direction.

My opponent fell onto his chest and I began trying to slip an arm in somewhere, but again had no luck. Finally I scooted off to one side hoping to get this thing called a cradle, but as soon as my weight was not completely on him, my opponent scrambled from beneath me. I lunged after him and caught hold of a leg. Then I reached around his belly. Suddenly his arm locked on mine and he broke hard sideways, tumbling us both. When we stopped rolling he was somehow on top of me. "Reversal. Two!" the ref yelled.

Since we were almost out-of-bounds, the ref stopped time. I huffed my way back to the center, then got down on all fours. Beneath me, beads of sweat struck the mat. They were falling from my forehead and face, collecting along the inside of the mask and dripping out through the mouth hole. Even my stomach now was moving in and out with the pumping of my lungs.

The other wrestler settled on top of me, one hand on my elbow and the other resting on my belly. With the whistle's blast I sat out, swinging my legs from beneath me to in front of me, going from all fours to sitting on my rear end. There was no resistance from my opponent, and instantly I knew why. He was still behind me but he had shuffled off to my right. His left arm looped around my neck and the other scooped inside my bent knee. He brought his hands together and my knee rose up to the nose of the mask and he rocked us both backward and just that quickly I was staring into Rocker's big center light.

I heard the ref begin to count out back points. Only my one leg was free, and all I could think to do was kick it back and forth, hoping maybe it might get me loose. But his arms held me fast. I got a hand onto the knee he had trapped and pushed but that did nothing, and when I grabbed one of my opponent's fingers, the ref made me let go before I could pull. Nothing I was doing was getting me free, and I was so tired I thought I might pass out, but I didn't stop moving because I knew I was close to being pinned.

Both my shoulders pressed against something, but I realized they weren't flat. My right shoulder was actually resting in the crook between my opponent's arm and his chest. When he'd rolled me back, he'd pulled part of me onto him. The Crusader coach yelled, "Watch your back! Shuck out of there!" and instantly my opponent began to worm out from underneath me, trying to slide my other shoulder down and pin me. It felt like he was about to steal something that was mine. Something precious. I began thrashing about without anything in mind more than breaking free, but then the voice came, so close at first I thought it was Michael. Then I realized it sounded more like Nicky. The voice said, "Be calm. He's out of position. What's his coach saying?"

The Crusader coach had been hollering all along, "Watch your back!" Suddenly I understood. Like mine, my opponent's shoulders were almost flat on the mat. I scooted farther up onto his chest, then lowered my free leg and planted my foot. I pushed down and leaned into him, and after all the flailing around I'd been doing, he wasn't ready for me to reverse engines. Easily, we tilted together back into him, and I heard a cry from someone in the crowd and the sudden whack of the mat and then the whistle.

Part of me wants to say I wasn't sure which one of us was pinned, but the truth is I knew I was the winner well before the ref took my hand and raised it over my head. The rush that I'd had yesterday when I kicked Nicky came washing over me. It swept me away and I thought for sure as I walked off the mat my body might slip into the air from its lightness. My eyes turned up, and when they held on the Wrong-Hearted Jesus I couldn't believe it. He wasn't looking at me. His eyes stayed fixed on the middle of the mat, and I knew the mask hid me from His sight as well as Michael's. I heard the words Nicky had said before the match. "It can happen." And staring up at the frozen face of the Wrong-Hearted Jesus, a plan of my own began to take shape in my mind.

Everybody patted me on the shoulders and Nicky burst past me onto the mat for his match. I sat on the floor behind the bench, gulping air. Angela handed me a towel that I draped over my head. Alone, I rested my arms on my knees, and it all came to me, clear as a holy vision:

I saw myself Saturday night in Rocker, wearing the mask during the match and keeping it close afterward. In the locker room, I slip it inside my gym bag, next to a couple pairs of jeans, some sweatshirts, my toothbrush, and my letters from Patrick. I tell Morgan that Van Fowler is giving me a ride home, then go upstairs and hide in the darkness of the upper bleachers above the locker room. I watch the wrestlers leave one at a time, climbing up the opposite bleachers toward the alley. Around 11:30, I slide the mask on and disappear from Michael's radar. I descend into the wrestling room and go to the boiler and crank it up till it's good and hot and then at about 11:45, I turn the steel wheel and trap the steam inside that big black egg.

Most of this has been part of the plan for a week, but this is where things change. Because with the mask on, I don't stay. I follow the same route out that Morgan and the rest of the team did, sneak along the back alley and through the faculty parking lot, down the steep grassy hill and then across the field where the students park, into the forest beyond. I crouch behind a tree, and when the explosion comes I'm the only one in the world waiting for it.

The sound is muffled because the boiler is so deep in the ground, but the vibrations reach me there in the forest and as my bones shake I picture the girders of the building buckle and give way. The columns directly next to the boiler go first, and two or three of the other ones crumble as well. And down comes the away-team bleachers and the balcony and the cafeteria and study hall. Even the chapel, with its holy stained-glass windows, has the ground taken out from beneath it, and finds itself hanging in midair for a heartbeat.

From the forest I see the building collapse straight down into its own crater. Some debris tumbles back into the faculty parking lot, right over the spot where Nathan came to earth. A few bricks cartwheel down the steep hill and come to rest on the dead grass, only a few feet in front of me.

Just when the noise dies down and silence fills the empty space left in the air, smoke floods down the hill in one great curling wave, and somewhere a church bell chimes out midnight. I rise and step out from the edge of the forest and the wind that comes rushes through the holes in the mask and cools the sweat on my face and lifts the mask miraculously free, and I step straight ahead into the wash of smoke and let it take me.

And when the smoke finally settles I'm sixteen, waiting for my bus to Philadelphia, and alive.

SITTING EIGHT SEATS BACK AND TWO ROWS OVER FROM
Angela in study hall, I was hard at work on a suicide note
that even Mrs. Shaw would've given an A-plus. It was all
about the life I wished Angela and I could've had together,
how I would've built her a house and how I would've made
her happy. "*But,*" I wrote, "*these things just can't be.*" I had
plans to mail it to her, but then I pictured her opening the
envelope and unfolding my letter. She'd be shocked, probably figure me for crazy, and start scanning her past for little
things she may have done wrong. I know about guilt, and I
don't want Angela blaming herself for whatever happens.

I wonder if they'll even bother to try and dig through the
rubble, or if they'll just have the mother of all bake sales and

rebuild Our Lady. Of course, whether my body will be buried beneath all those bricks or riding the bus to Philly is a good question at this point. No matter what, though, I want to leave a suicide note. It might get Dad in trouble, but it's nothing he can't handle, and I'm sure that if I disappear on the same night the school blows up, Dr. Connors will put two and two together.

I want to make sure they know it wasn't an accident, that everybody knows I did it.

During lunch, I wrote one to Dr. Connors, telling him I'd been crying out for attention all these years and what kind of a doctor was he anyway if he couldn't see what pain I was in. It was all a crock, but it was the kind of language he'd expect to see. I imagined him writing an article about my case for a magazine, then tore the note up and buried the pieces in my empty milk carton and crushed it.

In Father Jim's biology class, while he talked about the five stages of mitosis, I wrote him a letter explaining how I appreciated what he said about Nathan even though it got him in trouble, and how I thought what he said was right, and that his sermons were a lot more interesting than Father Halderman's and everybody said so. But then I figured he might get the idea that what he said made me think it was okay to kill myself. And I guess there's some truth in that, but there's no reason for him to know it. So at last bell I balled up his note and dropped it in the garbage can just inside the door.

During wrestling practice, I tried to write one in my head for Dad but couldn't get past *"Dear Dad."*

Afterward in the locker room, as everybody got ready for the showers, I tried to pick out a wrestler I could leave a note with. Nicky might not tell anybody. Van Fowler might not be able to read it. Then my eyes turned through the crooked door and fell on Morgan. He was wrapping a towel around his waist and cutting across the locker room. He'd make the perfect messenger, honor-bound to report to the higher-ups and proud in a fatherly kind of way that I had confided in him. Besides, I owe him something, since he'll need to get another ninety-eight-pound warm body once I'm gone.

That being decided, I figured I'd wait for my ride home with Morgan and get to work on the actual writing. I knew though that a note to him wouldn't take long, and I wondered how I should spend the rest of my last full night as Keegan Flannery. The house would be empty until eleven or twelve, since Dad's going to Hellman House after work. I wonder when he sees Mom if she asks how I'm doing. I wonder what he tells her.

Morgan disappeared into the hissing shower, and I noticed Kook, Van Fowler, and Bugalski move together into a little huddle. They were whispering, but I heard them well enough.

Bugalski said, "Look, I'm not saying I can't get it. I'm just saying we can't count on it. It's not a sure thing."

"This is brilliant timing," Kook said. "Brilliant."

"What's the problem?" Van Fowler asked.

"Mrs. Fogel's sister got sick, so the bridge game got moved to my house. Mom's having it in the back room. So if she's already set up when I get home, it might be hard to get at the stuff."

"Might be?" Kook said. "You should've stashed some this morning."

I stood up and walked over. They turned as I got close, then all looked at one another and back at me.

"What?" Kook said.

"I can get some," I said. "I'll need a ride."

He smiled.

And so a few hours later, after Morgan had dropped me off and I'd enjoyed a Hungry Man Salisbury Steak with Corn Niblets, I found myself crouching in front of my father's opened liquor cabinet, wondering which bottles to swipe. "Whiskey" was the first name I recognized, and then "rum." Both those bottles had a thin layer of dust on them, and I couldn't remember if I'd ever heard about liquor getting bad with age. I lifted them out and left clean circles on the floor of the cabinet, then spread the other bottles around. Only when I was closing the cabinet doors did I notice the vodka, forced into a compartment on the door that looked like it should be holding glasses. One bottle was half empty; one was full. Just then I heard a car horn in the driveway. I lifted the full bottle and slipped it into my bag, certain that Dad would miss it.

I figured Kook would head for the forest by the field where students park, so when he drove straight into downtown Allentown and parked the car not far from Hess's Department Store, I thought he was nuts. There was no place at all to hide around there, and I could see two cop cars just down the block. Kook walked around and up onto the sidewalk. "Lock it," he said. "And don't forget the bag."

I did as I was told and followed him toward Hess's. Just before we reached the entrance, he turned down an alley. I trailed behind him, past a few Dumpsters and a car with a ticket on its windshield. Then we cut onto an even smaller street and for just a second I thought this was a dead end and he was planning to mug me. He'd take the booze to where he was really going after he took care of me. "Hey," I said. "Where are we headed?"

"We're here," Kook answered, looking up at a sign that read, MR. B'S FINE HAIR SALON. Beneath the sign was a set of stairs leading down to a store with a big picture window covered with iron bars. After we went down the stairs, the alley was just above my head. Something ruffled the curtain in the window and the door seemed to open on its own. I stepped into the darkness behind Kook, and heard the click of the latch as the door was locked behind me.

Inside, dark shapes shifted against a green glow. Someone took the bag from my hand. "What've we got?"

It was Bugalski. As he began his inventory of the stolen goods, my eyes adjusted to the light of the "salon," more barbershop than beauty parlor. The square room had a low ceiling and two barber chairs bolted to the floor in the middle. Van Fowler was sitting in one of them, checking out his face in the mirror that lined the top half of the wall across from the picture window. The bottom half of that wall was one long cabinet, covered with a little skyline of hair spray bottles, with a cash register at one end. In the middle of the cabinet was a small light, next to a glass container with combs floating in green liquid. The light reflected off the mirror and gave the room a soft green sunset. Scattered against the remaining space were six other chairs, only two of which matched.

A yellowed five and a ten were taped up in one corner of the mirror. I had a little déjà vu, and then realized Mr. Frederick, my dad's barber, had money taped to the mirror at his shop in the lobby of the Ambassador Hotel. Dad used to take me there with him and every time I climbed up onto Mr. Frederick's chair, I'd wait for his big line. About ten seconds into his combing, he'd always say, "Boy, you've got your father's hair." Then he'd cut it to make it match Dad's, medium length, ears cut out, parted on the left. At the end when I was leaving he'd offer me a lollipop. When I was twelve he bent and held it out like a flower and I said, "I'm twelve." After that I never went back.

I tried to find a photograph of Mr. Bugalski along the walls, so I could see if his son had the same kind of hair, but there wasn't one.

Nicky sat in one of the unmatched chairs in the corner, holding something thin and square up to his face with both his hands.

Van Fowler swiveled in the barber's chair, like Captain Kirk on the bridge of the *Enterprise*. "So what've we got?"

Kook, who had taken the bag from Bugalski, said, "Whiskey, rum, vodka. Full bottles."

Van Fowler smiled at me. "Damn, Three-Quarters, you some kind of bootlegger?"

I laughed, though nobody else did, but it didn't bother me.

Bugalski looked into the empty bag. "Didn't you have any schnapps? I like to drink schnapps."

"Schnapps is for sissies," Kook said. He twisted the top

off the whiskey and took a draw, then passed it to Van Fowler.

Kook commandeered the other barber seat, and I pulled one of the chairs over so I was in the middle, though considerably lower. Bugalski dragged a chair too, but said under his breath, "We should get some mixers. I don't feel like throwing up tonight."

Nicky stood and walked over to a small plastic box next to the cash register. The top was open, and it was supposed to look like a treasure chest. Nicky dropped the square he'd been holding, then reached inside and pulled out another one. He turned around and hoisted himself up onto the counter, close to the light. His thumbs shifted along the square, and I realized he was working one of those puzzles with tiles set up on a grid like tic-tac-toe with nine spaces. If the tiles get arranged in the right order, they make a picture. But the most important tile is the one that's missing, because that empty space is what lets the other tiles move.

Van Fowler reached down and tapped the bottle against my chest. I held it for a moment before bringing the top to my lips. The liquor along the smooth rim had the taste of cough medicine, but I lifted the bottle and sent a splash of whiskey rushing into my mouth. The muscles in my throat kicked, and I almost spit the bitterness back out, but somehow my lips stayed closed. I forced a swallow and felt the movement of the liquor, a warm burning that lingered in the center of my chest.

Van Fowler smiled at the face I made and said, "Woof-woof."

Kook lifted the bottle away, gulped a quick one, and thrust it at Bugalski. "Come on, Bug, hair on your chest and all."

It was quiet for a bit, then out of the blue Van Fowler asked me, "You got a brother named Andrew?"

"Yeah," I said.

"He's a jerk."

"Yeah," I said again.

"What do you mean, 'yeah'? That's your brother."

I told them about Andrew chopping up my *Space: 1999* action figures with an ax, then blaming it on the lawn mower. I told them about him grabbing my comics whenever he comes home from college and wrecking the covers. I regretted saying that, thinking they might laugh that I read comic books.

Kook said, "Marvel or DC?"

"Marvel," I said.

"Damn." Kook shook his head. "Jerk."

Van Fowler swiped the bottle from Bug and said, "If that creep was still at school, I'd kick his ass next time I saw him. Just on principle."

He took a slow draw, and it occurred to me that he was serious. He really would pick a fight with my brother just because he had wronged me. I was glad I'd brought the booze.

"Time," Nicky said, looking at his watch. It was the first thing he'd said since I walked in. He put the puzzle back in the box and pulled out another one.

Bugalski said, "Hey, Nicky, hand me one of those."

Kook asked Van Fowler, "How's business with you and Angie?"

"Who knows."

Nicky spun a puzzle square at Bugalski.

I was happy Van Fowler answered that way. I didn't want to hear the intimate details of what he and Angela were or weren't doing. I didn't want to know if they were getting together again like everybody was saying.

"I wish we had a *Playboy*," Bugalski said.

Kook said, "That'd be great. I'd love to spend another night watching you drool over dirty pictures."

Everyone laughed. Even Nicky looked up, grinning. This was obviously referring to some previous episode, and even though I wasn't sure exactly what happened, I laughed as well.

Bugalski gave up on the puzzle he was working on.

Kook started a story about visiting his brother at Penn

State and watching a dirty movie projected onto a white bedsheet hung in a dorm study hall. The bad thing was that the sound was missing. Kook described the first scene — a rich man and a maid having sex on the kitchen table. After that she went to take a shower, and another girl got in the shower with her.

"Bull," Van Fowler said.

"Were they kissing?" Bugalski asked.

Kook grinned. "All over."

Bugalski giggled and asked if the girls were pretty.

"Well, sure," Kook said. "They were naked."

"Was this the one your momma was in?" Van Fowler asked.

All the while, Nicky kept working his puzzles, not paying too much attention to Kook's descriptions of the movie. Every now and then he'd snap, "Time," and check his watch.

We were about halfway down the whiskey bottle when Van Fowler said he wanted to play some game called "Alphabet."

Bugalski said, "Okay, but just for drinking, no hitting."

Kook punched him hard in the arm. "Whatever you say."

Bugalski massaged his bicep.

Van Fowler leaned over to me and explained that you had to name a band that started with a certain letter of the alphabet. If it was your turn and you couldn't think of one, you had to drink, and everybody else got to punch you in the arm. Then he asked, "You want in?"

I nodded my head, which was beginning to tingle.

They didn't ask Nicky.

The first time around Kook got America, then Bugalski said ABBA, then Van Fowler said the Allman Brothers, which was the one I had in mind. They pressed me for an answer and finally I came up with Alice Cooper, but Kook told me you could only use last names. Finally I offered my right arm and Kook, then Bugalski, then Van Fowler drilled my bicep. It's not like it didn't hurt, but it felt almost like a charley horse, like it was kind of funny.

Van Fowler was the one who ran out of B's. I had two good ones that round, the Bee Gees and Bachman Turner Overdrive. Kook punched him, then Bugalski. I stayed in my chair. Kook said, "Come on, whale him." And when I stood and drove my fist as hard as I could into this arm that was easily twice the size of mine, my eyes moved to Van Fowler's face and I saw he was looking at me, smiling with soft pain.

"Good shot," Van Fowler said, but it was strictly for my benefit.

So we played the game and passed the bottle and took turns stumbling to the bathroom no bigger than a closet. Whenever Van Fowler went, he didn't close the door, and the rest of us tried not to laugh at the sound. The whiskey ran dry somewhere around "V," by which time my head felt like it might float away. Bugalski didn't want to drink the rum straight. "I'm gonna go out and get some Coke."

"Where you gonna go?" Kook wanted to know.

"7-Eleven over on Linden. If it's the old guy he'll sell me a *Playboy*."

"Stop by Salvatore's and get me a slice of pizza. No anchovies."

"Yeah," Van Fowler said. "And get me a cheesesteak, everything, and some fries."

As a heavyweight, Van Fowler doesn't need to worry about his weight. I asked if anything was good to mix with vodka.

"Orange juice." That came from Nicky, who kept his eyes on his puzzle even as he added the name of the drink, "Screwdriver."

I reached into my pocket and pulled out the money Dad had left me to eat dinner with. I handed Bugalski two bucks and asked him to get me some orange juice.

Bugalski took it but started whining about how much he was going to have to carry. He wanted me to go with him, so I stood up. But halfway up I felt a rush of dizziness in my head and my knees went wobbly. I dropped back into my chair. "Sorry," I said, "but I don't think that would be a really good idea."

A chuckle came from Van Fowler. "Somebody's three-quarters gone."

"I'm not getting the pizza," Bugalski announced.

Kook got up. "Hell, I'll come with you." He grabbed his jacket and added, "Maybe see my ladies."

Van Fowler brightened. "Maybe your momma will be out tonight." He got his coat too. Linden Street is just one over from Sixth, where Allentown's few prostitutes keep patrol.

Kook gave him a dirty look, but then the three of them stumbled off together into the cold and just like that, I was alone with Nicky and his puzzles.

I'd been watching Nicky as we all drank. He didn't seem affected by the alcohol very much. It was very quiet in the shop, and for a long while I sat doing nothing. Finally I got to my feet, the floating in my head lifting my body as I moved, and took careful steps to the barber chair closer to Nicky. I reached down and picked up the puzzle Bugalski had given up on and started shifting the pieces around. It was a pirate ship or something, I couldn't tell. Again it was quiet for a minute or two, until Nicky said, "Get the corners first."

"Thanks," I said. Fearing the silence, I went on. "This some kind of hobby with you?"

"Not really. I'm testing my mental abilities."

I didn't ask.

"Usually these things take me four or five minutes. Tonight I've been right around two and a half."

"So you think booze makes you think better?"

"Hell, no." He dropped the finished puzzle in the box and didn't get another one. "What's the longest you've ever gone without eating?"

"I gave up chocolate for Lent last year," I said.

"Since Tuesday night I haven't eaten anything but sixteen saltine crackers, two oranges, water, and my share of this." Nicky pointed at the empty whiskey bottle, then added, "I'm not counting pig-out."

Pig-out is the ritual trip to McDonald's after each wrestling match. All the guys who suck weight go crazy on Big Macs and shakes. Bugalski told me he put on six pounds like that once. And since your body is so starved for food, the weight stays. But by morning of course, you're hungry, and the whole cycle begins again.

Nicky hopped down and opened the rum, took a shot, and passed the bottle. As my lips touched the rim, I got my first hint of rum. I didn't like it. I took a quick gulp and felt a spasm in my stomach. The liquor jerked back up into my mouth, and I swallowed again. It tasted no better the second time.

Nicky slid back up onto the counter. "The first twenty-four hours are the hardest. Your body keeps expecting more food. But once it gets the message, once it knows this is all it's going to get, your hunger just . . . goes. You might feel a little woozy on day two, and extra sleep's good if you can get it. Gotta watch out for muscle cramps. By day three, you're through the wall, and you start to feel really peaceful and smart. Like that bald guy who does kung fu in the Old West. You feel like you're out on the edge of everything looking in, and it all seems crystal clear. Everything." He glanced at the box of puzzles, now all perfect pictures — a lady pushing a baby cart, a house with flowers in the windows.

"I meant to thank you," I said. "For the other night. What you said during my match. About staying calm."

"During your match?" Nicky said. "During your match I didn't say squat. I was warming up. You must be hearing voices."

I chuckled to myself at his accidental wisdom. Sitting up on the counter, his face backlighted with the green shine glowing off the mirror, Nicky did seem very old and very wise. But he also seemed tired and worn out, and I wondered what price he paid for staying at 105. He could go up to 112 and be stronger and have more energy. So when I finally spoke, I asked him the same question I'd asked him in the boiler room. "Why do you do it?"

Nicky was quiet. He knew what I meant. A garbage truck rumbled outside. The men were laughing about something. "I'll tell you," Nicky said, "but then I got a question of my own."

I nodded.

He leaned back into the mirror and tilted his head up, like he wasn't really talking to me. "One-oh-five is mine. Everybody knows who I am. Nick Carpelli, that crazy Bulldog 105-pounder from Our Lady. Even the geek I beat at St. Francis knew me. When I step up on the scale everybody watches me because they all wonder if I'll make it or not. All those eyes, all that energy, is focused right on me. And then when I do make weight, I've earned something. The right to walk out on the mat. To stand out there alone with some guy I don't know and go at it. I make my weight, I take the mat, I kick some ass, or I get my ass kicked. No complaints. No excuses. That's who I am. That's what I got."

In the long silence that followed, I had no idea what I was doing in the place where I was. Then Nicky asked his question. "So what've you got?"

I had no answer. I knew that even if I blurted out all the great plans for tomorrow night they wouldn't compare.

Without the mask, I had nothing — my side of the scales was all but empty.

The patterns in the wallpaper seemed to be moving in and out as if the walls were breathing. I took a long drink of rum and felt another twinge in my stomach, stronger this time. I looked up at Nicky and saw my face in the mirror and heard myself say, "I've got my father's hair."

That made Nicky laugh, and the sound of his laughter made me laugh. "Well, hell," he said, "that's a problem I can remedy."

He scooted down and lifted something off the wall. There was a sudden buzzing sound, and Nicky moved behind me, a cord snaking from his hand to an electrical outlet. One hand pushed my head down, chin almost touching my chest, and I felt the tingling run over the top of my scalp. Passing before my eyes, a thick patch of hair dropped onto my lap. I laughed and Nicky told me to stay still. I closed my eyes and I think I would've fallen asleep but the feeling that the room was tilting came over me. I gripped the arm rests and opened my eyes and there were mounds of hair piled on my lap. A fresh clump fell and avalanched a bunch onto the floor.

I picked up some of the hair off my knee and rubbed it between my fingers and couldn't feel it at all. In the back of

my mind I wondered if this would help disguise me tomorrow night. I wondered too how Nicky would feel if I went
ahead and killed myself.

The buzzing stopped and I turned into Nicky's laughter
and the bottle of rum was in my chest. "Have a drink and
take a look."

I lifted my head and saw my face in the mirror and was
laughing so hard I had to close my eyes. There was still hair
on my head, but no more than a half inch all the way
around, like somebody going into boot camp. I got out of
the chair and tripped forward into the counter, and with my
face almost touching the mirror I saw blood spotting along
the edge of my forehead. I inhaled and caught a whiff of hair
tonic or something that made the muscles in my stomach go
tight. That sour taste flashed back into my throat. I pulled
my face away from the smell and the green glow, and my
head went light and I found myself on the floor next to one
of the barber's chairs. My knees hurt. Nicky helped me into
the chair and said, "You look like crap."

"Well," I said, "I feel worse."

I'm not sure how long I was sitting there, and I remember Nicky telling me to think about sand dunes for some
reason. Then I heard the door open and a wave of cold air
came in and all of a sudden the whole world reeked of
cheesesteak and pizza. The surge came rushing up from my

gut and I scrambled out of the chair and was on my knees
holding the cold sides of the toilet. My body was bucking
with the contractions of my stomach. Behind me Kook said,
"Hey, corn niblets."

They helped me up when I was done, and somebody
rubbed a towel across my face. Then somebody ran his hand
over my head. They laid me down in one of the barber
chairs and lowered the back and I felt the warmth of my coat
being laid on top of me. Just before I slipped away, I heard
Bugalski ask, "Is he gonna want this OJ?"

I don't know what time it was when they woke me up, but
the streets were pretty empty. I thought the car ride might
make me sick again but Kook said, "Hell. You pretty much
filled that toilet. It was a three-flusher. I doubt you'll even
have a hangover."

Somehow I felt remarkably calm — there was nobody
out and everything seemed very peaceful. Van Fowler kept
reaching back and rubbing my head. "You're gonna start a
fire," Nicky said. He was sitting next to me in the backseat.
I vaguely remember Bugalski being dropped off somewhere.
As the car moved down the streets of my neighborhood, I
heard enough to figure out that they weren't done yet. They
were going to a party someplace. I was going to tell them to
bring me along, and I'll bet they would have, but then I saw

the empty driveway and knew Dad wasn't home yet. "Anywhere along here is fine."

Kook pulled over to the curb and I opened the door. From the front seat, Van Fowler said, "Give your momma a kiss for me."

Nicky's hand shot out and smacked the back of Fowler's head. The heavyweight turned and said, "What?"

Nicky didn't actually speak; he only mouthed the words to Fowler, I guess so I wouldn't hear. But I read his lips just fine. "His mother is dead."

They all looked at me. I stayed silent.

"Hey," Fowler said. "I'm a . . . I'm sorry man, I didn't —"

I stepped into the cold and flipped the door closed behind me. I heard the engine idling as I walked up the empty driveway, and they didn't pull away until I was safe inside. Now all this should've probably rattled my chain good, but it only made sense. Rumors get started all the time at OLPH and nobody corrects them. But somehow I felt shame at what I hadn't said.

I pushed it out of my mind and got ready for Dad's arrival home. I went into the fridge and found some orange juice, then mixed myself a screwdriver with the half bottle of vodka I'd left in the cabinet. In the darkened living room I settled into his chair, watching the front door.

I knew what was going to happen, and I guess because I

was sitting there waiting for it, some part of me wanted it. He'd walk in and see me sprawled out on his chair, and he'd step closer and flip the light on and see my new haircut. He'd say, "What kind of a haircut is that?"

It would anger him that he couldn't do anything about it, and when he started yelling at me I would lift the glass from alongside the chair and raise it to my lips. I made it in one of the glasses he uses, so he'd recognize it right away. But still, I knew he'd ask, "What is that?"

And I thought up the perfect answer. "It's a screwdriver," I'd say. "Want one?" When he realized I was really drinking he'd go ape, maybe knock the glass from my hands, and I imagined the ice and the splash of orange hanging in the air.

He'd rage about me drinking while trying to hide his own breath. He always comes home a little lit up after he visits Hellman House, but I know it's not because of what he sees there. It's because of what he's got to come home to.

As I sat waiting in his chair, drifting in and out of sleep, I grew certain that tonight the truth at the center of his life and mine would be released at last. My father would finally let loose those words he's been keeping inside all these years. "You did this to me."

At the sound of the door opening I woke, just in time to watch him walk past me, completely unnoticed in the dark. He closed the bathroom door behind him and stayed in there for a long time. But I knew he hadn't passed out because every now and then I heard him humming, very low, a song I couldn't quite place. At the sound of the flushing toilet, I almost reached for the light myself, but I was still hoping he'd see me on his own. When he came out, though, he turned away from the living room and went into the kitchen. I waited for the sound of the refrigerator coming open but again I was wrong, and it took me a second to recognize the squeak of the hinges on the basement door.

I stood and moved quietly into the kitchen. The door leading downstairs was cracked open, and I put my face up to the opening. Looking down, I saw the movement of his angled shadow and heard a few cardboard boxes being shuffled. There was the sound of a table or chair being dragged, and then nothing for a long time and the whole house seemed unbearably quiet.

I thought maybe he'd passed out, but then a single, quivering note rose from the piano. The smiling one with the missing teeth. The deep note hung alone and filled the air. Then it sounded again. In the second's wake I heard him humming, the same song from the bathroom, and he began to play it, though very slowly, uncertain. After a minute or so, he became more confident in the song, and its tempo matched his humming. Although I still didn't know what song it was, it was clear some of the notes were missing, that the absent keys kept him from playing the song the way it was supposed to be.

I'd never heard him play before, and I couldn't imagine the sight of his fingers rising and falling along the keyboard. I wanted to go down the stairs and stand beside him, set my hand on his shoulder, but suddenly I felt almost embarrassed to be where I was, and I became afraid of being noticed.

I stepped away from the door and crept upstairs into my bedroom, and when my head sunk into my pillow I felt exhausted. I was confused by everything, and overwhelmed by the urge to be done with all my life's complications.

Even though the basement is far from my room, I could still make out the soft sounds of Dad's song. I knew his mind was with Mom and that touched me. I closed my eyes and imagined her sitting on the side of my bed, singing me the song he was playing, singing it to me like a lullaby.

DESPITE KOOK'S PREDICTION, I WOKE UP WITH A HEADACHE
and a heavy feeling I can only guess was a hangover. Around
ten, I crawled into the bathroom to get some Tylenol from
behind the mirror and ran smack into my new look. I
rubbed my hand over the fuzz on my head, and picked at a
few of the tiny scabs along my forehead. I heard Dad downstairs so I decided to go back to bed. I didn't think having a
fight over my new haircut was the best way to begin my last
day on Earth.

Next time I woke up it was close to twelve. My head
wasn't feeling quite like a bowling ball anymore, but I still
didn't want to go downstairs and find Dad. I wasn't at all
sure how I wanted my last scene to go with him, and lying

on my bed, I thought about the possibility of not having one at all. Just disappearing without a trace.

Eventually I rolled from my bunk and packed my gym bag with my wrestling gear and all the clean clothes I could fit. I counted all the money I had in my sock drawer. It came to seventy-two dollars. Both times. As an afterthought, for no reason I could think of, I stuffed in Patrick's drumsticks.

After I was done packing, I sat on my unmade bed and wrote the letter for Morgan, which took me a lot longer than I'd expected. I found myself running on too much and thought some of the things sounded suspicious. So I finally settled on this: "*Coach, I blew up the school from the boiler room because I'm upset about a lot of things. It isn't anybody's fault. Sorry. Thanks. Three-Quarters.*"

It wouldn't win any awards, but they'd get the message.

By then I was hungry, and my head was feeling as good as it was going to, so I went downstairs to face the man. He wasn't there. The radio in the kitchen was left on, and there was a note on the table. "*I had to go to the office. Be back in a few hours. Maybe we could go out to dinner tonight. Talk to you when I get back.*"

I read the note three times, then set it down.

We eat out every now and then. But it's never anything planned unless it's Christmas or some special day. I thought about the music he was playing last night and decided he had some kind of bad news about Mom.

I toasted the last Pop-Tart and threw away the empty box, then found *Jason and the Argonauts* on one of the channels we get out of Philadelphia. Watching those heroes search for treasure made me wish there was a way I could take a boat somewhere.

I wished I knew for sure where Patrick was.

Checking the Saturday afternoon schedule, I found three city buses that would get me to Rocker on time for the match: the 3:20, 4:20, and the 5:20. Weigh-ins weren't until 6:30, so even with the walk and stopping to buy the bus ticket to Philly in advance, I'd have enough time if I caught the 5:20. But Nicky was still a couple of pounds over last night and I knew he'd be in early trying to suck down. I decided I'd go in and work out with him, just let him throw me around some. It's better than jumping rope or jogging by yourself. I also had to worry about getting Patrick's letters from my locker and finding a good place to stash my note for Morgan. So at 3:00, right after Jason defeated the metal giant by unscrewing his ankle, when there was still no sign of Dad, I figured it was high time I set sail.

I took a pen and beneath Dad's note put, "*Wrestling match. Don't wait up.*"

* * *

I expected trouble at the bus station downtown, questions about who I was going to see or why a kid was leaving so late at night. But when I walked up to the glass booth, the man inside barely looked away from his tiny black-and-white TV. I peered in and saw Jason, fighting with the seven-headed hydra.

I said, "Philadelphia, tonight at 12:20."

He said, "Ten bucks."

I got to Rocker just before four. Nicky was running stairs, and when he saw me come in, he jogged over. His face was a burning red. "What'd your old man think of the haircut?"

"He loved it," I said. "Wants to know if you make house calls."

Nicky grinned and I asked him where he was at. "I'm golden. Twenty minutes ago I was 106 on the nose."

A pound wouldn't be hard to shed. He had two hours plus. He didn't need me. But he lifted his chin and said, "Want to work out some?"

I changed and we drilled for a while, mostly doing short buzzsaws. Basically it means you take turns doing moves, and your opponent lets you do whatever you try, then you return the favor. Like I'd shoot on Nicky and he'd let me take him down. Then he'd hit a switch to get a reversal and I wouldn't resist. Then I'd sit out, try to roll into a Peterson. The idea is for both wrestlers to keep moving, going from one move to the next. Nonstop motion.

Each buzzsaw lasted about three or four minutes, and Nicky would talk as we went from move to move, saying things like, "Look where you're at." "Where's my leg?" "Why were you open for that?" And in between, as we paced the walls to catch our breath, he'd tell me the things I'd done wrong and the things I'd done right.

After the last one, we leaned together against the wall opposite the Other Ten Commandments, sucking in deep gulps of air. I scanned the list and realized that here, in this wrestling world, I was sinless. But outside, I knew what the real Bible commanded: Honor Thy Mother. I thought of last night, how I had denied her. I turned to Nicky, sweat dripping from his forehead, and said, "My mom's not dead."

He looked at me. "Yeah?"

"Yeah. She's just real sick. She's in a hospital."

"That sucks," Nicky said. "I hope she gets better."

"Yeah," I said. And it was just that simple. Nothing dramatic changed between us. The heavens didn't crumble because I spoke the truth out loud.

He kicked off the wall. "Let's check my weight."

Accepting his invitation, I walked side by side with Nicky over to the locker room, hands on our hips, our breath slowly returning to normal. Nicky stripped and wiped the sweat from his body with a T-shirt, then stepped on the scale, already set to 105. The metal pointer lifted, tapped, and settled barely against the upper rim. Nicky said, "That's an eighth, maybe."

His prediction was accurate; when he tapped the countermeasure two notches over, the pointer eased down, and I saw light between it and the rim. That's all a ref needs. Nicky decided to sauna for a while, figuring that would take the rest of the weight off. There's no real sauna at Our Lady, sometimes they just carry a bench from the locker room into the shower and crank all twelve heads up to full blast. It gets hot pretty fast.

I helped Nicky set up, and even sat with him for a while. He lay down on the bench with a towel under his head and his hands draping off the sides. "Tell me what you had for breakfast," he said.

"Pop-Tart."

"What kind?"

"Blueberry."

"Toasted or raw?"

"Toasted."

He smiled. "I like mine straight."

With that smile on his face, he drifted off into a half trance, half sleep, and I decided to let him be. I dried off and got back into regular clothes. By now it was about 5:00. The other guys would start showing up in a half hour or so. I headed for my locker.

It was strange being alone in the school hallways, with only the light from the windows down at the end. I came up to my locker outside homeroom and again saw Nathan's empty locker. They just took away his books one night. I turned to my combination and rolled the dial, swung the door back for the last time. My geometry book spilled out and smacked the tile floor, sending an echo down the hallway. I knew the brown bag with Patrick's letters was probably way down at the bottom, so I started unloading stacks of paper and folders and books right down onto the floor. After tonight, who'd know the difference?

I spotted a tuft of brown paper and pulled at it under the mess of folders and books. As the bag came loose, a cigarette tumbled to the floor. But when I bent to pick it up, I saw that it was really a note. Kids roll them up like cigarettes so they can fit through the grates of the locker. I'd seen them before, but never gotten one. As I unrolled it, I imagined Angela secretly sneaking off to my locker and pushing this through the grate. The image gave me déjà vu, and when I saw the handwriting, I instantly knew why. The note was from Nathan Looby.

On his way to that fateful window, he had stopped not at his locker, but at mine. To deliver this message to me.

I turned around and leaned against the lockers, then slid onto the floor. I read.

Keegan,

When you read this I will be dead and gone. Even though we weren't really friends, you were always nice to me, so I thought I should tell you why I did what I did. The reason is very simple — I just don't like what I am.

Ever since I was little, the only way anybody ever knew me was "that poor handicapped boy." Nothing I did was ever going to change that, because those people were right.

Please tell my mom that it wasn't her fault I wanted to die. Tell her I'm sorry for all the trouble I put her through. Tell her she was the happiest thing in my life. But between you and me, she just wasn't enough. She tried to pretend I was normal and she was pretty good at it, but I always knew the truth. You can't change what you are.

> *Your friend,*
> *Nathan Looby*

I'd always understood why Nathan had committed suicide I guess, but having it spelled out like that, touching the very paper he'd held just before he died, was too much. I sat there stunned, frozen for a good five minutes.

When I finally snapped out of it, I moved quickly, stuffing the note deep into my pocket and double-timing it for the locker room. Obviously the thing to do was to get rid of it. Burn it. Flush it down a toilet. If I told anybody about the note now, there would be all kinds of questions and I'd get hauled down to the police station and all my plans for the night would be ruined. I'd never have the same chance again.

I got downstairs and slipped into the bathroom. Through the wall I could hear the shush of Nicky's sauna still going. Nobody else was around, but they would be soon. I went into the only stall with a door, and held the note over the still water. It was the same place where they'd dunked me, the same toilet where the pieces of Angela's note had fluttered down out of my shirt pocket. Again I mourned the words from that note that I would never know, and my mind turned to Mrs. Looby. I thought of her standing up during Father Halderman's sermon, her hand fisted inside the black glove. I wondered where she was at that exact moment. Sitting at home with a blanket across her lap, staring at nothing, with a glass of water beside her, untouched.

Nathan had asked me to do something to help his mother. He knew how upset she'd get. And I knew better than anybody where that kind of thing can lead.

I closed the toilet and sat down. I thought about the pay phone up on the court. I could make a quick, anonymous call and tell her the things Nathan wanted her to hear. There was a phone book in the coaches' office; the number would be there. But Marsha might answer and recognize my voice. And besides, I doubted anyone would believe a kid who wouldn't give his name.

Then I thought about leaving Mrs. Looby the note. I'd just pass it to Morgan with mine and he'd turn it over to Father Halderman who would give it to the police and sooner or later they'd let her read it and she'd know. But scanning the letter, I saw the sentence, *"But between you and me, she just wasn't enough."* That would kill her.

Scratching that sentence out might help, but then they'd question why I'd done it. And even if I did the same to my name, if it arrived with my own suicide note, they'd figure it out. I had to think of a way that the police could tell her the good parts of the letter without letting her see the bad parts. I wondered if the letter might not be her legal property, or if the police would hold it as evidence. The police might not care at all and tell her nothing. Or worse, tell her everything. I was out of my league, and I only knew one person who could help me. I looked at my watch. It was 5:25. I stood up and folded the note into my pocket, stashed Patrick's postcards in my gym bag, slid on my coat, and headed for the stairs.

The bus made good time, dropped me off at 6:15, three blocks from home. When I came in the front door, I heard

Dad in the kitchen. I could tell by his voice that he was on the phone.

I didn't have time to wait, so I walked through the dining room, then stood in the kitchen doorway, just behind him. He heard me there and turned, still talking. He stopped in the middle of a word that started off "tra-" and his mouth stayed open and his eyes grew large. He said to whoever it was, "I'll need to call you back."

He hung up and asked me, "Are you alright?"

I nodded.

"What happened?"

I told him one of the wrestlers had shaved my head last night as a prank.

He picked the note up off the kitchen counter and said, "Yeah, wrestling. I thought you had a game tonight."

"I do," I said. "A match."

I was still catching my breath after running from the bus. "I came back because I have to talk to you about something. Something important. But no matter what I say, can you give me a ride back to school?"

"Sure," he said.

All this time he'd been studying my face, and I realized just how different I must have looked to him. Along with my new haircut was a fresh mat burn across one cheek from the last buzzsaw. The skin was tender and red. And my nose was still a bit swollen from my match with Nicky, tinged with the blue-and-purple shade of bruises. Compared to two weeks ago, I looked like a different boy.

He stepped to the head of the dining room table and said, "Let's sit."

I sat on his right, where I used to when we had family dinners. He crossed his arms and leaned away from the empty table, and I put my elbows up and laid my chin into my folded hands. There was nothing to keep me from telling him about the note in my pocket and all that went with it. But when I finally broke the silence, my words surprised me. I asked, "How is she?"

"The same," he said. "No change."

These were the exact words I'd heard before, whenever Andrew asked about Mom, or when Dad was on the phone with family on the days following his visits. I had no idea what the words meant. But he remained frozen as a statue, straight-backed and arms crossed. Now at least I understood his silence. He couldn't start talking about her because if he did, his truth might slip: He knew I was to blame.

The crush of guilt pressed in on me, and I thought of my plan and the only way out. Taking a deep breath, I reached into my pocket and pulled out Nathan's note. "I found this in my locker today."

He took the note and held it with the tips of his fingers.

291

His eyes moved slowly back and forth across the lines. When he finished he said nothing. He only looked at me and waited, and his eyes on my face felt like a descending gray sky.

I could have turned away and held my silence, but instead, without really knowing why, I started telling him the whole story. I looked him straight in the eye and gave him every detail I could remember, from seeing Nathan's hearing aid on the cafeteria table to the thick pink scar around his neck to writing the message on the board to hiding in the bathroom. He asked no questions as I spoke.

I told him how I found out about the turtlenecks and what happened with Mrs. Looby the day of the memorial service. I told him about how people started thinking Nathan got pushed and how I was probably the prime suspect.

Then I realized what the next part of the story was and I stopped. I couldn't look at him and say what I had to say. So my eyes moved to the empty kitchen when I said, "After the police talked to her, Nathan's mom had kind of a breakdown."

Even on the edge of my sight, I saw him react to the word. Breakdown. Like a live wire.

I turned to him again, but now he looked away, toward the doors of his study, a place where he could hide from all that this was becoming. I pressed on, knowing that if I stopped I could never start again. "I'll bet she blames herself for her son's death."

Again we were silent for a long time, neither of us saying what we were both clearly thinking.

Finally, I said, "I think part of this note might help her."

He turned back to me. "It might."

"But if she sees all of it, it'll just make things worse."

"I think you're right."

"So what I need to know is, how do I do this without getting in trouble with Detective Dougherty?"

He went perfectly still, then held the note up in one hand. "Can I have this?"

I told him he could, instantly, and just as quickly he said, "Dougherty won't bother you again. I'll see that Mrs. Looby gets a copy of this, slightly edited. I'll tell her the original had that line scratched out."

I couldn't believe what he'd just said. For my father to lie, on any level, was inconceivable. It just wasn't the way things were. But he went on. "I'll tell her the identity of the student is being protected because he's a minor, but that I personally verified the note's authenticity. I'll make sure she gets Nathan's message and I'll keep your name out of it."

It was too much for me to process. My father seemed suddenly like a different man than the zombie I'd lived with for years. He must have read the surprise in my face as uncertainty because he leaned forward and said in a smooth, steady voice, "I promise."

I vaguely recall nodding my head, feeling almost dizzy. The clock in the living room started chiming out, and before it finished, the phone rang.

He stood and moved into the kitchen. As if from a great distance, I heard him say, "Yes . . . No . . . This is his father. . . . He's here. . . . I understand. . . . He'll be there in twenty minutes."

In a daze I followed him out to his car, and just like that we were rolling down Chew Street, headed for Our Lady. I watched the parked cars whizzing past and felt lost in the flow of my thoughts. I knew his plan was genuine; he would do exactly as he said. But why would he do such a thing? They'd guess where the note came from, and if he tried to silence Dougherty, it might lead to real trouble. Surely he saw this possibility too. Yet he drove without speaking, unnaturally calm. His face seemed softened somehow, and he was almost smiling. He did know what would happen, but he was prepared to bear all the suffering. That word "suffering" actually came through my head, and it made me think of the saints and how they atoned for their sins. I wondered what made Dad so eager for penance.

The car stopped. We had come to an intersection.

I said, "You think it's all your fault, don't you?"

He looked both ways and accelerated without looking at me. "I think what's all my fault?"

"Her," I said. "Mom."

His face jerked to me, but then went back to the traffic. "The doctors can't say for sure why it happened. It was probably just —"

"Stop it," I said. "You don't believe that. I can see it in your face."

I was right, and he knew it. We passed the bus station in silence.

I found myself tapping my forehead against the window. I wanted to stop thinking. I wanted to be gone. Dad told Ernie that Mom was dead because he feels guilty. Not because he doesn't love her. Not because he blames me.

The car rolled down the hill and he cut into the alley that leads to the faculty parking lot. He pulled up to the curb, but I didn't move. I stared out the window, at the place where Nathan had come to earth, and I wondered if Nathan had ever come close to talking with me like I wanted to talk then with my father.

"This is so crazy," I whispered. "All this time . . ."

"All this time what?" He turned the engine off.

The glass was cool on my forehead. "I always figured you were mad at me."

He said nothing. It was like he knew I wasn't finished. I heard the voice of the mask inside me. And the words rumbled around like an explosion until I turned and said, "I thought you blamed me."

He understood. That much I was sure of instantly. It was cold in the car now and when I said those last words, a long trail of air rolled out of his mouth, like a dying breath, and his face turned down.

He took his gloves off and reached over and laid his bare hands on either side of my face. His palms were warm. He tugged me over into him and pulled my face into his winter coat. I felt his chin cross back and forth on my scalp as he shook his head and said just one word: "Never."

His hands guided my face up, and our eyes came together. Then he pressed his lips to my forehead and kissed me there, as if I were a child.

The door to the school burst open and I saw Bugalski scramble out into the cold. Even through the frosted windows he saw me and yelled something, but the only word I could make out was "forfeit."

Without saying anything more to my father, I pulled away and jumped out. Bugalski was holding open the school door for me, but being on the verge of Rocker snapped me back to where I was, and what all my plans were, and I realized with a start that I might never see my father again. I leaned back into the car and I said, "What happened to Mom. It wasn't your fault."

He was looking away from me, out his window. And though he didn't face me when I offered absolution, his head nodded just enough so I knew he heard.

From there it's strange the way I remember the next hour or so. Things moved fast, and I couldn't keep my mind on where I was. Time seemed to jump and skip, and right from the beginning I had the feeling that I was riding some strong current.

Morgan met me on the basketball court and his hands gripped my shoulders, pushing me forward. Mock applause broke out when I came through the locker room doors and hands ran over my scalp, and the other team's assistant coach made a big fuss about the time and regulations. After the ref told me to get on the scale and confirmed I was under ninety-eight, the assistant coach demanded an exact weight. Some of the wrestlers nearby chuckled, since my weight has always been the same, and I didn't even watch the ref tap the countermeasure down the metal numbers. Then he stopped and said, "Call it ninety-seven even."

Then I was lying down on the bench by my locker and had the feeling that if I fell asleep I'd stay out for a long time. I touched my fingers to my forehead and tried to remember the last time he'd kissed me.

Nicky came over, scooping the last of some cold spaghetti noodles from a Tupperware bowl. He told me he ended up a quarter-pound under, and said he checked out my opponent at weigh-ins.

"He looked familiar. Maybe I saw him at a tourney somewhere, but that doesn't sound right. Anyway, the thing is he's small. Small like you."

Sometime after Nicky left I rolled off the bench and opened my gym locker. With my suicide note folded in the palm of my hand, I walked into Morgan's office. His gym bag was on the desk right in front of me. When he looked up I told him I was sorry about almost missing weigh-ins. I don't even know what he said. The bag had a small pocket facing me, and while he wasn't looking, I slipped in my note.

We warmed up in the wrestling room and I kept looking over at the black boiler-room door, knowing what was waiting behind it. It didn't make me nervous at all, but the sensation that something nameless was coming my way grew in my gut. Like steam building inside me.

Angela came down to tape up McMillen's knee. On her way out she walked by me and told me good luck and I saw her lips say that but I heard instead, "This one's a goner," and the pieces of her note fluttered out of my pocket and into the toilet.

Morgan came down and led us up onto the court and the

crowd gave a yell. The national anthem played and I swore some of the notes were missing but no one else seemed to notice.

Angela settled the mask over my face. Shovels of dirt came in on my grave. All aboard for Philadelphia. Behind the bench they pressed against me and the chanting began. People in the bleachers banged their feet and the team clapped their hands in unison. The clapping went faster and faster and I felt caught in a trance. Nathan stepping into the window. The broken sledgehammer. The stained-glass Hell. My face on Mom's stomach. Her breath on my neck at the water fountain. Dad's eyes in the rearview mirror. SICK CHILD carved in the wood. Frankenstein's heart in my hand. The browned leaves of Mom's plants. Pictures of me burned onto film. My hair drifting past my eyes. The gypsy's crystal ball in midair. My hands grabbing Michael's ankle in the womb. Nathan's empty window.

This final image lingered in my mind, and with it came the sudden silence of that room when the fire alarm quit. The sounds of the crowd were gone, and when the team parted to clear a path I felt the breeze come through the window and caress my face inside the mask. I lifted my eyes and looked through the eyeholes and just as I began jogging forward I saw my opponent waiting for me. I felt no surprise at all. He'd come here himself to finish the job in case I had second thoughts. In the middle of the mat, wearing a head-gear with a mask just like mine, stood my brother Michael.

I didn't have any chance to really think about what was happening. The referee pulled our hands together for the shake, and then we were circling each other. Through the mask, I could see Nicky was right. The muscles in Michael's arms and legs were about the same size as mine. We locked up and pushed into each other, the foreheads of our masks ramming together. I kept expecting him to talk to me, to taunt me somehow, but he said nothing.

We stepped in unison, jabbing forward and pulling back, testing each other for the first part of the period. Then I saw his leg out in the open and I shot. But by the time I got to where it had been, it was all but gone. I felt his weight on me as he sprawled, and although I got both my hands behind his knee, they weren't touching. I tried to pull his leg toward me so I could lock my hands, but his weight pressed down on my bent back and my grip slipped up his leg as he worked it away from me. Soon I was on both my knees, my head forced into the mat, his hips on my shoulders. His leg came free and he spun around behind me to score the take-down.

I got up on all fours but only for a second. His right arm swung inside my right elbow and knocked it up and out, then he drove me forward and I dropped onto my belly, pinning his arm beneath me. I felt it squirming but knew it couldn't hurt me. His free hand pressed my head into the mat as he shifted his weight up. His stomach came down on the back of my head and I felt him arching his back as his heels dug and kicked at my thighs. He wanted me to lift a knee so he could throw in legs, but I stayed flat. Better to get called for stalling.

But then I realized that he didn't want legs at all. It was a distraction. Not just for me, but for the ref and the crowd too. Nobody was paying any attention to the hand trapped under my chest, including me, until the fingers wormed their way up and formed around my throat. No one else knew. I was so flat I couldn't get my hands back to try and peel his fingers. They dug into my flesh. He was holding my windpipe in his hand and squeezing. I couldn't cry out, couldn't take a good breath.

I guess I must have lifted one of my knees. All at once he shot his leg inside and his hand let go of my neck. It squirmed up to lock with his other hand, forearmed down on the back of my neck, and when he cranked hard to one side, I rolled to my back like a dead fish.

The period ended. He got his back points. I got the message.

The second period started with me on top. He escaped without much trouble and immediately shot in on a fireman's carry. I snapped over his shoulder and if the mask wasn't on, my nose would've hit the mat before any other part of my body. Clearly he'd been baiting me when we started. He was better than me, and not just a little bit. I don't even know what moves he was using to turn me; one minute I'd be on all fours, struggling to break free, then the lights would be above me, and the ref counting out back points. He wasn't trying to pin me at all, he just wanted to humiliate me before the end.

We tumbled out of bounds at one point and I glanced over at the scorer's table. 15–0. Somebody yelled ten seconds. The second period was almost over, but Michael had the whole third period to keep punishing me. When we got back to the center I got on all fours and focused myself. I wanted things to change. I pictured the escape in my mind and thought, *It can happen.*

He settled on top of me, one hand resting on my elbow, one on my belly. Off the whistle I drove my left knee up and grabbed the hand on my belly and suddenly we were standing, him behind me. Half the move had worked. But when I tried to pop my hips and break away, his grip was too tight. His hands wrapped into each other, and squeezing into my stomach, they forced the breath out of me. He lifted me without effort, and the ref shouted something. An explosion

beneath me rocketed my body into the air. Through the eyeholes flashed Morgan, the Wrong-Hearted Jesus, the big
light over the mat, and in the next instant my world was upside down. The top of my head crashed into the mat, my
neck buckled, there was a shot of pain, and then darkness.

I couldn't have been out for very long. Even before I
opened my eyes, I felt hands on the headgear and heard Angela's voice. "Don't move him."

I opened my eyes and Morgan and Angela and the ref
were in the eyeholes, looking down. The crowd was totally
silent. Angela spoke again, this time to me. "How does your
neck feel?"

It hurt a lot, but I gave a shaky thumbs-up. The ref stood
and shouted, "Roll injury time. One point Bulldogs."

He had penalized my opponent for not bringing me
down safely, or after the period ended. I couldn't know
which.

I heard the ref again, "Two minutes, Coach."

The other coach answered, "Come on, he's fine."

Morgan called for water.

Angela said, "Lie still."

Bugalski showed up with a water bottle, and Morgan
went over to talk to the ref and the other coach. I heard
yelling.

I shook the water off. Bugalski leaned in close and whispered, "That was illegal. If you're hurt bad and can't go on, you win. Six team points."

Angela shot him a look. The next part he only mouthed, but I read it just fine. "Stay down. Don't fight it."

As the injury time ran, the fans got involved with what the coaches were saying. They started shouting back and forth across the mat, right over my body.

"Faker! Get up."

"Cheap shot artist."

"Baby!"

"He should win an Oscar!"

"Go on, play dead!"

My eyes moved to Angela, once again haloed by the big gym light. Here we were, in the exact same place we'd been two weeks ago, only this was no simulation. Michael was out to kill me. He could do it.

I found myself wondering suddenly if Dad had stayed. If he was watching me right now from the stands.

Angela said nothing and Morgan reappeared. "Thirty seconds. What's it gonna be?"

My eyes closed and I tried to block out the crowd. But they were too loud. I didn't even know why I was thinking. The pain was growing sharper and throbbing. If I got up and went on, I knew what would happen. Instead, I could be a hero to the team by doing nothing. By being nothing. It was exactly what I'd always wanted, the answer to all my prayers.

Then came the calm voice, so calm at first I thought it was my father's. Then Nicky's. Then Michael's. Then the mask's. But it wasn't coming from the crowd or anywhere else. And the voice said, "Rise."

And I did.

The crowd clapped and I nodded at Morgan and then at the ref, who signaled the injury time to be cut. The score was 15–1. Angela picked up her box and started to move away from me. I saw my arm reach out and take hold of hers. The calm voice spoke again and the words came through me. "The mask," I said. "Take it off."

Angela didn't ask any questions. All that remained clear to me was that if Michael was going to try to kill me, I was going to fight it, and I wanted to do that face-to-face. But even more, I wanted all those people shouting in the crowd to know who it was that was getting up and taking the mat. That this was me.

I wasn't expecting any miracles, and none came. The third period wasn't as bad as the first two, but I still couldn't score. He let me up, took me down, let me up, and did the same again. Though when he tried to turn me I was able to block him once or twice. After my mask was gone, I noticed other things too. The fake to the right before he tried to go left. The shine of sweat on his shoulders. The tape on his fingers. The scuffs on his sneakers. This was no avenging angel.

Michael wasn't my opponent. He never had been.

The final score was 25–4, but as we shook hands at the end, the other guy said through his mask, "Good match."

When I jogged back to the bench Nicky was waiting to go out. Our eyes came together for a moment, but it wasn't the time for words. He marched out and kicked his opponent's ass. Bugalski got pinned in the second period. Flynn won. The Grieber brothers split their matches. McMillen tied. Kook was ahead by four points when he got pinned. Van Fowler roared out to a big lead, then held on to win by a point. When all was said and done, we lost 25–22.

In the locker room everybody acted like they were mad we lost, but it was a good match and everyone knew it. People came by and patted me on the back. Nobody blamed me. On his way into the showers, Nicky stood over me and said, "Way to stick it out. Woof-woof." I forced a smile and barked back, then watched him disappear into the steam.

I went ahead with my plan and told Morgan I was getting a ride home with Van Fowler. I'd already seen him leave with Angela.

I climbed up into the bleachers and hid in the darkness where no one could see me. I watched the wrestlers come up one and two at a time, walk across the court, climb the far bleachers, and disappear into the stairway leading up to the faculty parking lot. When I was finally alone, the gym felt a lot like a church. Much more than when we have masses. Morgan was the last one out, and after he hit the switch, all that was left was the light above the Wrong-Hearted Jesus. Until my eyes adjusted, everything else was completely black, and it seemed like Jesus Himself was hanging there in space. In that near silence, I could hear the low rumble of the boiler every few minutes, like a beast clearing its throat. It occurred to me that I might say a prayer for guidance, but really I'd known what I had to do the second I'd known to stand up and finish the match.

I could just make out the outline of the steps as I walked to the pay phone. I reached in my pocket and touched my suicide note. I'd gotten it from Coach's bag when he was in the shower, and on the back of the note I'd copied the number from the phone book. The dime made a quiet click and I dialed, counting with the tips of my fingers. The sensation that I was in a holy place was very strong, and I cupped one hand over the receiver, like someone else might hear. When Mrs. Looby answered I knew her voice immediately. "Hello," I said, more in a whisper than anything else. "You don't know me, but I was a friend of Nathan's."

She asked, "Who is this?"

And I said clearly, "Keegan. Keegan Flannery." Nothing else.

But when the sound came out of me it was no whisper at all, and it rose into the darkness and returned off a distant wall somehow magnified. I recognized it as familiar, this sound from inside me, and all the voices that have come to me, Michael's and the mask's and the calm one tonight, all seemed sudden echoes of something else. Something real and alive.

I spoke calmly then to Mrs. Looby, giving her all the details I thought right. She didn't say much as I talked, and at the end I told her that Nathan's last words were about how much he loved her. She cried and couldn't speak but it was a happy crying I was sure. I told her I would bring the note by her house tomorrow. I'll fix it myself.

Then I called home and Dad picked up on the very first ring. He didn't say a word about the match, but I got the feeling he'd seen it. I asked if he could come get me at school and he said, "Sure." There was a long silence before we said good-bye but nothing else could really be said, not over the phone. The talk we both felt coming would be one we had to have face-to-face.

He's probably upstairs at the curb right now, waiting in the car. I should've gone up right after I called him. But some part of me wanted to stay here and lie motionless on this bench and do nothing, one last time. That feeling is gone now, as if it had belonged to some other person, a confused boy with longer hair who lived too much in the past.

I'm afraid of what we'll say, of how things will change between us. Maybe we'll start right away and maybe we'll wait till we're home. Maybe he'll want to stop at a diner and eat or maybe he'll want to drive around. I can't imagine the words that will pass between us. But what I do know is that when I speak to my father, long into the night, as the darkness gives way to the dawn of my sixteenth birthday, I will speak with something real and alive, somehow old and somehow freshly born — something for my side of the scales. The voice I've found that all along was mine and mine alone.

SUNDAY	MONDAY	TUESDAY	WEDNESD

This book was edited by Zehava Cohn and designed by Elizabeth B. Parisi. The art for the jacket was created by Greg Spalenka, using mixed media, created digitally. The text was set in Adobe Garamond, a typeface designed in 1929 by Frederic W. Goudy. The display faces were set in Heliotype and Cezanne Regular. The book was printed on 50 lb. Renew Antique paper and bound at Berryville Graphics in Berryville, Virginia. Manufacturing was supervised by Angela Biola.